Ally fe

She woke a few hou⬛wondering alternate⬛get along at all or wh⬛⬛⬛ ⬛⬛uld get along *too* well. Had she leaped out of the frying pan and into the pressure cooker, so to speak?

Would that be so bad?

She let her imagination run rampant, and the mental images got her so hot she threw off the covers. But while the fantasy of making love with Ben held some appeal, she felt instinctively it would be a mistake to take up with him on the rebound. She needed to figure out where she kept going wrong with men before she embarked on another romance.

Engaging in sex without love would cloud her judgment and delay finding Mr. Right. She was too old to waste time on Mr. Right *Now*.

Dear Reader,

Just as food nourishes the body, so does love nourish the soul. In *Party of Three,* Chef Ben Gillard seduces Ally Cummings with food and nourishes her with love. Gradually she rediscovers her passion for life, and in doing so opens up a whole new life for Ben and his son, Danny.

I had a ball writing this book. I was given the opportunity to observe the inner workings of a restaurant kitchen, take part in an olive harvest and spend a romantic weekend in the country with my husband, all in the name of research.

Party of Three takes place in a resort town in my adopted country of Australia. It was a pure pleasure for me to use a local setting. So make yourself something good to eat, pull up a chair and have a few laughs with Ally and Ben.

I love to hear from readers. You can write to me at P.O. Box 234, Point Roberts, WA 98281-0234 or visit me online at www.joankilby.com.

Sincerely,

Joan Kilby

PARTY OF THREE
Joan Kilby

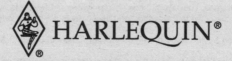

HARLEQUIN®

TORONTO • NEW YORK • LONDON
AMSTERDAM • PARIS • SYDNEY • HAMBURG
STOCKHOLM • ATHENS • TOKYO • MILAN • MADRID
PRAGUE • WARSAW • BUDAPEST • AUCKLAND

ISBN 0-373-78069-9

PARTY OF THREE

Copyright © 2006 by Joan Kilby.

www.eHarlequin.com

Printed in U.S.A.

Books by Joan Kilby

HARLEQUIN SUPERROMANCE

*The Wilde Men

I'd like to thank Chef James Redfern of Montalto Restaurant for allowing me to observe his kitchen during lunch service and giving so generously of his time, experience and expertise. Thanks also to the rest of the staff of Montalto Restaurant and Winery for their help in answering my many questions.

I'm very grateful to George Mistriotis and his family for a warm welcome and a most enjoyable and informative day on his olive farm.

CHAPTER ONE

EVERY MORNING at precisely seven forty-five Ally Cummings tapped the glass of the antique brass ship's barometer that hung in her house high atop Wombat Hill. George, who was always trying to psychoanalyze her, claimed she was anal retentive with father issues, but she simply liked to know what lay ahead.

Tap, tap. The needle swung left; the barometric pressure dropped twenty millibars.

Change was coming.

Deep inside, a tiny voice insisted, *About bloody time.*

Then her eyebrows drew together in a frown and her lips pursed as she brushed that thought aside. She didn't care for surprises.

George walked past, flipping the wide end of his blue silk tie through the loop and pulling it tight. "Are you working late to-night?"

Every Friday like clockwork George asked her that same question. Every week she gave her standard answer. "I have to stay to close the office at eight. Will you be all right on your own until then?"

"I'll manage," he said and headed for the kitchen.

Ally twisted the diamond engagement ring on her left hand. Ever since George had moved in she'd had that horribly familiar sinking feeling their relationship was doomed. Surely it couldn't be happening *again*. George was perfect for her—predictable, reliable, as wedded to routine as she was. Yet, inexplicably her feelings had cooled.

This wasn't the first time she'd lost interest once she had the man in the bag, so to speak, but it was the first time she'd gone so far as to get engaged before dumping the guy. What was wrong with her? She wasn't cruel or callous; she didn't *want* to hurt people.

She followed George out to the kitchen and put on a pan of water while he read the paper. She wasn't much of a cook but she always made breakfast because she liked her eggs done just so, the whites set and the yolk soft, but not too soft. A lot of people felt like that; it wasn't only her.

George usually fit easily into her routines but today he grumbled when she put his poached egg in front of him. "Don't feel like this. I'll just have toast."

"But, George, Friday is Egg Day." Mondays, Wednesdays and Fridays were Egg Days. Tuesdays, Thursdays and Saturdays were Muesli Days. It was called having a balanced diet. Sundays she left open just to show George she could be spontaneous.

"Egg Day," he admonished her from behind the business section of the newspaper, "is a construct of your id, an attempt to impose order on a chaotic universe."

Ally suspected he made things like that up but she couldn't ever be one hundred percent sure. *She* hadn't spent seven years studying psychiatry, as he was all too fond of pointing out. His perfectly cooked eggs cooled on the plate while he spread boysenberry jam on a piece of wholewheat toast.

The waste killed her. "We should get a dog."

"Don't want a canine," he mumbled around a mouthful. A dab of jam trembled on his bottom lip and fell onto his white shirt. "I'm a cat person."

Siggy, George's gray Persian, lay curled in the clean cast-iron frying pan. Lazy, selfish, pampered beast. For one glorious Walter Mitty moment Ally saw her hand turning the gas up high and Siggy leaping off the stove with an outraged yowl.

Ally blinked herself free of the image. What deeply repressed psychosis would George diagnose from that? As if she would harm an animal. Scooping up the cat, who mewed in protest, she deposited him gently on the tiled floor. He stalked off, tail upright as a flagpole, tip twitching.

"In a few years you can have a baby," George offered magnanimously.

Ally itched at the patch of dry flaky skin on the inside of her elbow where her eczema was playing up again. The doctor said skin conditions were often stress-related and she was beginning to think he was right. She wanted children but she no longer wanted to have them with George.

When she didn't reply George lowered his newspaper and peered at her. He had soft brown eyes that she used to think were sensitive but now realized were merely near-sighted. "When are we going to get married?" he said. "It's time we set a date, especially now that I've moved in with you."

"There's plenty of time," she said, fiddling with her ring.

"You're always living in the future," he complained. "Why can't you be like Kathy and inhabit the moment?"

Inhabit the moment? Was this some new psychobabble buzz phrase? "I can't believe you're comparing me unfavorably to your secretary, the woman you call Jezebel behind her back. She'd try to seduce the Pope if he came to town."

"At least she doesn't dress like a nun in civvies."

Ally glanced at her white blouse, navy skirt and low comfortable shoes. Good quality, neat and clean. What was wrong with that? She wasn't like her sister, Melissa, who wore silks and satins from the vintage dress shop where she worked, or her mother, Cheryl, *Vogue* elegant in all black, all the time. She definitely wasn't like her father, Tony, who used clothes the way an actor did costumes, with a different getup for every role he played in his various money-making schemes.

Ally was the ordinary one in her family, the sensible one. The only whimsical note in her conservative style was her colorful collection of brooches. "There's nothing wrong with the way I dress."

George checked his watch and with an impatient sigh, tossed down the newspaper, which slipped off the breakfast table in separate sheets. "Now I'm going to be late," he said dabbing ineffectually at the purple jam splotch on his shirt. "I have a lot of work to do before an important meeting this afternoon."

The implication that this was somehow her fault strengthened the traitorous thoughts that had been tiptoeing through her mind for weeks. She didn't want to marry George. She'd made a huge mistake. If she needed proof, there was the fact they hadn't made love in months and she didn't care. That couldn't be right.

She worried all through breakfast and getting ready for work. A breakup was inevitable. Working up the guts to say she wanted out was hard but had to be done, and soon. It was only fair to George who, like his predecessors wasn't a *bad* man, just not the right one for her.

Who was? And why did she keep making mistakes when it came to men?

As she passed the barometer on her way out the door she stopped and contrary to her usual custom, gave it a second tap. The needle fell another twenty millibars toward Stormy.

George, briefcase in hand, touched his lips to her cheek leaving behind the faint scent of cloves. When was the last time he'd really kissed her? she wondered, and a mocking internal voice replied, *when was the last time you wanted him to?*

This made her sad. Once upon a time they'd been in love—or at least she'd convinced herself they were. Suddenly she needed to know. "George…" She flung her arms around his neck and planted her mouth on his. Incredibly, he resisted at first. She persisted and finally he opened his lips. His tongue bumped blindly against her teeth like a warm slug. So much for excitement. She felt nothing inside, not even a flicker of tenderness.

Drawing back, she avoided his eyes and handed him a furled black umbrella from the hall closet. "Take this. There's a storm coming."

"You and your barometer." He chucked her under the chin and favored her with a gently patronizing smile. "Look outside— the weather's perfect."

Through the lounge-room window she could see the town nestled in the valley below, red tile roofs and church spires sticking up through the gray-green eucalyptus trees and darker pines. On the far side of the valley, clear to the distant rolling hills, the sky was a pale crystalline-blue, not a cloud in sight. For a split second the gap between hard scientific evidence and what she saw with her own eyes gave her a queer feeling in her stomach, as if she'd been turned upside down.

But she knew what she knew. Change was coming.

Taking a deep breath, Ally said, "When I get home tonight, we have to talk."

"Fine," George replied, unconcerned. Either he didn't know the underlying meaning of the expression or he didn't give a rat's you-know-what about anything she might say.

Ally retrieved her own umbrella and locked the front door behind them, then waved goodbye to George as he backed his cream-colored Mercedes-Benz out of the driveway and drove off to his office, thirty miles away in Ballarat.

Every day, rain or shine, she walked the seven blocks down the long hill into Tipperary Springs. She had a car, small and nondescript, tucked away in the garage, but Ally liked listening to the birds and seeing the flowers bud and bloom in people's gardens. This morning the air was heavy and still. The noisy rainbow lorikeets that fed in the flowering gums outside the Convent Gallery were silent, and in the center of town the purple and yellow pansies that filled the planters along Main Street were wilting after days of heat.

Ally passed her mother's art gallery.

Through the open door she saw Cheryl setting out the guest book on the front desk. She lifted her sleek champagne-colored head, saw Ally and smiled. Without breaking stride, Ally waved. A few weeks from now her parents would celebrate their thirtieth wedding anniversary. Ally was in charge of ordering the cake, sending out invitations, arranging for food and drink. Her family tended to rely on her for things like that but she didn't mind; organization was what she did.

Ally headed toward the rental agency where she worked. The agency acted for cottage owners who rented out their properties. Tipperary Springs's population of four thousand swelled on weekends and holidays when city dwellers and tourists flocked to the resort town, an hour west of Melbourne. Besides taking bookings, Ally made sure there was a bottle of chilled champagne, complimentary chocolates and fresh-cut flowers in every cottage.

Every morning Ally opened the office, which occupied the ground floor of a heritage-listed building. She'd brightened up the stone pillars, marble floors and high ceilings with colorful posters and potted palms. Along the walls, wooden racks displayed pamphlets of local attractions—wineries, lavender farms, glass blowing, ballooning—you name it, Tipperary Springs had it.

Ally was checking her e-mail when Lindy came in and dumped her purse on her desk. "It's hot!" she said, pulling her damp blouse away from her chest. Perspiration ringed her armpits and her filmy skirt was stuck to her thighs. "When is this weather going to break?"

"Later today. We're in for some rain." The phone rang and Ally reached for it. "Tipperary Springs Cottage Rentals. Ally Cummings speaking. How may I help you?"

"Ally, it's Olivia. How's everything going?"

"Ticking along nicely," Ally replied. Olivia owned the Cottage Rentals plus she ran a travel agency in Ballarat. She frequently dropped into the office unexpectedly to ensure Ally was maintaining her exacting standards. "What's up?"

"I just got word the American tour group is leaving New Zealand a day early and arriving here tonight," Olivia said, getting right down to business. "Will the cottage they're booked into be available?"

"Let me check. That was Kingsford Cottage, if I remember correctly." Ally drew up the page on her computer. "Yes, it's empty. There's no problem with them coming tonight."

"Excellent," Olivia said. "By the time they get through customs and drive to Tipperary Springs it'll be at least seven-thirty."

"No problem," Ally assured her employer. "I'll be here until eight o'clock as usual. If they can't make it before then, tell them to give me a call and I'll wait."

"These people are from travel agencies in Los Angeles," Olivia said. "If we make a good impression, who knows how much extra business will come our way. Put out the twenty-dollar bottle of champagne and the liqueur chocolates instead of the plain ones."

"It'll be my pleasure," Ally said. And truly, it was.

She wasn't finding a cure for cancer or building a rocket to the moon but she liked to think that because of her attention to detail, her experience and her caring, stressed-out couples who picked up their keys on Friday night went back to their ordinary lives on Sunday rested and invigorated, ready to face life again. Rich or poor, important or not, she gave everyone first-class service.

Around noon a few high white clouds were piling up over Wombat Hill Botanical Gardens. Treetops fluttered in the breeze. By midafternoon the blue sky had all but disappeared and at precisely 4:05 the sun dimmed, throwing the office into shadow. Ally rose from her desk and walked to the door to look outside. Black thunderclouds filled the sky and a gust of wind set the gum leaves rustling.

Next door at the recently refurbished restaurant, Mangos, another landmark building of the last century, workmen were pushing dollies loaded with boxes through the propped-open doors. Their hurried movements seemed somehow connected with the impending storm.

"What's happening at Mangos?" Ally asked Lindy.

Lindy joined her at the window. Short and

compact, the top of her pale head barely came to Ally's shoulder. "The grand opening is tonight. Didn't you see the flyer that came around?" She went back to her desk and brought over a menu. "It looks fabulous. You and George should go."

"George doesn't like to eat out." Ally glanced at the colorful flyer with its mouth-watering descriptions; she had to admit, the menu sounded appealing. "Are you going?"

"Wouldn't miss it. Ben Gillard, the head chef, came here from a top Melbourne restaurant."

"Is he the man with the spiky blond hair I see going in and out?" A couple of times he'd passed her on the street, nodding hello with such friendly confidence that she'd actually turned her head to look at him over her shoulder. Once she'd found him staring back and for the rest of that day she hadn't been able to get him out of her mind.

"That's him." Lindy blew back her straight bangs and peered up at the sky. "Would it be okay if I leave early? I don't want to get caught in the storm."

"Sure, go ahead," Ally said, her gaze

drawn back to the entrance to Mangos. Ben Gillard had just emerged. He was pacing outside the restaurant, gazing up the street at the crest of the hill as if waiting for something. Or someone.

Sure enough, as she watched, a car came through the roundabout and pulled up to the curb. A woman in a sleeveless dress got out and embraced Ben. A towheaded boy of about eleven or twelve years old, all knobby joints and spindly limbs, scrambled out next. Ben gave him an awkward hug then went to get the luggage out of the trunk. All three disappeared into Mangos.

"What's so fascinating?" Lindy asked, coming out of the back room with her purse slung over her shoulder.

"Ben Gillard has a girlfriend. Or a wife. And a kid. I suppose she could be a sister."

"What do you care?" Lindy teased. "You're engaged."

Ally's lips pursed in a smile. "So I am."

After Lindy left, the office seemed unnaturally quiet, the streets outside all but deserted. Shopkeepers folded up their sandwich boards, pulled their racks of clothes and tables of merchandise in from the footpath and closed their doors. Like birds going to roost before a storm, the town was shutting down and withdrawing inside.

Ally rubbed her arms and shivered, an uneasy feeling skittering through her. The change was on its way.

"THIS IS THE PLACE you rented for our son to live in? It's a dump. And so hot! There's no air-conditioning. Do these windows even open or are they painted shut?"

Ben's ex-wife, Carolyn, strode through the apartment over the restaurant, high heels rapping hollowly on the bare wooden floors, her disgust echoing off the cracked plaster walls as she gazed about her in disbelief. "I'm not sure I want to hand my baby over to your care."

"Danny's my son, too. He's twelve years old, hardly a baby. I'm going to buy a house of my own as soon as I have a chance to look around. Besides," Ben dropped his voice, mindful of the boy exploring the back bedroom, "you were quite happy for him to come live with me after you and Ted got married."

"When are you going to buy more furniture?" Carolyn went on as if he hadn't spoken. "You've been here a month and so far you've got nothing but a shabby couch, an old dining table and a TV."

Danny wandered out of the back bedroom. "Where'll I put my computer? I don't see a phone jack anywhere. I'm not staying unless I have the Internet."

"You let him spend too much time playing computer games," Ben said to Carolyn. "I thought we talked about that."

"I had to promise he'd have his own computer," Carolyn countered. "How else can he occupy himself? He doesn't know a soul and won't meet anyone until school starts. What is he going to do while you're at work?"

"He'll be fine. The restaurant is directly below us, with a stairway from the kitchen to the door."

"There isn't even a backyard for him to play in."

"There's an Olympic-size swimming pool literally around the corner," Ben said.

"What about my computer?" Danny persisted.

"I'll put a jack in," Ben told him. "Meantime, you can set up on the dining table. What do you say, mate?"

Danny shrugged. "I don't have any choice, do I? Mum doesn't want me around now that she's married again."

"You know that's not true—" Carolyn began.

Ben dropped to a crouch so he could look into his son's eyes. "Your mother loves you, Danny. So do I. She's had you for five years and now it's my turn. I'm really glad you're coming to live with me."

"Only as long as Danny's happy and there are no problems," Carolyn reminded him. Danny went back down the hall to his room again and Carolyn resumed her inspection, craning her neck to study the large crack from one corner of the ceiling to the central plaster rosette. "Does this roof leak? Because I think it's going to rain."

"Are you about finished?" Ben said, glancing at his watch. "I hate to rush you but I'm opening tonight and I've got a few things to do."

"Are you going to leave Danny alone on his first night here?" Carolyn demanded.

Ben cracked the knuckles on his right hand. Patience wasn't his strong suit and he'd always needed bucketloads when dealing with Carolyn. "The restaurant is right below, with a stairway leading to the kitchen. I'm there if he needs me. *You* chose to bring him this weekend so you and Ted could fly to Bali for your honeymoon. *I* wanted to wait a few weeks until the restaurant was up and running and I was more settled. But if you're worried about Danny you're welcome to stay a few days. There's a spare bedroom. I'll need to find an extra bed but—"

"You know we're flying out tonight. This was the only time Ted could get off work." Carolyn fished in her purse and pulled out several folded sheets of paper, typewritten, single-spaced. "I've set out a schedule for Danny and some instructions. He needs regular meals and adherence to an established bedtime."

Carolyn and her nine-to-five routine. He'd never been able to fit the mold, which pretty much summed up why they were no longer married. "Kids are more flexible than you give them credit for."

"If you want to have Danny live with you, you've got to stick to the rules," she said, handing him the papers.

Ben resisted the urge to crumple them into a ball. "All right. Fine."

"Next, I insist you move out of this dump, and I mean right away."

"The apartment is convenient."

"See those dark circles on the ceiling? That's where the roof has leaked. Promise me you'll find a more suitable home."

"Maybe."

"Promise."

"Whatever you say, Carolyn," he said. "Aren't you going to be late for your plane?"

"I'm not finished. Keep Danny away from the restaurant kitchen. I don't want to come back to find my son swearing like a chef." She grimaced. "Gord is a disgrace."

"He works like a mule and is utterly loyal," Ben replied. The sous chef also drank like a fish and yelled at the staff. Occasionally, Ben wondered if he'd been insane to hire someone so volatile, then he remembered

Gord's genius with sauces and told himself the man was worth the hassle.

"Speaking of working too much," Carolyn went on, "you need to spend time with Danny. You can't work sixteen hours a day, six days a week when you're a single father."

"I *know* that," Ben assured her. "I discussed it with Steve and made it a condition of my employment that I get time off to spend with my son."

Ben's ambitions were simple—he wanted to cook good food and make a life for himself and Danny. Steve, the ex-lawyer and self-proclaimed gastronome who owned Mangos, wanted nothing less than a chef's hat from the *Good Food Guide*. He'd hired Ben to get it for him and to that end had made concessions not normally given to a head chef.

Carolyn moved toward the door. "One more thing…"

"What is it?" Ben said with exaggerated patience.

"The parade of women through your life has got to stop. If he sees a different woman in your bed every weekend he'll get confused."

"You flatter me," Ben said dryly. "But there won't be a parade of women. There won't even be *a* woman. Whatever spare time I've got I'm going to focus on Danny."

"I hope you mean that. As much as it pains me to admit it, Danny's at an age when he needs a father more than he needs me right now. More than anything, I want him in a happy, stable environment. Don't blow this, Ben."

"I've been waiting for the opportunity to be a full-time dad for years," Ben said. "Nothing and no one will come between me and my son."

CHAPTER TWO

ALLY WAS SUFFOCATING in the heat despite the floor and ceiling fans whirring away. She undid her top button, lifted her ponytail off the back of her neck and fanned herself with a brochure for Lavender Farm.

Outside, the sky was nearly black and the shopfronts across the street glowed with a weird yellow light. Papers blew along the footpath ahead of a little whirlwind of dust that rose from the gutter. It was going to rain—

Oh, no, she'd left laundry on the line. Would George think to bring it in? She glanced at her watch and picked up the phone. Ten past five. He should be home.

No answer. He must have been delayed.

She dropped the receiver back in the cradle. The door opened and on a gust of warm wind, in walked Ben Gillard.

Ally sat up so fast her chair shot forward and her bare toes flattened against the marble floor. "Hi."

"G'day." His dark gold hair, tousled from the wind, was lighter at the spiky tips. He had deep-set green eyes under straight thick brows and a jutting jaw that might have looked aggressive if it weren't for the smile on his face. He reached across her desk to shake her hand. "I'm Ben."

"Ally." Her eyes widened at the sight of his forearm scarred with knife cuts and burns. Then her hand was enveloped by a callused palm that sent a jolt of electricity up her arm, and it took all her professional training to stammer, "O-on behalf of Tipperary Springs merchants may I wish you every success on your opening."

"Thanks." His smile twitched at her little speech. Casually he picked up a brochure and started to thumb through it. "I'm hoping you can help me. I'm renting the apartment above the restaurant but I need a better place to live."

"As much as I'd like to assist," she said primly, "the real estate agent across the road is the person you ought to speak to. We cater to the tourist industry."

"I realize that but I'm talking short-term, until I buy a house," Ben explained. "The real estate agents all want a minimum one-year lease."

"I could make inquiries." Ally pulled out a pad of paper, thinking one of the cottage owners might welcome a couple of months guaranteed income. "What are your requirements?"

"Two phone jacks," Ben said. "According to my son life isn't worth living if he can't be on the Internet."

"Two phone jacks," Ally repeated, writing the words. "What else?"

Ben shrugged. "Just your basic house. Nothing fancy."

"How many bedrooms?" Ally persisted. "Do you want built-in wardrobes? Gas or electrical kitchen? How big a yard? Do you need it fenced?"

"Hey!" he said. "I just want a roof over my head."

"Perhaps your wife has some ideas?"

Ben threw her a swift glance. "My *ex*-wife

has a great many ideas but she's going off on her honeymoon. *I'm* the one paying the rent."

"So it's just for yourself and your son. Two bedrooms." Ally made a note on her pad of paper. "You'd probably like to be in town so your restaurant is within walking distance for your son."

"Good idea. I didn't think of that." Ignoring the visitor's chair, Ben perched on the side of her desk and peered at her list.

"Perhaps a yard so he could play outside?" Ally suggested.

"Anything to get him away from the computer."

Big yard, Ally wrote. "Do you cook at home?"

"Of course."

"Then a decent kitchen with a gas stove." She glanced up at him. "Electricity is so slow."

"I agree." Ben's gaze drifted from her notepad to her chest. "Gas is hotter. Faster."

Ally belatedly recalled her open blouse. With an effort, she resisted glancing down and drawing attention to herself. She was suddenly aware of his tanned arm with its smattering of golden hairs lying across his thigh. She could casually lean back, discreetly button up—

"Interesting brooch," Ben commented.

"I beg your pardon?" She blinked up at him. He wasn't looking at her breasts, after all.

"Your brooch. The little person with the pink hair sticking straight up."

"Oh!" Heat flooded her cheeks as she stroked the long fringe of soft pink atop the silver and blue figure. "It's called Bad Hair Day."

"I bet you've never had a bad hair day in your life."

Instinctively, Ally touched her long, smooth ponytail held in rigid obedience by a battery of ties and clips overlaid with hairspray to stop flyaway stragglers. She gave a nervous laugh. "I like to live vicariously."

"I hope that doesn't apply to your love life," Ben said with a wink and a smile. He pushed himself off the desk. "I have to get back to the restaurant. Drop by later."

Ally got up as he walked out and hurried to the window to watch him until he disappeared inside Mangos. *I like to live vicariously.* What on earth had possessed her to say that?

She went back to her desk and tried calling George again. Still no answer. Where was he? Ally paced the office, her gaze flicking constantly to the window and the coming storm. She could run home, take the laundry off the line and be back in less than twenty minutes. Plenty of time before the Americans arrived.

Thunder rolled across the leaden sky as she hurried along Main Street before coming to the side road that led up the hill. With her umbrella tucked under her arm she tugged her skirt down and leaned into the buffeting wind. Finally, she turned onto her street. Down the side of her house, between the fence covered in jasmine and the white weatherboards, she glimpsed the backyard and clothes flapping wildly on the line. She pushed through the iron gate and it was whipped out of her hand by the wind to clang shut behind her.

George's Mercedes was in the driveway. So he *was* home. He must have just got there.

She ran up the steps and across the veranda to turn the front door handle.

Locked. How strange. She and George never locked the door when they were at home during the day. She fumbled in her bag for her key chain and opened the door. The lounge room to her right was dark from the approaching storm but light spilled down the short hallway from the kitchen, along with the sound of voices.

George. And Kathy, his secretary.

Ally set her umbrella by the door and moved through the dim house, her footsteps drowned out by the wind keening through the trees and a branch banging against the corrugated tin roof. Overhead, a loud clap of thunder shook the heavens.

She stopped in the doorway. George and Kathy were seated at the breakfast table over cups of coffee in a scene that was oddly domestic. George looked uncharacteristically relaxed with his shirt untucked and his hair messed up. Kathy's short brown curls were ruffled, her mascara smudged and her lipstick worn right off.

"Hi," Ally said. "What's going on?"

George jumped, his eyes widening. "Ally! What are you doing here?"

"I ran back to bring in the laundry. I called not fifteen minutes ago. You didn't answer." She hadn't meant it to sound like an accusation but it came out that way.

Outside the kitchen window, a streak of jagged lightning split the black clouds, followed immediately by another deafening crack of thunder. A few fat raindrops splatted against the pane. She spared a fleeting thought for the clothes billowing on the line and turned to Kathy. "What are you doing here?"

"I, uh, came by to drop off some papers George forgot at the office. He, er, offered me a cuppa." Kathy's fingers crept to her lacy blouse and did up the top button. She could simply be suffering from the heat or…

"Where are your shoes?" Ally asked her. An idea was growing, an evil idea she found difficult to accept and impossible to let go. Before Kathy could answer Ally turned to George. "How was your meeting this afternoon?"

George swallowed and took out a white

handkerchief to blot his temple. "I didn't go. I wasn't feeling well. I think I have a fever."

Ally pressed the back of her hand against his forehead. "You feel clammy to me."

"Really, Ally, I'm not a child." The irritation in his voice was the first ordinary note in the whole surreal exchange.

"I'm going to get the laundry in." It was all she could think of to do. Numbly, she walked into the hallway and stopped dead.

High-heeled shoes lay on the floor in front of her bedroom, a hand-painted silk scarf beside them. Ally recognized the scarf as one she'd given to Kathy at Christmas. Well, she'd picked it out; George gave it to her. Forgetting all about the laundry, Ally stepped over the shoes and reached for the doorknob.

"Wait!" George cried out. "Don't go in there."

Her hand on the knob, she turned and regarded him with an eerie calm. "Why not?"

George was half out of his chair, his mouth opening and closing like a dying fish. "Because, well, it's a mess. I went to bed when I got home. Before Kathy dropped over." He exhaled heavily. "Yes, that's it. I was sick. I got under the covers. Alone. I haven't remade the bed."

For a so-called intelligent man he was really botching this. "You never make the bed, George."

Feeling strangely detached, Ally contemplated strangling Kathy with her own scarf. "You two are having an affair."

Kathy walked over to pick up the scrap of silk and wind it around her neck, oblivious to the danger. "George is going to leave you and marry me."

George made a strangled noise and sat back down on the kitchen chair with a thump. "Let's not be hasty, Kath."

Maybe Ally was forgetting to breathe, causing a lack of oxygen to her brain because she blurted, "You could at least have taken the clothes off the line!"

"Who cares about the laundry?" George said. "For God's sake, Ally!"

"I'm sorry you had to find out this way," Kathy said, not sounding sorry at all. "But really, you bring these things on yourself. If you'd come home when you were supposed to, everything would have been tidied up and we could have sat down and talked it out."

Oh, so this was all *her* fault, was it? "How long has this been going on?"

"Not long," George muttered.

"Six months," Kathy corrected him, and said to Ally, "Remember when your uncle died and you stayed with your aunt for a week to help her with arrangements for the funeral? That's when it started."

Ally recalled Kathy's promise to look in on George while she was away and remembered thinking how kind she was, especially since George never said anything nice about her. All an act. Both of them.

"You stole my fiancé out from under my nose," Ally said, still calm. "You're a home-wrecker." And a very convenient excuse to call off the engagement. "We're through, George. Get out."

"Now, Ally," he began in his most soothing couchside voice. "Let's talk about this."

"Do you love her?" Ally was merely curious. His answer, either way, wouldn't make any difference to how she felt.

"Love is a complicated emotion, meaning different things to different people," he replied in typical George fashion.

"Do you love *me?*"

"A part of me will always love you, Ally."

Which part, she wondered. His earlobes, his liver? It certainly wasn't his you-know-what. "Why did you ask me to marry you?"

Perplexed, he wrinkled his brow. Then he gave up and shrugged. "You seemed so normal."

But she wasn't normal. She was a serial dumper who'd just got dumped herself. Karma was having a field day.

Ally marched back to the bedroom, intending to get out his suitcase and throw his clothes into it, the way she'd seen in the movies. She actually snarled at Kathy and the secretary jumped out of her way. Ha! *Now* Kathy was afraid of her.

Then she entered the bedroom and was confronted by rumpled sheets and Kathy's lacy black panties lying on her pillow. *In her own bed.*

For a moment, Ally thought she might throw up. No doubt George would have a scientific explanation for the sudden onset of nausea, but she didn't want to know. The room would have to be fumigated before she could sleep here again.

"Never mind, *I'm* leaving." Pushing George aside, she strode out the front door. George followed. On the veranda she stopped and while the wind howled around her, she yanked his ring off her finger. She stifled the urge to throw it at him, but instead dropped it in his shirt pocket. "But I'll be back. And when I am, I want you gone. Do you hear me? Every CD, every dirty sock, every issue of the *Australian Journal of Psychiatry. Especially* the *Journal of Psychiatry.*"

"Yes," George said meekly.

Kathy rolled her eyes, pulled George inside and slammed the door.

Alone in the wide empty street, shock set in and to Ally's horror and disgust, she began to cry great gulping sobs. It was only shock, she told herself, but that didn't stop the tears. Tears of anger or anguish, she couldn't tell, but they were uncontrollable all the same. She started to run, trying to outstrip her emotions.

A small detached segment of her brain insisted she should be happy, that she'd wanted to break up with George. Not like this, she moaned. Not humiliated and betrayed, lied to and cheated on. It wasn't just George she was crying over, it was her whole life. She wanted love, marriage, children, but she just could not seem to get it right. Why, oh why, did love always end badly for her?

She slipped and slid down the unpaved footpaths in her headlong flight down the hill. Branches reached out to scrape her cheek and tear at her blouse, already soaked by the rain. As she turned the corner onto Main Street the glowing plate glass windows of Mangos spilled light onto the shiny pavement. She was almost at her office....

IN THE RESTAURANT kitchen Ben ripped the order ticket out of the printer and shouted over the hiss and clatter, "Table Seven—prawns, risotto entrée-size, veal times two."

Opening night was every bit the challenge Ben had anticipated. All forty-five tables were occupied and half a dozen customers waited in the small lounge by the fireplace.

Ben's long-sleeved white chef jacket was buttoned to the neck and sweat beaded his forehead as he separated the different colored copies: pink to Baz, the pimply-faced apprentice who was working the entrée station, yellow to Beth, the sweet round-faced pastry chef on desserts. The white ticket he hung on the slide above the sauté station for himself and Gord.

On the stovetop half a dozen sauté pans sizzled and small saucepans were situated according to their heat requirements. Ben called, "Fire on twenty-six," and Gord slammed a couple of seared fillet mignons into a hot oven to go with the tuna Ben placed in the bamboo steamer, heaped with chili and garlic, lemongrass and ginger.

"Someone stole my effing spoon!" Gord roared suddenly. "Baz, was it you? I told you to keep away from my meez!"

"Sorry." Baz slid Gord's favorite slotted spoon across to him then looked to Ben. "What's meez again?"

"*Mise-en-place*, your station prep, your

assembled ingredients, condiments, tools," Ben explained as he swiftly stacked slices of rare lamb fillet atop a puddle of buttered polenta. "Everything at the ready, the squeeze bottle of sauce placed just so, the metal pans of chopped condiments arranged in a precise order so that you can reach for a specific item without looking." He wiped the rim of the plate with a clean rolled napkin and sprinkled on chopped parsley. "You don't mess with another chef's meez."

Ben slapped the lamb on the pass-through win-dow next to a veal marsala. "Pick-up on fifteen!"

Across the steamy kitchen Gord, his face as red as his flaming hair, berated Mick, the dishwasher. "Get those effing plates washed or I'll shove them up your effing arse."

Ben spotted Danny sitting on a sack of rice in a corner, munching on garlic prawns. While Ben swirled butter into a demi-glace heating in a saucepan he said, "How's it going, mate? How are the prawns?"

Danny shrugged. "You need kid food on the menu."

"There's no such thing as kid food, just uneducated palates," Ben told him. "Why, I was eating Szechwan and loving it when I was your age."

"Ben!" Julie was shouting at him through the serving window as she stacked plates of seafood risotto on her arm, ready to whisk away. "Cassie's way out of her depth and going down for the third time. Where did Steve get her, Hungry Jack's?"

Not far off. Cassie, the maître d' Steve had hired because she was his wife's cousin, had last hosted at a family restaurant in suburban Melbourne. "Cut her some slack, she's new."

"We're all new here," Julie said bluntly. "Table Six wants to compliment the chef." She lowered her voice. "It's the mayor."

"I'll be right there." This was no time to be away from the kitchen but he couldn't ignore the mayor. She'd been very helpful about Mangos's liquor license.

He turned back to Danny. "Go on upstairs. Take something from the pastry cart if you want."

"When are you coming home?" Danny said. "I don't like it up there by myself."

"I'll make it up to you, I promise. Tomorrow

we'll go swimming." Ben gathered his son in a rough one-armed embrace. "Turn on the TV but don't watch garbage. I'll be up to check on you as soon as I can."

He pushed through the swinging wooden doors that led into the dining room and wove his way through the tables, smiling at unfamiliar faces and calling greetings to those he recognized.

Table Six, next to the window, held two women in their late fifties, both blond, well-dressed and well-preserved. To Ben they looked almost identical. A panic-stricken thought swept through his brain—which one was the mayor?

"Evening, ladies," he breezed, automatically making a mental note that the woman on his right hadn't touched her kipfler potatoes. He directed his next words to her. "I hope you're enjoying your meal."

"The steamed tuna was delicious," she said.

Above the aromas of food and wine, the scent of White Diamonds tickled his sensitive nose, triggering a memory of their earlier meeting. "Thank you, your Honor. I—"

A movement outside caught Ben's attention. Through the window he recognized the priggish young woman from the cottage rental agency next door stumbling along the rain-soaked footpath. Her sleek brown hair had fallen out of its tight ponytail and was plastered to her cheeks in wet ropes. Even through the blurred glass he could tell she was crying.

Leave her be, Ben told himself. She wasn't his problem. God knows, he had enough of his own waiting for him in the kitchen or upstairs. Then she turned her head and he saw her contorted face. Something shifted inside him, and he couldn't ignore her pain.

"Excuse me," he said to the mayor and her guest. "There's something I have to attend to."

The next instant he was out the door, grabbing Ally, whirling her to a halt. "Whoa! What's your hurry, sunshine?"

She struggled in his arms, kicking at his shins. "Let me go."

"Ow! Stop that," he said, ignoring her request. "Ally, are you hurt? Tell me, so I can help you."

Hearing her name, she stopped struggling

and pushed back her lank hair to peer at him. "Oh, it's you."

"Yes, me. You've lost a shoe." For some reason this sparked a torrent of verbal abuse directed at men in general and some poor sap named George specifically. Ben took her by the shoulders. *"What is it?"*

Ally took a huge gulping breath. "I went home and found my fiancé and his s-s-secretary drinking c-c-coffee together!"

"Sorry, I'm not getting it," Ben said with what he thought was commendable patience while the rain soaked through his chef whites. "What's wrong with that?"

"Her underwear was on my p-p-pillow! They're having an affair." Ally gave a violent shiver and her teeth began to chatter. She bent over and started retracing her steps, looking for her missing shoe.

He swore under his breath. "You'd better come in out of the rain or you'll catch your death."

"I *want* to die," she said fiercely.

"Not outside my restaurant, you don't. People will blame the seafood." He found her shoe floating in the gutter and plucked it out just before it was sucked down the storm drain. Handing it to her he offered his arm to lean on while she put it on.

"Come inside," he urged, intending to park her in front of the fireplace with a glass of brandy until she calmed down and dried off.

"I can't go in there," she wailed. "I don't want everyone in town seeing me like this."

"You've got a point. We'll go in the back way." He started to tug her around the side of the building. "I'll take you upstairs to my apartment."

"I don't know you," she said, resisting.

"Trust me, I'm not going to attack you."

"Why should I believe that? I saw the way you looked down my blouse this morning." She was shivering and soaked to the skin, her arms crossed protectively over her chest. The rain had rendered her blouse transparent, revealing a plain cotton bra, about as alluring as her pinched white face, although the nicely rounded breasts that filled it had potential.

"In the name of Good Samaritanism I'll do my best to resist. Anyway, I have to get back to my restaurant."

"But—" She broke off to sneeze violently.

"Come on, at least you'll be warm and dry. My son is up there. I'll send up some food. Are you hungry?"

She'd started to shake her head when her stomach gave a rumble that was audible over the drumming rain.

"When did you last eat?" he persisted.

"A salad at lunch."

"I thought as much. Do you like pasta?" Reluctantly she nodded. "Creamy chicken and wild mushroom sauce?" She swallowed, as if salivating already. Ben took her arm and tugged gently. "Sun-dried tomatoes, avocado, parmesan…"

She let him lead her past the Dumpster and the empty produce boxes, past Baz sneaking a smoke outside the back door and up the steep narrow staircase to the apartment.

Ben gave his coded knock, three short, two long. A moment later, the latch turned and Danny opened the door.

"What the—?" Danny's wide-eyed gaze took in the pair of them.

"This is Ally," Ben told him. "She got caught in the rain. She's going to stay here for a bit and dry off." Beneath his arm he could feel the faint tremor in her shoulders. "You okay?" he said to her.

She nodded, and Ben steered her into the lounge room. On the TV, Sharon Stone was undressing in front of a mirror while a man looked on in the background.

"For crying out loud, Danny," Ben said, switching it off. "What did I tell you?"

"You told me not to watch garbage. This movie got four stars in the TV guide."

"Don't be a smart aleck." Ben left Ally and rummaged in his dresser for track pants and a T-shirt. He threw them onto the bed and then found a towel and handed it to Ally. "You'd better change before you catch pneumonia."

He ran downstairs, ordered a meal for her and came back with a bottle of Remy Martin. Ally emerged from his room, dwarfed in his clothes, her hair wrapped in the towel. He poured out half a tumblerful of cognac and handed it to her.

She took a gulp of the thirty-year-old liquor and choked.

"Easy. Pace yourself," Ben said.

Ally took another sip and with a deep

shudder, swallowed the fiery liquid. "I'm going to get blotto."

"Oh, I don't think that's a good idea."

"On the contrary, it's the best idea I've had in a long time." She drank again then held out her glass. "More." Hiccup. "Please."

CHAPTER THREE

BEN SPLASHED A SOUPÇON more cognac into her glass, only too aware of a still wide-eyed Danny avidly watching the proceedings. He'd better not blab to his mother....

"I'll call a taxi to take you home," Ben informed Ally.

She tilted the bottle and gave herself another five or so ounces. "I don't want to go home. Not until George has had time to pack and leave."

The alcohol had to be hitting her empty stomach like a ton of bricks. As she took a swig, her eyes began to glaze.

"I need to get back to work," Ben explained. "Do you have a friend or a relative you can call to come and get you?"

"No, no, don't want to cause a fuss." Ally

suddenly noticed the glass in her hand and raised it to her lips. "This is *good.*"

"Are you sure I can't take you home?" Ben was starting to feel desperate.

"I have no home," she declared melodramatically.

"You've had enough cognac, that's for sure, at least until the food's ready."

Ally twisted away before he could take her glass and moved unsteadily across to the window overlooking Main Street. The storm was directly overhead; wind gusts rattled loose windowpanes and spattered them with rain.

Ben went to the side table that held the phone and the local directory. "What's George's last name?"

"No!" She whirled around, arm outstretched as if she was a wizard about to smite Ben with her staff. "I forbid you to call him."

Oh, boy. What had he gotten himself into? Ben led Danny out of Ally's earshot and into the cramped kitchen with its old-fashioned appliances. "I'm going to run downstairs, check on the staff and pick up her dinner. Take care of her for a few minutes, okay?"

Danny's eyes widened. "What am I supposed to do?"

"Don't let her go back out in the storm."

"I'm just a kid. How can I stop her?"

"Lock the door after I leave."

"What if she's crazy and chops me up into little pieces?"

"She's not crazy. She's upset."

"You can't leave me alone with her," Danny said, obviously panicking.

He was probably right. Ben went back to the lounge room. Ally had collapsed on the overstuffed couch and was refilling her glass. Amber liquid slopped over the rim and she licked it off her hand. She raised her glass to him with a giggle. "It's not the drinking that'll get you, it's the steady sip, sip, sip."

Ben checked his watch. He'd been away from the restaurant for over half an hour. Anything could have happened in the kitchen in that time. Gord was a volcano waiting to erupt, especially when he got into the bottle of vodka he kept hidden in the walk-in freezer.

Ben paced the wide space between the couch and the fireplace, trying to come up with a plan. Who could he call? He didn't know anyone in town well enough to ask them to babysit a drunk woman.

He felt a tug on his sleeve. "Dad?"

"Shh, Danny, I'm thinking."

"Dad, never mind." His son pushed him around to face the couch where Ally lay sprawled, eyes shut, one arm clutching the bottle to her chest, the other dangling above the floor, clinging to the empty glass. "She passed out."

Ben walked over and with a sigh, removed the glass. "I guess she can stay here tonight."

WHEN ALLY AWOKE her head felt as though it was gripped inside a vise being screwed tight by some sadistic monster while a dozen tiny hammers pinged on miniature anvils. Scrunching her eyes shut she tried to slip back into oblivion.

"Water?" asked a voice floating above her.

"Go away," she muttered. Something awful swam just below her consciousness, something too terrible to acknowledge, too enormous to confront.

"You really should take liquid after drinking alcohol," the annoying voice persisted.

"I don't drink," she croaked. Then she became aware her throat was dry, her skin burning hot. She opened one eye. A man loomed over her, holding out a glass.

He had streaked blond hair and was somehow familiar.

Memories of yesterday flooded through her like an injection of poison. George. Kathy. The storm. Cognac.

"Ohhh," she groaned, and curled into a fetal ball. George had cheated on her. With Kathy.

The bed creaked and sank beneath a weight greater than her own. A hand gently grasped her wrist and pulled her arm away from her face. Ben's jaw appeared, bristly with golden stubble, his hair tousled from sleep.

"Drink this," he said, propping up her pillow. "You'll feel better."

She pushed back the rumpled chocolate-and-cream-colored duvet and sat up. Then she saw the source of the pinging; leaks from the roof were dripping into pots at various locations around the room. Talk about Chinese water torture. Her right shoulder was damp where she'd been dripped on in bed.

"Is the storm over?" she asked, accepting the glass of water with shaking hands.

"Pretty much. The rain is easing." Ben placed his cool fingers over her feverishly hot ones to steady them. Ice water slipped down her sore throat, easing the dryness. "You must feel awful," he added.

She nodded, which made her head hurt so much she decided not to risk speaking.

"A broken heart is just about the worst thing going," Ben went on, smoothing her hair off her face. "Trust me, anyone who would cheat on you isn't worth having."

He thought she was sick over losing George. Ally sipped more water, taking a moment to examine her feelings. Was she heartbroken? No…relieved described it better. Her pride was badly dented but George was out of her life without her having to be the bad guy, or worry that he'd be lonely. In fact, things had turned out pretty well. She was free. Her lips curved in a tremulous smile.

"That's the spirit," Ben said, rewarding her

with one of his own warm smiles. "But remember, it's okay to cry. If you want my shoulder, I'm here."

"Thanks," she rasped. "I feel better already."

She glanced around the room. An old-fashioned wardrobe leaned against the wall, the door open to reveal a rack of men's clothes. A wicker chair in the opposite corner was draped with her skirt and blouse. Apart from her clothes, nothing looked familiar. "Where am I?"

"In my apartment above the restaurant."

"Whose bed am I in?"

"Mine."

"We didn't…" she croaked in alarm. "Did we?"

"No." He seemed faintly amused. "I spent a rather uncomfortable night on the couch, if it makes you feel better."

"Much, thank you." She preferred to be conscious when making love. Then she glanced at the clock on the bedside table and gasped. "Is that the correct time?"

Ben checked his watch. "Yep. Just after eight-thirty."

"Oh God, oh God, oh God. I'm late for work." She ran her fingers through her snarled hair and threw aside the covers. Her thighs were bare and she wore nothing but a man's T-shirt. Quickly she tugged it down. What had happened to the track pants?

"The sky won't fall in if you're a few minutes late," Ben said, getting out of her way.

"I'm not so sure about that." Her feet hit the floor and she stood up, her stomach lurching. "Lindy doesn't have a key. She'll be waiting outside for me to open the door—" She groaned as further recollection of last night hit. The Americans!

"Are you going to be sick? Here's a bucket." Ben produced the receptacle from beside the bed and shoved it under her nose.

Swallowing hard, she waved it away. "I'm fine. I just have to get to work."

"I'll make you breakfast," Ben said as he moved to the door. "Nothing like bacon and eggs to cure a hangover."

"It's Saturday—" she began "—Muesli Day," but he'd already left.

She staggered over to the chair and

reached for her blouse. It was damp and wrinkled but it would have to do. Shivering, she buttoned it on in front of the mirror. For a moment she didn't recognize her own reflection. Her puffy bloodshot eyes looked more muddy than hazel, her skin was blotchy and somehow her hair had turned lackluster and stringy overnight.

Outside the door she could hear Ben speaking to his son. "I know I promised to take you swimming but it's just not going to be possible."

"You always break your promises," Danny said matter-of-factly. "Just like Mum says."

"That's not fair," Ben replied. "And please keep your voice down. *She* can hear you."

Danny whispered something Ally didn't catch. She tiptoed to the door to listen.

"Last night while I was out of the restaurant the soufflé situation turned into a complete disaster," Ben said in a lower voice. "I have to work this morning. It's not a whim."

Her escapade had had consequences for both Ben and his son. The sooner she got out of here, the better for everyone.

"I'll just play on the computer," Danny said, subdued but apparently indifferent. "It's okay."

"No, it's not okay. The pool's just around the corner," Ben went on. "Why don't you check it out?"

"Mum would never let me go by myself," Danny said. "Don't you know anything about taking care of kids?"

"This is a small town, not Melbourne."

"Bad things can happen anywhere," Danny said, clearly repeating a favorite phrase of his mother's. "You said you wanted to spend time with me."

"I do. You just need to be patient."

"Good morning!" Ally entered the room, a big smile plastered on her face. She found her purse on the floor beside the couch and sailed toward the door. Ben and Danny stopped their bickering as she slipped her feet into shoes that squelched. "I'll be going now. Thank you so much for having me."

"You haven't had breakfast," Ben said.

"I don't need anything, thanks. Except…" She glanced around the room. "Do you have a barometer?"

"Barometer?" He laughed. "I barely have furniture."

"Then how do you know what the weather will be?"

Ben walked to the window overlooking the street and glanced out. "The rain has stopped. I reckon the clouds will burn off before long."

In other words, he had no idea. She pursed her lips and smiled tightly. "Thank you. Goodbye."

"Where are you going?" Ben said. "What are you going to do?"

"I told you," she explained patiently, "I'm going to work."

He came closer. "I mean about your fiancé."

"Oh, that. I'm sure it's all for the best."

He just looked at her, frowning.

"Something wrong?" she said, a touch defensively. She knew she looked a wreck.

"Take it from me, you shouldn't ignore your feelings about your breakup. You'll get over him faster if you allow yourself to be angry."

"Oh, I'm angry. He lied to me and cheated on me." Mostly she was angry at herself for getting engaged to a man who it turned out she didn't love. But how could she explain that to Ben when she didn't understand it herself? "Thanks for everything. I'll be fine. And I'll check into that cottage for you. You really can't stay here with this leaky roof."

Clutching the banister for support she hurried down the stairs and slipped past the kitchen—where a gangly teenager with acne was chopping mushrooms at the stainless steel bench—and out the back door.

The side street was empty, desolate as the morning after. Sporadic raindrops rippled the puddles lying in the gutter. The paperbark tree next to the footpath had been torn in the wind; a broken branch hung forlornly, tattered layers of bark fluttering in the cool breeze.

Ally turned the corner onto Main Street and her heart dropped to her feet. Olivia's cherry-red Mazda was out front of the agency. For her to have driven from Ballarat this early on a Saturday morning was not a good sign. Then Ally noticed something worse. A minibus was parked in front of the Mazda and emerging from it was a group of groggy, disheveled men and women in wrinkled clothes.

She hurried past them and went inside. Olivia was seated behind Ally's desk, her black hair pulled back severely, her narrow features set in icy disapproval. Ally caught a fleeting glimpse of Lindy's anxious expression before her assistant swiveled to face her computer.

Ally's stomach started to churn and she wished she'd taken Ben up on breakfast. Her shoes made squishy noises as she crossed the marble tiles to stand before her employer. "I'm terribly sorry—" Ally began.

"Did you see those people on the street?" Olivia demanded. "They arrived last night under the impression they would be warmly welcomed to an idyllic weekend getaway. What did they find? The office shut and locked. Unable to obtain other accommodation, they spent the night in the minibus. In a thunderstorm."

"It's entirely my fault—"

"Were you ill?"

"No, I—"

"Were you struck by lightning?"

"No, but—"

"Were you kidnapped and held against your will?"

"Olivia!"

"What possible excuse could you have for not being here during stated business hours to hand over the keys to guests you knew were arriving?"

Ally heaved a large sigh. "I broke up with George last night, got drunk and stayed in a strange man's apartment."

"If you think a recap of your sordid love affairs is going to get you off the hook, you're wrong," Olivia said, tapping her pen against the desk in a jackhammer beat that bored into Ally's splitting head. "I have no choice but to let you go."

"What!" Ally felt her jaw drop. "You can't do that."

"I'm sorry. I simply can't afford to have someone in charge who isn't responsible."

"But I've worked here for three years and there's never been a problem before."

"That's not strictly true, you know." Olivia's gaze was accusing. "Six months ago you left the office unattended for a whole afternoon. Your sister had some crisis, I believe."

Melissa had called Ally in hysterics after she'd singed both her eyebrows off while trying to light a cigarette at the gas burner on her stove. Ally had applied aloe vera and told her sister to quit smoking. It was one of the few times Melissa had acted on her advice.

"Then there was the time you had to bail your father out of jail," Olivia said.

"His arrest was a complete misunderstanding." At least that's what Tony claimed. Generally speaking her father squeaked in on the right side of the law in his business endeavors.

"Excuse me, ladies." One of the men from the minibus poked his head through the door. "Is there a washroom?"

"On the next block," Ally said. "Right beside the Tourist Information office."

When he'd gone, Olivia went on. "The first two incidents I let pass. I even hired Lindy to assist you so there was always someone here in the event of an emergency."

"It won't happen again," Ally promised.

"You're correct, it won't. Three strikes, you're out. This is the height of the tourist season. I need someone I can count on. And just look at your appearance…."

Olivia's voice rolled over her, a steady stream of criticism and chastisement. Suddenly, Ally couldn't take any more. She turned and walked out of the office with Olivia still talking. All she wanted to do was go home. To crawl under the covers and sleep for a million years. And when she woke her life would be back to normal.

Except that George would be gone.

Well, they said every cloud had a silver lining.

The hill had never seemed so steep as that morning. Evidence of the storm littered the road—fallen tree limbs, knocked-down fences, overturned rubbish bins. Luckily, her own property was intact, barring a cracked window.

The first thing Ally did was bring in the laundry. Most of it had been torn off the line by the wind and flung in the mud. She carefully separated out George's socks, underwear and shirts and placed them, still filthy, in a black plastic garbage bag. Upon reflection she decided to add a poor dead mouse that had drowned in the water barrel. A treat for Siggy. Then she tied the bag up tight and left it in a patch of sun on the veranda for George to collect. Just because he'd brought another woman to her bed didn't mean she couldn't act civilized.

Her own clothes she put back in the washing machine and waited until it filled. Then she had a long hot shower, washed her hair, put on a clean skirt and blouse and sat down at the breakfast table with a bowl of muesli. Getting back to her routine made her feel a little better. Food helped, too, although she couldn't help but think wistfully of the hot breakfast Ben had offered.

Doggedly, she chewed and contemplated her situation. Losing her job left her feeling adrift in a way that losing George could never do. Worse, the loss of income caused a big financial problem. With no salary and no George to contribute a share of the mortgage, how was she going to make payments on her house?

She loved her home and didn't want to give it up. It represented both stability and independence. Besides, she really, really hated moving.

The phone rang.

"Ally, it's me, Mel." Her sister sounded agitated. "I called your office and Lindy said you were fired and that you'd broken up with

George. Sorry to hear that but thank God you're home. You've got to come quick."

"Slow down. What's up?"

"Tony and Mother had a big fight. Mother left him and she's over here. With her luggage. That's suitcases, plural. Her entire set of faux Louis Vuitton. The last time she did that she stayed a whole month."

"Calm down, Melissa," Ally said. "She can't leave him. Their wedding anniversary is in three weeks and I've got it all organized."

"What she can't do is stay with me." Melissa lowered her voice, but her tone was increasingly urgent. "I only have one bedroom and I met this cool guy from the Cirque du Soleil. You know how men always get that nudge, nudge, wink, wink, smile about women gymnasts? Well, now I know why. You've got to convince her to go home."

"Can't you stay at your boyfriend's place?"

"It's not just that, it's…you know what she's like."

Ally couldn't blame her for not wanting Cheryl moving in. As much as they both adored their mother, she was the roommate from artist hell. Painting, pottering, fixing, fussing, arranging, changing, moving, improving—she engaged in an endless quest for visual perfection, right down to repositioning the kitchen utensils in a jar.

Fifteen minutes later Ally walked into Melissa's renovated miner's cottage and picked her way through the tiny lounge room crowded with brown-and-cream-patterned luggage. In the kitchen, Melissa, in a burgundy lace top over a black satin slip dress, was making tea. Black filigree earrings dangled from beneath impossibly red hair and, even at ten in the morning, her deep blue eyes were lined in black with dark silver shadow.

Cheryl, slim and attractive in a black linen sheath and fine gold jewelry, was standing on a chair to reach a leadlight suncatcher hanging in a window charmingly framed with ivy.

"Leave it there, Mother. I like it," Melissa said.

"Red and blue doesn't go with the teal on your walls, darling. While I'm here I'll help you redecorate."

Melissa turned her desperate gaze in Ally's direction. "Tell her, Ally."

"Well, it does kind of clash—"

"No, I mean how she loves Tony no matter what he does. And she should go back to him now and save me, I mean *them,* a lot of heartache."

Cheryl succeeded in unhooking the sun-catcher and climbed off the chair. "Never mind that. How are you coping, Ally, darling? Mel says you and George have split up and you've lost your job."

"Yes, but I'm fine, honestly."

"You can always get another job," Melissa said. "But quick, change the locks before George changes his mind."

"He can't," Ally said flatly. "I kicked him out."

Cheryl patted Ally's hand. "Good for you."

Was her mother being supportive or had she always disliked George? Ally decided there was no point in knowing. "What has Tony done this time?"

"He refinanced the art gallery to take out a loan. I knew I should have had it in my name but he needed the tax write-off so on paper, it's his." Cheryl set the suncatcher on the table and gazed around the room as if looking for further insults to her sensibilities. "I'd just knocked the mortgage down to a reasonable level and now suddenly I owe twice as much as I did five years ago." Her nostrils flared in a refined quiver of rage. "I could kill him. Boil him in his own olive oil."

"Olive oil?" Ally took a sip from the teacup Melissa handed her. She was starting to feel vaguely human.

"He bought a majority stake in an olive grove along the Murray River," Cheryl explained. "Turns out there's no water lease for irrigation. The company is struggling to survive."

"Fancy Tony getting into farming," Melissa said as she rehung the suncatcher. "I can see him now in a flannel shirt and Akubra hat with his faithful dog at his heels."

"You're thinking of sheep farming." Ally turned back to her mother. "At least the deal sounds legitimate."

"No irrigation means a poor harvest," Cheryl informed her gloomily. "I could lose the gallery."

"I've got mortgage problems, too, now that George is gone," Ally commiserated.

Melissa looked from her sister to her mother. "Hello! Obvious solution here. Mother, if you want to make Tony sweat awhile longer, and frankly, it would do him a world of good, move in with Ally. You two can split costs."

"What a great idea!" Cheryl said, taking up the suggestion enthusiastically. "I've been dying to do something with that house of yours, Ally. I know you think you've got it the way you want it but you haven't heard my ideas yet. Now that stick-in-the-mud George is out of the way I can really let loose. Oh, I can't wait. We'll have a ball, won't we, Ally?"

If there was any justice in the universe the look Ally threw her sister would have been fatal. For years she'd been collecting furniture and artwork for the time when she had a place of her own to decorate. Since she'd moved into her house she'd worked her way through each room, painting walls, polishing floorboards, sewing drapes and cushions. She'd scrimped and saved so she could have the kitchen and the bathroom renovated. Now her mother was proposing moving in and changing everything. Over Ally's dead body!

"There's just one problem. I, uh…." She racked her brains for inspiration. "I have a roommate already."

"Oh." Cheryl looked disappointed. "Who?"

Ally crossed her fingers in her lap. "Ben Gillard, the new chef at Mangos."

"Wow," Melissa said. "Fast work. I'm impressed."

"Yeah, well." Ally tried to look modest.

Now all she had to do was convince Ben to move in with her. It shouldn't be too hard; her house easily fulfilled his requirements. Plus, she had something he didn't even realize he needed—a barometer.

CHAPTER FOUR

"TIPPERARY SPRINGS Restaurant thinks it's the only fine dining establishment in town. We'll show them." Steve stroked his trim silver goatee and paced the kitchen floor in front of the serving window. He wore a navy cashmere jacket and designer blue jeans pressed with a knife-edge crease. Upper crust effing nerd, Gord called him. "I must have that chef's hat," Steve went on. "Ben, you will create a new dish using…scallops." He stroked his goatee some more. "Yes, scallops are good. I *like* scallops."

Ben just nodded and took out his frustrations on a batch of sourdough, pummeling it beneath the heel of his hand. There was no more demanding employer than a frustrated amateur cook. "Scallops it is."

Over by the sink, Baz was hulling strawberries destined to be made into a coulis for

Beth's panna cotta dessert special. Gord was throwing roasted chicken bones and roughly chopped vegetables into the enormous stockpot simmering on the stove. The yeasty scent of the sourdough, the chicken stock, the aniseed aroma of tarragon clinging to the cutting board, created a pleasing melange of smells. The radio was tuned to popular music, loud enough for everyone to hear over the clang of pots and slam of oven doors.

Out in the restaurant, the phone rang. Steve roused himself from his reverie about scallops and went to answer it.

What had happened to Ally? After breakfast, Ben had wandered past the Cottage Rentals and poked his head through the glass door, but she hadn't been at her desk. Instead, an evil-looking crow of a woman had glared at him over the top of narrow glasses. He was pretty sure he'd interrupted her in the middle of putting a hex on the other girl, the stocky blond one. By now, she'd probably been turned into a toad.

"We have a problem, gentlemen," Steve announced on his return to the kitchen, adding belatedly, "er, and Beth."

"What is it?" Ben rubbed at his nose with the back of a floury hand.

"Cassie," Steve said. "I did her a favor hiring her and already she's quit."

Gord threw double handfuls of fresh thyme, parsley and rosemary into the stockpot. "Good riddance. Did she give a reason?"

Steve turned to the sous chef. "As a matter of fact, she did. She didn't like your attitude, Gord."

"What the hell does she mean *my* attitude?" Gord growled.

"Maybe she means you telling her to get her fat arse out of the kitchen and to the front of the house where she belonged." Baz's fingertips were red and a telltale dribble of crimson juice stained his chin.

Gord turned on him. "*You* keep your effing mouth shut. And stop eating them berries or they'll come out of your effing pay."

"Stow it, you two," Ben said. "Steve, can you hire someone else in time for tonight?"

"Julie will have to cover for her," Steve replied. "I've given Cassie until the end of the week to change her mind, otherwise I'll never hear the end of it from my wife." He sighed. "If anyone needs me I'll be in my office nursing a migraine."

A busy waitress doubling as maître d'. Ben shook his head and folded over the wad of dough, slamming the heel of his hand into the yielding softness till the compressed gas bubbles squeaked. This was a surefire recipe for disaster.

ALLY PUSHED THROUGH the front door of Mangos into the dining room. The twelve-foot ceiling and padded high-backed wooden bench that ran along two walls gave the bistro a European flavor, while the marble fireplace, crisp white linen and mismatched wooden chairs lent the room a funky elegance. A huge vase of fresh flowers sat at one end of the polished mahogany bar. The only jarring note was the expanse of bare gray walls devoid of decoration.

A woman with shoulder-length auburn hair and a lean swarthy man with a shaved head were setting the tables with cloth napkins, cutlery and wineglasses. They must be the waitstaff. Ally recognized the woman as Julie

Marsden, a school friend of Melissa's. "Hi, Julie," she called out. "Is Ben here?"

"Hi, Ally. He's in the kitchen." Julie gestured to a short hallway to the left and behind the bar. "Go through."

"Thanks." Ally went in the direction Julie had indicated and found herself in the serving area of the kitchen. Heat radiated from the bank of ovens in the center of the room. A short man with wiry red hair was cursing at a spotty-faced youth, and a young woman with wispy blond hair was mixing what looked like cake batter in an enormous stainless steel bowl.

Ben was shaping dough into mini cob loaves, cutting off even-sized lumps with a pastry knife and rolling them into smooth balls between his palms. Ally found herself mesmerized by the sensual movements of his scarred hands. Her gaze followed his fingers up forearms taut with muscle and sinew to broad shoulders, to his full mouth, strong nose and forehead frowning in concentration.

No one had heard her come in over the

sound of the music. She cleared her throat. "Ahem."

Ben glanced up and his expression lightened. "I was just thinking about you."

Ally looked at the mound of creamy dough in his hand and couldn't help but blush. "Can we talk?"

"Sure. Just give me a minute to finish this." With speed and dexterity he shaped the remaining loaves and placed them on flat pans to proof. Moving to the sink, Ben washed his hands with soap and hot water and dried them on the towel tucked into the waistband of his apron. "Let's go into the dining room."

Ally followed him out to the bar and hoisted herself onto a stool.

"Brandy?" Ben asked innocently.

Ally shuddered. "No, thanks—" she began, then noticed his grin. Her lips tightened in disapproval and she drew herself upright. "I have a place for you and Danny to live. It's a house, not a cottage, but there's no fixed-term lease."

"When can we move in?" Ben picked up a swizzle stick from a glass container and twirled it between his fingers.

"Right away, but there's a catch," she added. "You'd have to share. You see, it's my house. I live there, too."

"I don't know…"

"There are three bedrooms," she added hurriedly. "We don't have to share in *that* sense."

The swizzle stick snapped between his fingers.

Shut up, Ally. Shutupshutupshutup—

"This is the first time Danny's lived with me since my divorce five years ago," Ben explained. "I was planning on it being just me and him."

"I understand." She'd scared him off with her crazy talk about sharing. Gathering up her purse she prepared to leave. "I'll see what else I can find for you."

"On the other hand." Ben flashed her an easy grin, "I'm flexible."

Ally gave him a strained smile. "Have a look and then decide. I can take you there now."

"Great. I'll just let Gord know I'm going." Ben slid off the stool and headed for the kitchen, untying his apron as he went.

Ally picked up the broken pieces of the

swizzle stick and found a rubbish bin on the other side of the bar to dispose of them. Behind the counter little metal containers of green olives, cocktail onions and maraschino cherries were neatly lined up in the drink mixing area. The olives were just a touch out of alignment so she nudged the container into place.

Hearing footsteps behind her she turned. Ben was back with Danny in tow. The boy regarded her warily. She guessed she couldn't blame him. "Hi, Danny."

Danny said nothing until Ben nudged him. "Hi."

She wanted to tell him she wasn't really a dipsomaniac but felt it beneath her dignity to explain herself to a twelve-year-old. Besides, if they moved in with her the boy would soon see how upright and responsible she was.

Ben followed her in his battered blue utility truck and parked behind her in the driveway. He got out and turned slowly, taking in the view of the town and the distant hills. "This is fantastic."

Ally was used to it but she knew what he meant. His prediction about the clouds burning off had come true. The rain had washed the air clean and every leaf and blade of grass was etched against the brilliant blue. The air was fragrant with jasmine growing over the back fence.

She hurried him inside before the wind changed and he got a whiff of the farm on the other side of the hill. She didn't mind the smell of cows and horses but Ben was from Melbourne and if she'd learned anything from renting out cottages, it was that most city people could only handle the country in small, sanitized doses.

"Nice house," Ben said, gazing around at the saffron walls with the triptych of moody clouds-at-sunset photos, the overstuffed maroon sofa covered in pink and persimmon silk cushions and the orange tulips in a glass vase on the walnut coffee table. Ally especially loved this room at the end of the day when it glowed with the sinking sun.

"The bedrooms are this way," she said, leading them down the hall. Every room had a different theme color, tied together by glossy white trim. Ben's room, painted a warm cobalt-blue, contained a double bed and not much else besides a chest of drawers and a chair. Ally threw the curtains back on the north-facing window and the room was flooded with natural light.

"I like this," Ben said, nodding.

"Danny can sleep in here," she said, leading them across the hall to the study. It was the most utilitarian room in the house because she'd shared it with George. She was annoyed to see that although her ex was gone his things weren't. "There's a single bed under all those binders and the rest of this will go," she said waving at the filing cabinets and bookshelves. "Well, the computer is mine but I can put it in my room."

"I don't mind if you leave it here," Danny piped up.

"Why would you want it?" Ben said. "You've got one."

"I can network the two and play games against myself." Danny's bright blue eyes glazed over at the thought. "I've always wanted to do that."

"We're not talking chess, are we?" Ben asked.

"Search and Destroy," Danny said enthusiastically. "Command and Conquer. Gory and Gorier."

"I'll move the computer into my room," Ally said, settling the matter. "Excuse me a moment. I need to make a phone call."

While Ben and Danny moved on to the bathroom Ally called George's mobile and got his message bank. "I'm renting the spare bedrooms so you need to move your things out," she said. "Today."

She snapped the phone shut with a smile. That felt good. Draconian but good. Exhilarating, even.

When she got back to the others she found Ben inspecting the plastic trays in which she stored her bits and pieces, each neatly labeled; first aid, hair accessories, makeup, etceteras.

"Very organized," Ben observed.

"I have more of these trays," Ally told him. "You and Danny can have your own."

Ben exchanged a glance with his son then smiled at Ally. "That won't be necessary."

"It's no trouble at all," she assured him.

"Can we see the backyard?" Ben asked.

She'd been hoping he wouldn't ask that but she headed down the hall to the kitchen and the sliding doors that led onto the back deck. "Right this way."

Put mildly, the yard was a shambles. Oh, it was big enough, huge, in fact. There was a large grassy area, some shade trees, an old veggie garden she'd never gotten around to cultivating and a tumbled- down shed. The lawn hadn't been mowed in weeks—okay, months. The weeds were waist-high and just thinking about what might be lurking in the heap of rusted metal and wood scraps tossed in one of the back corners made her shudder.

Ben was entranced. He didn't even seem to mind the barnyard odors now wafting their way. He strode over every inch of turf making excited noises. Ally followed, treading heavily to frighten away snakes.

"You could grow anything in this soil—herbs, veggies, anything." He dug into the dirt and watched it sift through his long fingers like gold dust. Shaking off the remaining particles he strode over to the derelict shed. Ally had stored gardening tools there until she'd encountered a redback spider. After that she'd erected a new pre-fab shed.

Ben seemed to think the old shed was still good for something. "With a little work we could convert this to a chicken coop."

"Chickens?" Ally said dubiously.

"Fresh free-range eggs," Ben said, already in chef nirvana. "What do you think, Danny? Shall we live here?"

Danny shrugged. "It beats the apartment."

"We'll move in today," Ben said to Ally. "If you're sure you want us, that is. Maybe you'll reconcile with your fiancé."

"No chance," she said firmly. "Today, it is."

Ben and Danny went away and returned that afternoon, the back of the ute loaded with suitcases and boxes. The furniture belonged to the apartment, which was just as well since Ally didn't have room for it. What Ben did have a lot of was kitchen gadgets.

There was a pasta maker, espresso machine, commercial juicer, industrial-strength electric mixer and what looked like a nuclear-powered food processor. Then there were copper-bottom saucepans, heavy-gauge roasting pans, Italian casserole dishes, French cast-iron grill pans, stainless-steel mixing bowls—the largest of which Ally swore she could have taken a bath in.

While they were unloading the ute George showed up. He didn't look happy when he saw Ben and Danny. Ally wasn't happy that George hadn't brought a truck. She met him on the veranda. "You're supposed to be moving your stuff out."

Ignoring her, George jerked a thumb over his shoulder. "Who are they?"

"My new tenants, Ben and Danny." Ally shifted impatiently. "I need you to move those filing cabinets."

"I'm not moving the cabinets," George said, his jaw jutting forward.

She used to think his stubbornness showed strength of character but now she saw he was merely inflexible. "Then why are you here?"

"Excuse me." Ben edged past them up the steps, carrying two heavy suitcases in each hand. Ally's gaze followed him. All that whipping and beating certainly put muscles on a man.

"Yesterday morning you wanted to talk,"

George said, forcing her attention back to him. "I'm here to talk."

Ally stared. He was serious. "It's an expression, George. It means, *I'm breaking up with you.*"

"Why?" He saw her gaze stray back to Ben and a knowing expression lit his nearsighted eyes. "Oh, I get it. I've been feeling guilty about having an affair and here you've been having it off with the cook all along."

"Shh," she hissed as Danny, carrying a huge cardboard box that blocked his vision, felt his way up the steps.

Danny paused and rested his box on his bent knee to say to George, "Don't let him hear you call him a cook. He'll go after you with his cleaver."

"You're having sex with a maniac!" George grated under his breath.

"He's not a maniac!" Ally said. "You call yourself a psychiatrist? You can't even tell when a boy is making a joke. I am not having sex with Ben. I only met him yesterday."

At the top of the stairs Danny turned. "I wasn't joking. He's a chef, not a cook."

"Yesterday!" George dragged her to the

other side of the veranda, out of Ben and Danny's earshot. "Yesterday you were going to marry me. I know you still love me," he said. "You're upset over Kathy and now you're acting out. I don't blame you. But I'm telling you, she's nothing to me. I'll stop seeing her. In fact, I'll fire her."

Ally couldn't believe what she was hearing. Was this what he imagined would appease her? If possible, George sank even lower in her estimation. "Don't you dare fire her. Not even Kathy deserves that kind of treatment. Look, George, I don't want to fight. I just want you to get your things and get out of my life."

"Where do you expect me to go?"

"If Kathy won't have you, the apartment over Mangos restaurant has recently been vacated."

"Can't we talk this over?" he pleaded. "Things are happening too fast."

Events *were* unfolding quickly. After living in slow motion for the past year the current pace of her life was a bit unnerving. But now that she'd involved Ben and Danny she couldn't turn back. "There's nothing to discuss," she said. "You're moving out."

"Are we still going to your parents' anniversary party?" He was starting to whine.

"I'm going—you're not." Arms crossed, she waited for the light to dawn on him that he was no longer welcome around her house.

Still he wouldn't leave. "Did you type up my speech to the psychiatry symposium?" he asked sullenly.

"You know, George, you're really making this easy for me." She turned him and pointed him in the direction of his Mercedes with a little shove. "I'll give you until the middle of next week to get your things. After that, I'm calling the Salvation Army."

Back stiff, George stomped down the gravel driveway past the ute, casting Ben a vile glance on the way.

Ben responded with a cheery smile. "Stop in at the restaurant sometime."

"Wait!" Ally said, running after George. "Your key."

As he painstakingly wound the front door key off a spiral metal ring she almost felt sorry for him. Then she remembered Kathy's panties on her pillow. Six months he'd been cheating on her—every Friday afternoon.

Ally turned straight around and held out the key to Ben. Keeping a tight grip on it, she said, "We should have a probation period. Say, three months."

"Fair enough," Ben said, grinning. "Who knows? We might drive each other mad."

Madness with Ben was looking better than sanity with George. Ally released her grip on the key and let it fall into Ben's palm. The deal was done.

Ally left Ben and Danny to settle in and drove the few miles out of town to her parents' home to try to talk sense into her father. Heronwood, a two-story Victorian on a couple of acres, was a monument to Cheryl's good taste, filled with artwork, fresh flowers and antiques.

Ally found Tony in the kitchen where the afternoon sun softened the white tiles with a golden glow and warmed the touch of Delft blue in the ceramic canisters and the frame on the picture hanging over the breakfast table.

Tony was seated at the table dressed in baggy rustic pants and an open-necked shirt with a red scarf knotted around his neck.

With his dark hair tinged with silver and his handsome face he looked like an Italian heartthrob playing a noble peasant.

"Ally!" he said. "Just the person I wanted to see. I'm conducting a tasting of extra virgin olive oil from my grove. Try some."

Lined up in front of him were five slender, dark green bottles. Beside each bottle was a shot glass one quarter full of viscous greeny-gold liquid.

Ally approached warily and sat down opposite her father. Maybe things weren't as bad as Cheryl had made out. "You mean the grove is actually producing?"

"Of course it's producing. This oil is from last year's harvest, which netted eight tons of olives. We're expecting even more this year."

"Did you buy the whole farm? Wouldn't that cost a lot?" She swirled the shot glass and sniffed. It smelled like olive oil.

"I bought a controlling share and the owner stayed on as manager. We've got twelve-hundred established trees of various strains of oil-producing olives plus five hundred kalamata saplings planted this year," he said. "Did you know that olive oil is what the

Greeks called 'nectar of the gods?' Go on, taste it."

Drink oil? She'd as soon mainline peanut butter. "About you and Mother—"

"Your mother will come home when she's over this snit she's in," Tony said. "Go on, try it."

"This is more than a snit. She feels betrayed," Ally said. "She could lose her gallery if this olive grove goes belly-up. Why did the owner sell if oil is so profitable?"

"I'm doing this for us," Tony said, ignoring her question. "For your mother and I. The olive grove is our nest egg, our retirement fund."

"You said that about the hydroponic tomato growing operation and before that, the Indonesian furniture import business. You never admit the possibility of failure until the bailiff is knocking at the door." Ally sighed at the futility of reminding him of the past. "If you would just talk to her."

"Go on, take a sip. It's liquid gold. Tears of Italian virgins pining for lost loves."

Ally swirled the oil in her tiny glass, putting off the awful moment as long as she could. One glug and it'd be gone, but she couldn't seem to bring herself to do it.

"We've got the Mediterranean climate and all the space you could ask for to grow olive trees," Tony expanded. "We'll beat the Italians and Spaniards at their own game, not to mention the Californians."

"How are you going to irrigate, Dad? That land along the Murray is dry as a dead dingo's you-know-what if you don't have a water lease."

"Donger," Tony supplied. "Dry as a dead dingo's donger. If you're going to use an expression you might as well say it, Ally. Get earthy. We're people of the land now."

"*I'm* a person of the town and you're evading the issue."

"Naturally I have the water problem all figured out," Tony blustered.

"Tell me." Ally held up the shot glass, demanding he convince her before she tasted.

"Why do you think I was able to buy into the grove at a bargain-basement price?" he said. "The government is taking water out of irrigation licenses for environmental flows to save the river red gums. The newest licensees lost out, including my olive grove. But there are organizations that broker water. It's possible to buy and sell megalitres of Murray irrigation water, almost like the stock market. I'm on the Internet daily, searching out the best deal. It won't be a problem, you'll see."

"Mother seems to think it's a problem," Ally said. "What if you can buy water one month and not the next?"

"I'm on a waiting list for a permanent irrigation license. Getting it is only a matter of time. Meanwhile, I can access all the water I need in temporary sales. It'll happen, Ally," he said, eyes bright, smile gleaming. "You have to have faith in the big picture."

Just for a moment she did. Tony had an enormous zest for life that she envied and admired. He radiated a confidence that had convinced many a gullible soul before her to believe in him. His secret to swaying people was that *he* believed whatever plan he was hatching was the best plan in the history of the world. Or at least in the history of Tipperary Springs.

On the other hand, their family had suffered in the past for his pie-in-the-sky schemes. Her nanna had paid the ultimate price. George had been right about one thing—she had conflicting feelings about her father.

"If you can't guarantee a water supply, how can you guarantee the crop and by extension, the mortgage on her gallery?" Ally demanded.

"It's so simple it's sinful." Tony leaned toward her to whisper, "I'm trading in water futures. I know a fellow in the meteorology department of the Victorian government who's feeding me long-range weather projections." Tony leaned back and smiled. "I stand to make millions."

"Is it legal?" Ally said.

"Now why is that always your first question when I come up with something really groundbreaking?" Tony complained.

"Because so often your schemes are somehow illicit," she replied. "Is this? Allowed, that is?"

"There are no laws against it," Tony hedged. "As far as I know."

"As far as you know," she repeated skeptically. Selling water futures sounded far-fetched, even for Tony—more science fiction than agricultural fact.

"Enough talk." Tony put his hand on hers and lifted the glass to her mouth. "Taste."

Ally put her mouth to the rim and held her nose. She'd do this for Mother, just to find out how far into trouble he was headed. Too many of Tony's plans had ended in spectacular failure, and she had a really bad feeling about this one.

Finally, she tilted the shot glass and the oil slid over her tongue, filled her mouth and oozed down her throat. "Agh! Yuck! Ugh!" Ally slammed the glass onto the table. "I can't believe you made me drink that stuff."

"It's luscious and well-balanced with fruity, grassy flavors and just a hint of citrus," Tony insisted. "At least that's what the tasting notes say." He pushed another glass toward her. "Try this one."

"No way!" Ally got to her feet, swallowing repeatedly to remove the oily taste from her mouth. "I'm leaving."

"Ally! Take a bottle with you. Try it on a salad."

"No, thanks!"

Tony followed her to the door and tried to

push it on her. "You can use it in cooking, dip bread in it."

Ignoring the oil, Ally shook her head, furious. "You better not have screwed up your marriage completely this time. Mother loves you. I know you love her. It's time you got your priorities straight."

"I didn't ask your mother to leave," Tony said. "She'll come back when she's ready, as she always does. Once she sees how rich this olive grove is going to make us she'll be thanking me."

"Should I tell her you want her to come home?" Ally asked. "You do love her, don't you?"

He looked at her as if she was demented. "Of course, I do. Go ahead, tell her she can come back. Anytime. I'd like her to taste these olive oils."

"I don't think she's too keen on anything to do with olives at the moment." Berating him hadn't worked, so Ally tried appealing to reason. "In fact, given what you've been telling me, don't you think you might want to reconsider this whole venture? If you really do love her."

"Ally, I know when I'm onto a good thing. If your mother loves *me,* she'll believe in me and what I'm doing." Tony swung the knot in his scarf to one side and managed to look even more like Marcello Mastroianni. "*Cara mio,* take the olive oil. That's my girl."

Ally refused to be charmed but she knew he'd be after her until she complied. Grabbing the bottle out of his hand she stomped off to her car.

"Mother's staying at Melissa's," she called to Tony. "If you want her back I suggest you bring her chocolates, not olive oil."

CHAPTER FIVE

POOR ALLY, Ben thought as he unpacked his suitcase and stowed his clothes in the chest of drawers and closet. She must be going through a tough time having her heart broken like that. After George had left she'd taken off, too, her face a picture of trouble and woe. The only cheery note about her was the fluoro pink and green ladybug pinned to her blouse.

Ben got Danny to help him move George's filing cabinet and boxes of binders onto the wide, covered front veranda. What Ally needed was something to take her mind off her broken engagement. Women liked chocolate, he knew, especially when they were down. "Hey, Danno, how about helping me bake a cake for Ally?"

"I want to put my computer together,"

Danny replied. "Anyway, you said we'd go swimming."

"It's too late for swimming now, and you can put your computer together later," Ben said. "We could whip up a chocolate torte before I have to go to work."

Danny groaned. "Cooking is so *gay*."

"It is not!" Ben protested. "Not that I have anything against being gay—"

"It's an expression, Dad."

"The point is, I'd really like you to spend some time with me."

Danny heaved a sigh and rolled his eyes and hung his head, the picture of misery. "Do I *have* to?"

"I know it's torture but yes, you do," Ben said. "If you don't want to cook, we can go out back and throw the football around."

Once outside Danny was no more enthusiastic. "I'm not going in that grass. There might be snakes. I saw Ally stomping around this morning, trying to scare them away."

"I suspect Ally was just being cautious. Snakes are more afraid of you than you are of them."

"I doubt it," Danny said, immovable.

"You're in the country, now. You have to learn to get along with snakes." Ben waded into the long grass, trying to look fearless.

"You don't get along with snakes," Danny replied. "They bite you and you die."

"You've never heard of antivenin?"

Danny crossed his arms over his chest, jaw set.

"Okay," Ben said, giving up. "We'll mow the lawn."

Easier said than done.

He opened the door on the prefab garden shed. A wobbling stack of what seemed like five hundred empty plant pots fell on his head. Undeterred, he battled on, having glimpsed the mower buried behind a wheelbarrow, a shovel, a rake and a hoe, all of which conspired to either smack him in the forehead or fall on his toes as he was pulling them out. Finally, he wheeled the mower onto the grass, only to discover the fuel tank was empty. Danny sat glumly on the veranda, head propped in his hands, while Ben siphoned petrol out of his ute into an old fizzy drink container, then used his good kitchen funnel to transfer it into the tank. After about a thousand pulls of the starter cord he got the motor running.

"Here we go, Danny," Ben said, grimly cheerful. "We'll be playing footy in no time." He rammed the mower into the thick bed of tall grass.

Phut. The engine died. Ben patiently started it again, only taking eight hundred pulls this time. With cautious jabs he nibbled at the edge of the grass with the mower. So far, so good. He pushed farther in—*phut.*

Ben let loose a string of expletives.

"Mum said you're not supposed to swear around me," Danny called from the veranda.

Ignoring his son, Ben took hold of the starter cord and began to haul on it for the third time. On about the sixty-fifth pull, when his shoulder was screaming with pain, Danny called out again. "It's five o'clock."

Perfect. He had to go to work.

"Can I put my computer together now?" Danny asked, already halfway inside the screen door.

"No," Ben said. "You're going to have to put all this stuff away for me."

Danny groaned. "Thanks for the quality time, Dad."

THE MOMENT Ally got home she tossed Tony's bottle of olive oil into the rubbish bin between the stove and the fridge. Good riddance.

Then she looked around at all the appliances cluttering up her once tidy kitchen and her heart sank. Ben had had two hours to put things away and he'd done nothing. It wasn't that she didn't appreciate the contribution an electric garlic press would make to her home, but she needed orderliness. And peace. From down the hall she could hear Danny blazing away at the enemy with bazookas and flame throwers.

Saturday night dinner was Leftover Night. But she didn't have leftovers because she hadn't been home last night to cook. Nor did she have a contingency plan. Ally opened the fridge door and stared at the contents, hoping inspiration would strike.

All she could think about was where she was going to get another job. There was another cottage rental agency in town, or maybe she could try for a position at the hotel.

"You're letting the cold air out," Danny said behind her.

Ally jumped. How long had she been

standing there, communing with the lettuce and cheese? "Are you hungry?"

"Dad said to come to the restaurant and he'd feed us."

After the stresses and strains of last night and today all she felt like doing was curling up in front of the TV. "Would you mind if I didn't go?"

"I don't mind. Can I stay here, too?" Danny asked. "I get a little tired of garlic prawns and foie gras."

"Sure," Ally said. "Call your dad and let him know we won't be there. I'll make dinner."

She couldn't compete with a chef, so she decided to make what she felt like—comfort food. They ate tuna casserole with crushed potato chips on top while curled up at either end of the couch watching an American sitcom.

"How come the Americans call this room a 'living' room and we call it a 'lounge' room?" Danny asked during a commercial break. "Which one's right?"

"They're both right," Ally said. "Depending on where you live."

Danny's brow wrinkled as he thought

about that for a minute. "I reckon we're *more* right. You 'live' in every room—unless it's a funeral home and you're the corpse—but the room with the comfy furniture is where you 'lounge' around."

"Maybe *some* people lounge around," Ally teased. Smiling, she tossed a cushion at Danny who ducked and grinned. Then she rose to take their plates.

Danny grabbed at the cushion, his eyes brightening. "Can we have a pillow fight?"

"No," she said, and yawned. "I'm going to bed."

"Thanks for dinner. That was yummy," Danny said. "I'm going to stay up and watch a movie. Don't worry, it's one I've seen before with my dad."

Ally fell asleep quickly then woke a few hours later, her mind churning, wondering alternately whether she and Ben would get along at all or whether they would get along *too* well. Ben had a casual charm, a sexy confidence that made her think women rarely said no to him. What if he took it for granted that room and board included sex along with gas and electricity? Had she leaped out of the frying pan and into the pressure cooker, so to speak?

Would that be so bad? She let her imagination run rampant and the mental images got her so hot she threw off the covers. But while the fantasy of making love with Ben held some appeal, she felt instinctively it would be a mistake to take up with him on the rebound. She needed to figure out where she kept going wrong with men before she embarked on another romance. Engaging in sex without love would cloud her judgment and delay finding Mr. Right. She was too old to waste time on Mr. Right Now. Someday she might settle for Mr. Whatever, but she didn't think so. Dogs were probably more affectionate and definitely more loyal.

The digital clock on the nightstand read one-thirty by the time she heard the front door open. She lay rigid in her bed like a spinster schoolmarm while Ben crept past her room and opened Danny's door to check on him. Straining her ears, Ally heard Ben return to the lounge room and the soft creak of the couch springs. She had to go talk to him and clear the air or she'd never get to sleep.

First she brushed her hair and tied it back in a ponytail. Out of habit, she started to pick up her lipstick, then hastily put it down. Makeup at this hour would look too odd. Her nightie became transparent under certain light conditions so she put on her wool dressing gown, even though the night was warm. And in case he was turned on by a shapely ankle, she slipped her feet into a pair of Ugg boots. Sweating from heat and nervousness, she made her way down the hall.

A single table lamp glowed behind his head and he was leaning back against the cushions, one bare foot resting on the coffee table, a beer bottle in hand. His hair was damp with perspiration and sticking up and his T-shirt was stretched across his chest. When he saw her he straightened. "Hope I didn't wake you. Want a beer?"

"No, thank you." She sat on the extreme end of the couch, conscious of the late hour, the darkness and his long fingers wrapped around the bottle. Now that she was here, what she'd planned to say seemed presumptuous. "How did it go at the restaurant tonight?"

"Full house. Was Danny okay? I hope you didn't think I expected you to babysit. He's old enough to stay on his own. God knows, he did it all the time at his mother's."

"Danny was fine." She wasn't, though. She was boiling in her heavy robe and the wool was making her eczema itch. "It's a warm night." She loosened the belt and pulled the lapel away from her shoulders. Ben's eyebrows rose fractionally and his eyes seemed to take on a gleam. Uh-oh. He might not have been thinking anything before but now he was, she could swear it.

"I made you something," Ben said. "I was going to save it for tomorrow but since you're up…" He rose and went out to the kitchen, leaving Ally sitting on her own.

A moment later Ben was handing her a fork and an entire chocolate tart topped with whipped cream. "This is a thank you for taking me and Danny in, and commiseration for your breakup."

"You shouldn't have," Ally said, wondering if you had to count kilojoules eaten in the middle of the night.

"Dig in," he urged. "Go on."

"Maybe just a sliver." Carefully she began cutting a section from the crust so as not to break up the dark silky surface any more than she had to.

Ben grabbed the fork from her and jabbed it straight into the middle of the tart. Ally opened her mouth to protest and he filled it with chocolate and cream.

"Mmm," she moaned, unable to speak. "Oh, oh… *Oh!* This is…this is…you-know-what."

"Orgasmic?" Ben supplied. He held out another forkful.

"Wait! I'm going to end up with it on my dressing gown." She slipped her robe off her shoulders and pushed it aside, trying to ignore the way her breasts pressed against the thin fabric of her nightie and the way Ben's gaze drifted downward. If he attacked her now it would be her mother's fault. Only Cheryl would buy her a designer dressing gown that needed dry cleaning.

"I can feed myself," she insisted, trying unsuccessfully to take back the fork.

"Nope. You'd eat a dainty tidbit and chew it twenty times. What you need is to wallow. Open up."

She obeyed, and he gave her a second heaping forkful. Her eyes closed as the rich chocolate flavor and velvety texture traveled a direct path to the pleasure center of her brain. Unable to help herself, she moaned aloud.

"Look out, a bit dropped on you." Hands full with the pan and the fork Ben nodded to a creamy morsel above her right breast.

Ally glanced down at herself, half-naked and flushed with heat, and at him, all broad shoulders and tousled hair, leaning toward her. She wiped the chocolate off her skin. Good grief, where was this heading?

Abruptly, Ben put the chocolate tart on the coffee table. "Ally, since we're going to be living under the same roof there's something I ought to tell you."

He had insatiable appetites and needed sex five times a day. He was into bondage and whipped cream—

"I'm not interested in getting involved with anyone."

Ally felt a chill despite the warm night. Did he think she was coming on to him, and was he rejecting her before she got any more carried away? How humiliating. She drew her dressing gown back over her shoulders and pulled it tight.

"Good," she said. "Because frankly I'm a little vulnerable right now." Vulnerable like a Sherman tank. Since she'd gotten rid of George she'd felt invincible.

"I know and I don't blame you," he said. "I'm not one to take advantage of a situation. What kind of guy would move in and immediately start hitting on his landlady?"

A guy with really gorgeous green eyes might get away with it, she thought wistfully.

"I need to concentrate one hundred percent on Danny," Ben went on. "I've wanted custody for years and this is my chance to have a real relationship with him and to prove to my ex-wife that I can be a good dad."

"Haven't you had access before now?" Ally asked.

"Oh, sure. I lived nearby and saw him all the time. Carolyn never made any difficulties about that. But we don't communicate. I don't want to just go to movies on the weekend or see him for a few hours at a time. I want to be a real dad, take him to soccer practice, help him with his homework and just hang out talking guy stuff."

"I understand." He wasn't interested in her as a woman. Fine. No, *good*. She wasn't ready for that anyway. She hadn't had time to sort out her problems and Ben sure didn't fit the profile of her perfect man. "I should go back to bed. Thanks for making me a tart."

Then, blushing furiously, she muttered a hasty good-night and scurried back to her room.

Ben clamped a hand over his mouth to keep from laughing, but he sobered quickly. That had been a bit too close, he thought, recalling how tempted he'd been to lick the chocolate off her breast. Thank goodness he'd restrained himself. His focus was on Danny and only Danny.

Ally had surprised him, though. Nobody who enjoyed the pleasure of taste that much could fail to savor the other senses. Was it possible that somewhere beneath her prim and earnest exterior lurked a sensuous woman?

MONDAY MORNING Ally woke up at 6:58, as usual, two minutes before the alarm. She used those two minutes to stretch out spread-eagled in her queen-size bed, savoring George's absence. The second before the first warning beep, her hand shot out and hit the button. Sleepily, she rose, put on her white blouse and gray skirt and pinned an iridescent blue sailboat to her chest. She left her room quietly, glancing at the two shut doors in the hallway. It felt strange to have other people sleeping in her house.

In the bathroom she reached for her hairbrush, only to find she'd picked up Ben's electric shaver. She looked at the counter in dismay. Danny's toothbrush wasn't in the toothbrush holder and neither of her new tenants had used the containers for personal items she'd left out for them. She was probably being anal again but honestly, life was so much easier when people followed simple rules of organization.

Monday was Egg Day. Moving about the kitchen on autopilot, she reached into the cupboard to the right of the sink for the small pot she used to boil eggs. The pot wasn't there. Eventually she found it in the cupboard beside the stove, but not before she'd lost five minutes searching. Not being a morning person, she needed to have everything in its proper place. A routine helped immensely when it came to getting to work on time. And she particularly wanted to get to the office early today because—

Wait a minute. She wasn't going to the office. She'd been fired. A wave of panic threatened to overwhelm her. How could she have forgotten she no longer had a job?

Abandoning her boiled egg she went to the lounge room to stand before the barometer. The needle rested on Change. Tap, tap. The needle didn't move. Her mouth pursed as she frowned. Tap, tap. The barometer was definitely stuck on Change. Well, that was no good. She'd had enough change, thank you very much. Fair would be good. Even Rain would be preferable.

After another tap, Ally, completely unnerved, gave up and went back to the kitchen. She sat down at the table and stared unseeingly at Ben's kitchen gadgets that still hadn't found a home in her cupboards.

It was hardly surprising her mind couldn't function when her surroundings were in chaos. Her barometer was broken. She had no work to go to. She had no compelling reason to have breakfast. She could go back to bed and stay there all day if she wanted to. No job, no fiancé, no life. What was the point of anything?

"Good morning," Ben said, coming into the room. "What's for breakfast?"

"It's Egg Day," she said in a monotone, not giving a rat's you-know-what. "Boiled, poached, fried, scrambled, whatever."

"You've mentioned that before. What *is* Egg Day?" he asked, opening the fridge to look inside. "Some sort of local custom?"

"It's my personal system to reduce choles- terol and increase dietary fiber. It's not in the lease agreement or anything so as a tenant you're not obliged to participate."

"That's okay. I could go for some eggs." He got out a frying pan and a carton of eggs, a mixing bowl and chopping board.

"I'll do it," Ally protested, but he waved her away.

"Make coffee. I'm no good until I've had an espresso."

"You want me to make espresso?" she said. "I don't have a machine."

"Over there, behind the rice cooker," he said, nodding toward a stack of small appliance boxes.

"Do you really use all these appliances?"

"Most of them were gifts from friends," Ben said, cracking eggs one-handed into a mixing bowl while he reached for a whisk with the other hand. "What do you give a chef for Christmas? Anything to do with food, apparently. They never think I might like a set of golf clubs or a fishing rod, something to take me *away* from work for a change."

"It's too bad one of your friends didn't give you a barometer," she said. "I think mine's broken."

"Why, what's wrong?" he asked.

"I tapped it this morning and the needle didn't even flicker. Usually there's at least a tiny movement."

"That's probably because I already tapped it," Ben said casually as he chopped parsley. "I woke up early, came out for a glass of water, tapped the barometer and went back to bed."

"You already tapped it!" Ally exclaimed. "You can't do that. It's *my* barometer. *I'm* the tapper. Do you have any idea of the havoc you've created?"

Ben went very still, as one does when confronted by a dangerous beast or the criminally insane. "I just tapped."

"You've upset my whole routine," she yelled. "The bathroom, the pots, now the barometer. *You're not allowed to tap!*"

"Okay!" He threw up his hands. "I'll never tap again."

"Thank you." Ally put her head in her hands. What had she gotten herself into?

"Er, are you still going to make coffee?" Ben reminded her cautiously.

"Of course," she said with dignity. Did he

JOAN KILBY 121

think she would forget her obligations?
Honestly.

By the time she had the espresso machine
set up and plugged in, with water in the res-
ervoir and coffee in the holder, and was
reading the manual for the fourth time, Ben
had made the perfect omelet.

Golden brown, it was fragrant with fresh
herbs and butter, oozing cheese and mushrooms and crisscrossed with crisp strips of
pancetta. Beside it on the plate were two
thick pieces of sourdough bread, grilled, not
toasted, and dripping with real butter.

"Wow, this is great," Ally said, her mouth
watering. She felt bad now for yelling at
him. "A person could gain weight just
looking at this."

"Don't you want it?" Ben's hand hovered,
ready to take away the offending plate.

Ally gripped her fork, prepared to stab his
wrist if he tried to remove so much as a
mushroom. "No, it's fine."

"By the way, where'd the olive oil come
from?" Ben asked, sitting down with his own
plate.

"Mfph?" Ally mumbled, her mouth full, eyes closed with bliss.

"The olive oil?" Ben repeated, pushing across the bottle Tony had given her. The seal was broken and the level had dropped.

Ally opened her eyes and focused. "Where did you get that?"

"I found it in the rubbish bin yesterday. You must have thrown it out by mistake."

"I did it on purpose. It's terrible."

"It's premium quality extra virgin," Ben said. "There's a handwritten label, but all it says is 'koroneki,' which is a type of olive. Is it from around here? I'd love to get my hands on more."

He liked Tony's oil. Obviously she knew nothing about olives if she couldn't tell premium quality from motor oil. Maybe there really was a market for the stuff. Maybe Tony was onto something big. Cheryl's gallery would be saved and he'd make a fortune.

But wait, she was forgetting. This was Tony. Supply wasn't guaranteed. She winced at the thought of Tony convincing Ben to buy dozens of cases for the restaurant then being unable to deliver. Too embarrassing.

"Fly-by-night operator," she said, waving a hand dismissively. "Not worth your time."

"WHERE'S MOTHER?" Ally breezed into Melissa's lounge room then stopped short. A lithe, muscular man in an iridescent green leotard was standing on his head in the corner where a potted corn silk plant used to be.

Melissa was draped over a chintz-covered love seat in front of the fireplace, looking like a lingerie model but for the large bandage on her right thumb. She waved her cup of tea in the green man's direction. "Ally, this is Julio. He's from Argentina."

"Buenos días," Julio said with an upside-down smile.

"Er, hi," Ally replied, tilting her head sideways. She straightened and looked at Melissa's heavily bandaged thumb. "What happened to you?"

"Sliver." Melissa shuddered. "I can't look at it."

"Is it infected?" Ally asked, sitting beside her on the couch. "That could be bad." Not the wound but the huge fuss her sister would make.

"No," Melissa admitted reluctantly. "But it's red and swollen. Do you think I have blood poisoning?"

Taking Melissa's fears seriously usually saved time in the long run, so Ally grasped her sister by the wrist and inspected her inner forearm. "There are no red streaks running up the skin. I think you're safe for now."

"Were you looking for Mother? She's around somewhere," Melissa said.

Cheryl's presence was evident; she'd replaced Melissa's ceramic cow collection with an abstract rusted iron sculpture and brought in an area rug with a geometric design to cover Mel's stained carpet. The area rug was actually quite nice but Ally missed the cows.

"I'm here," Cheryl announced, coming into the room and greeting Ally with a kiss on the cheek. She had on a black sleeveless top and a black and white skirt.

"Tony's pining for you," Ally said. "He begged me to ask you to come home."

"I doubt he's even noticed I'm gone," Cheryl said, sniffing. "That man takes me for granted, thinks he can do anything and I'll forgive him endlessly. Well, I've had enough. If he's willing to risk losing me over some stupid olive grove then I can live without him."

"Apparently Tony's oil is phenomenal," Ally said. "He should have no trouble selling his product."

"Has he actually sold any yet?"

"Not that I know of," Ally replied guiltily. "Mel, help me here!"

"You could at least wait to leave him until after your anniversary party, Mother," Melissa said languidly. "Ally's gone to a lot of trouble organizing it."

"I'm not going home until the mortgage has been repaid and the gallery signed over to me." Cheryl pushed her pale blond hair off her forehead and glanced around at the cozy room. "Melissa, darling, have you thought about knocking out that wall and extending? French doors leading onto a patio would change this room completely."

"I know, so don't even think it," Melissa said.

"I'm not talking about the party," Ally said. Although it *was* a consideration. That was *her* signature on the deposit for the spit roast and the marquee. "I'm talking about thirty years of love and commitment. Sure, Tony's made mistakes, but you always told me marriage requires work."

"If marriage is work, I need a vacation," Cheryl declared. "On our latest bank statement twelve- hundred dollars was deducted for the month of January as payment on the second mortgage. I'm lucky if I clear that much a month during the summer tourist season. What's going to happen during winter?" She shook her head. "We can still have a party but we'll call it a divorce celebration."

"That's not what it's going to say on the cake," Ally protested.

"Maybe Ben would be interested in buying Tony's oil," Melissa interjected thoughtfully. "Ally could sleep with him as an enticement."

"I am not going to prostitute myself for olive oil," Ally said. Not even if she had a choice in the matter.

"Too bad, Ben is hot." Mel picked at her bandage, then added, "I saw George in the supermarket. He droned on for fifteen minutes about what a mistake you made in throwing him out and made me promise to put in a good word for him. So here goes. *Dull*. Dull is a very good word for George. Rigid or set-in-his-ways would also work."

"Dull?" Ally repeated. "Is that what you think of him?" She knew her family hadn't liked George much but she'd thought it was because of his tendency to act superior.

"All your boyfriends have been dull," Melissa said. "Who were they again? I seem to recall an economist."

"Edward," Ally supplied. "Before him I went out with Thomas, a professor of ancient history at the university and before that, Robert, who worked for the government doing—" She broke off, frowning. "I never could figure out exactly what his position entailed but he's been doing it since he left school."

"And will probably continue until the day he retires. They were all dead-boring and without a spark of spontaneity," Melissa declared. "I've never wanted to hurt your feelings but you could do much better."

"They were solidly respectable and financially secure men with whom I had every reason to expect a stable relationship," Ally protested. Except that it turned out she hadn't loved them.

"George wasn't so bad," Cheryl said, clearly forgetting her antipathy toward him in her desire to see the good in anybody besides Tony. "He has nice eyes."

"Bonking Kathy in Ally's bed is the most interesting thing he's done," Melissa insisted.

"Don't talk to me about Kathy," Ally said darkly. "I had to buy new sheets."

Over in the corner Julio's feet rose a few inches; he'd lifted himself off his head and onto his hands. With a polite farewell waggle of his toes he walked out of the room.

"You think you've got it rough," Melissa said, gazing after him. "Julio's leaving for Adelaide in a month. I'm thinking of running away with the circus."

"Don't you dare," Ally said. "We need you here."

"Julio says he could teach me to do that bungee thing they do swinging from the rafters."

"Are you mad? You're afraid of heights!"

Ally picked up her purse. "I've got to go put in job applications."

"When *are* you going to sleep with Ben?" Melissa asked.

"Never, and I mean that. Why does everything come down to sex? Can't a man and a woman just be friends?"

"Sure they can, but the first hot guy you've met in ages moves into your house and you're not even a little bit interested? George's dullness has rubbed off on you. When are you going to learn to listen to your gut? That's what's wrong with the world, not enough people follow their instincts."

"Too many people do," Ally replied. "And *that's* what's wrong with the world."

"Ben could liven things up," Melissa persisted. "Why have him move in if you're not going to take advantage of the situation?"

"Rent money. Nothing more, nothing less," Ally added firmly. "Ben's devoting all his spare time to his son and I'm swearing off men until I can figure out how to tell Mr. Right from Mr. Wrong *before* I get involved."

"Darling," Cheryl said. "If a woman could

tell that, half the therapists and counselors in this country would be out of business."

"Not to mention writers of self-help books," Melissa added.

"Daytime talk show hosts…" Cheryl said.

"Divorce lawyers…"

"Makeover consultants…"

"I'm going now." Ally headed for the door. This could go on for hours.

"Dating services…"

"Sex toy parties…"

"Hire A Handyman…"

"Hire A Handyman?" Melissa repeated. "I wouldn't have thought of that."

Even Ally paused to listen.

"Ruth from the health food shop hired one to fix her fence after her husband ran off with the nanny," Cheryl explained. "Andy, the man's name was. Ruth said he was really… handy."

"Handy Andy," Melissa exclaimed, delighted.

"*Goodbye,*" Ally said, rolling her eyes even as she gave an involuntary smile. "Mother, will you *please* just look in and say hello to Tony?"

Cheryl sighed deeply. "Well, I suppose I should go and see if he's remembering to water the house plants."

CHAPTER SIX

BEN WIPED DOWN his station at the end of a busy Saturday night, listening with only half an ear to the edgy banter among the kitchen crew. In spite of Mangos's instant popularity, the restaurant would soon be in trouble if the maître d' situation wasn't rectified.

Steve went past the kitchen on his way to his office. Ben hailed him. "Julie's finding it tough-going waiting and doing the maître d's job. You need to hire someone."

"I'm already in deep trouble with my wife for letting Cassie quit," Steve said. "I'm trying to negotiate a return to work but it's not going well."

"That's crazy. This is a business," Ben said. A business he had shares in. "My land-lady's looking for a job. She used to manage a cottage booking agency and is highly organized." Was *that* an understatement.

"I'll think about it, but I promised my wife I'd give Cassie a few more days to change her mind," Steve said. "Listen, I have exciting news. I heard a rumor that the restaurant reviewer, I. Lemke, who recently joined the *Good Food Guide,* will be heading our way soon. This is our big chance to win that chef's hat."

"Don't stress over this," Ben warned. "It's not good for you. Or the rest of the staff."

"Stress? I don't stress. What are you talking about?" Steve said, chewing a hangnail. "How's that new scallop dish coming along?"

"I'm, uh, working up some ideas," Ben said. "By the way, I'll need to take tomorrow off to be with Danny. He's not adjusting well to Tipperary Springs."

"Lemke's coming," Steve repeated.

"Any compelling reason to think he'll be coming tomorrow?" Ben asked.

"No," Steve admitted reluctantly.

"Then I'm taking tomorrow off. Monday we're shut and Tuesday's quiet so I won't be back until the dinner service." Ben untied his apron and chucked it onto the pile of dirty linen. Before Steve could argue, he left.

Ben could have slept all the next day but he got up at ten to find Danny watching cartoons and eating sugarcoated crapola. He was about to tell his son to turn off the TV and eat a decent breakfast when through the lounge-room window he spied Ally struggling to unload a giant Whipper Snipper from the roof rack of her car.

"I'll be back in five," Ben said to Danny.

Danny mumbled something unintelligible, and Ben went out the front door in his pajama bottoms and T-shirt. Although it was early the sun was already hot. They were into another five-day cycle of rising temperatures that were so common in summer.

"Let me get that," he called to Ally. "You'll brain yourself."

"I got it up here," Ally puffed. "I can get it down—Whew!" She swung it down from the roof, nearly taking off Ben's head. On the ground the machine was almost as tall as she was and probably weighed as much.

"Do you have a license to operate one of these babies?" Ben asked.

"I rented it from the hardware store. Guaranteed to cope with your basic African savanna." Ally reached back into her car and emerged with goggles, earmuffs, leather gauntlets and shin guards. She put the goggles on and looked at him. "How would you feel about going in front and beating the ground for snakes?"

"When you start that motor up, any self-respecting snake for miles around is going to go bye-bye. Give me a few minutes to have breakfast and I'll cut the backyard."

"Relax. It's your day off." Ally started dragging the Whipper Snipper down the driveway to the rear of the house.

There was no point in arguing, Ben decided. He'd just eat, talk to Danny and go out later. He grabbed a piece of toast and a cup of coffee and plunked himself down in the chair next to his son. "Sorry about yesterday."

Danny shrugged but didn't take his eyes off the screen. "Mum called from Bali last night."

"What did she say?"

"Hi."

"That's all? Just hi? What did *you* say?"

"I told her I'd reached the top level of my new game."

"Danny, will you please look at me when we're talking."

Danny glanced over, crunching on a mouthful of cereal. Drops of milk oozed from the corners of his lips. He blinked as if he'd never seen Ben before and wasn't quite sure who he was. *"What?"*

"Do you want to do something together?"

"Not if it involves the kitchen."

"You wound me, son."

Danny shrugged.

"Ally and I are going to cut the lawn then we'll be able to throw the football around," Ben said.

"Whatever," Danny muttered, and turned back to the TV.

Ben threw his hands up. It was bad enough his child didn't care about learning to cook, but he didn't even want to do traditional father-son activities. Was it already too late for him and Danny to form a real relationship?

Outside, Ally was rigged up in gauntlet and goggles and hauling on the starter cord of the Whipper Snipper. Petrol fumes hung in the air. Ben watched in silence as she struggled, wondering if she was the kind of female who would be offended by an offer of assistance. He'd met them before and frankly, such an encounter wasn't on the top of his list of fun things to do on a Sunday morning.

Finally, she pushed the goggles to the top of her head in exasperation. "D'you think you could give me a hand?"

"No worries. I said I'd do it."

"What about Danny?"

"Danny's busy." Ben gave the cord a sharp yank and the machine roared to life. All that practice with the lawn mower had paid off.

He lowered the cutting edge and waded into the grass, clearing a very satisfying swath as he went.

"Go back and forth in a line toward the back fence," Ally instructed him. "Or you could go up and down in line with the side fence."

Ben didn't mind being told *what* to do but he didn't like being told *how* to do it. Just to be ornery, he walked in vague circles around the yard, mowing a path before him in a random pattern. Through the earmuffs he dimly heard Ally calling to him but if he kept his head down he could pretend he didn't.

Another loop around and he began to forge a path through the last large stand of long grass. Danny had come out of the house and was throwing handfuls of cut grass at the magpies who'd swooped down to pick off exposed insects. Ally stood on the veranda with her hands on her hips, shaking her head.

Without warning, a snake shot out of the grass. Ben saw it in his peripheral vision and spun to see the animal slithering away from him, toward Danny. The snake was a meter long, thick in girth and striped dark brown and golden. Tiger snake. Aggressive and highly venomous.

"Don't move!" Ben shouted.

Danny froze. Ally screamed. Ben charged at the reptile, brandishing the Whipper Snipper. The snake shot between Danny's open legs. Ally screamed again. Ben knocked Danny to the ground as he pushed past in pursuit of the reptile, visions of slicing and dicing the snake into canapé-size pieces dancing in his mind's eye. Just as he was stretching the Whipper Snipper forward the creature slithered beneath the pile of wood scraps and rusted metal.

Ben shut off the motor. The silence was deafening. He helped Danny up and dusted him off. "You all right?"

"I saw where he went," Danny said eagerly. "He's under all that junk. Let's get him."

"I thought you didn't like snakes," Ben said. "What happened to 'they bite you and you die'?"

"That was before I saw one up close." Danny's eyes were shining. "Wait till I tell Mum. That was so cool when you went after it with the Whipper Snipper."

"It was nothing," Ben said modestly. "Although you might not want to mention it to your mother." Then he decided that with his filial approval rating at an all-time high he more or less had to cement his macho image. "I'll see if he's still there."

He'd started toward the junk pile when he realized Ally was jumping up and down on the veranda. "Get away. Get away from the junk," she shrieked hysterically. "You've made it angry. It'll come back out. It'll bring its friends and attack us all."

"I don't think so," Ben said. He was no expert, but nothing he'd ever read about snakes suggested they were vengeful creatures, or even capable of formulating a plan of action. He turned to Danny. "She's a bit upset. Maybe we'd better leave it alone for now. Let it catch its breath."

"Aww," Danny groaned.

Ben walked over to Ally, who was hyperventilating. Even in a heightened state of panic and consternation she was immaculately groomed, not a hair out of place. "Do you have a phobia about snakes?"

"Tiger snakes are deadly," she squawked. "It is *not* unreasonable to be afraid of a poisonous animal."

"Petrified, you mean," Ben said. "Rationalization is a sign of neurosis."

Ally's eyes narrowed in suspicion. "I thought you were a chef." She crossed and uncrossed her arms, then crossed them again. "I do not have a phobia."

"Don't worry," Ben said. "You can overcome this."

"I wouldn't need to overcome anything if you'd cut the grass in a straight line," she pointed out. "The snake would have gone through the back fence into the neighbor's yard."

"Do your neighbors know you have it in for them?" Ben asked.

Ally kept casting anxious glances at the junk pile. "Now I'll spend the rest of my life worrying about when that snake is going to reappear."

"Tell you what," he said. "Tomorrow I'll clean out the scrap, load it into the back of my ute and take it to the rubbish tip."

"Really?" she said. "You would do that?"

"Absolutely."

"Thank you!" Her shoulders slumped in relief.

Today she had a cloisonné kite pinned to her lapel, its dangling chain-link tail punctuated by brightly colored enamel bows. The brooch looked incongruous against her crisp tailored blouse but it gave Ben an idea.

"I've been trying to think of fun outdoor activities to do with Danny," he said. "Do you know where I can buy a kite?"

Her fingers went to her brooch, flicking the tail before she dropped her hand. "I don't know any stores in town that carry kites, but I guess you could borrow mine."

"*You* have a kite?" He didn't mean to sound skeptical but it slipped out. Prim white blouses and roped-off hair didn't seem to mesh with the mindless abandon of kite flying.

"It's a good one," she said, misinterpreting him. "The best place to fly it is Wombat Hill Botanical Gardens. There's an open grassy area at the top and it's usually windy."

"Do you want to come?" he asked. "It would be fun. You, me and Danny. How about it?"

She bit her lip and scooped an invisible strand of hair behind her ear. "My sister Melissa comes over every Sunday afternoon. George always played golf, you see, so she and I watch a week of taped *Coronation Street* episodes together. We never miss it."

She was starting to look a little stressed at the thought of changing her routine and he didn't want her hyperventilating again. Besides, she was vulnerable and he wasn't getting involved. "That's cool. Danny and I will go alone."

"Okay." She breathed out and smiled that tight little smile of hers.

Ben was surprised to feel just the tiniest bit flat knowing she wouldn't be coming with them. Didn't *want* to come in spite of the fact she was clearly a kite aficionado. That was silly; he was going kite flying to bond with his son. If she came she would just distract him.

Putting an extra ounce of cheer in his voice, he called, "Come on, Danny. We're going to Wombat Hill."

CHERYL OPENED the door to her house and stepped inside. The lounge-room curtains were still drawn though it was nearly noon, and dirty plates and cups were stacked on the coffee table. Tony obviously hadn't done a lick of housework since she'd been away. "Hello?"

No answer.

She stuck a finger in the dirt of a potted cordeline and frowned. Dry as a dead dingo's you-know-what. "Tony?"

Gathering what dishes she could carry, she

moved through the house. Where was he? And why had he taken down the Brett Whitely print from above the dining table? The whole color scheme was thrown out of balance. And what were all those boxes doing on the table itself?

Cheryl dropped the dishes in the already-full kitchen sink and glanced around in dismay. Cardboard boxes were piled three high and two deep around two sides of the room. She pried open a flap. Inside, separated by pieces of cardboard, were gallon jugs of olive oil.

A quick glance out the back door showed no sign of her husband but there were more boxes, dozens of them, piled up on the covered patio. The door of the garage they'd made into a games room was open and inside she could see still more boxes. Why not just drain the pool and fill it with oil? she thought bitterly. Even assuming their anniversary party went ahead, there would be no place for their guests to congregate.

She continued toward the master bedroom. Half afraid of what she would find, she slowly opened the door.

Cheryl blinked, mouth agape. Bright white light filled the room from newly installed overhead fluorescent strips. A humming sound emanated from two computers. The monitor of one computer showed bands of clouds stretching across a map of Australia just like on the TV news.

Her ebony statue from Thailand had been removed from the dresser and shoved in a corner to make way for books and papers. The painting on the far wall had been taken down and a white board with columns of Tony's illegible scrawl put in its place. Her antique hand-sewn quilt was covered in untidy piles of papers, and in the middle of the bed sat Tony, clipboard on his knee, pen clutched in his mouth, a mobile telephone pressed to each ear.

Spitting out the pen he glanced at her over the half glasses he used for reading. "Good, you're back. We're out of milk and the bread's gone off. Could you pop down to the shop? I'm a little busy."

Cheryl's heart stopped at the thought of ink marks on her priceless quilt, then lurched into palpitations. It was worse than she'd thought. He was possessed. Any minute now the bed would rise off the floor and his head would spin around.

"Have you gone completely mad!" she exclaimed. "First you put my gallery in danger of foreclosure, now you're destroying our house."

"I'm doing this for us, darling," he said with cheerful confidence. "My plan is unfolding beautifully. Who knew you could have this much fun with water without getting wet? You're looking particularly fetching today, by the way. I'm so glad you're back."

"I. Am. Not. Back!" Cheryl felt tears of anger spring to her eyes and she squeezed past the computers to get to the bathroom for a tissue. There she was struck with fresh despair. Her lovely cream-colored towels had been replaced with aqua ones and paired with the crimson bathmat from the guest bathroom. Dangling from the gold faucet was the frayed brown facecloth she'd consigned to the ragbag.

If Tony had thought long and hard about what she'd hate the most and deliberately set out to make it happen, he couldn't have wounded her more. But he didn't think. He *never* thought. He just blundered through life, dragging her along on a roller-coaster ride that never ended. Why, he'd even used her expensive bar of special face cleanser. It was covered with grime and, and— *What was that in the sink?*

"I'm *never* coming back," she sobbed as she rushed from the room. "Never, never, never."

Tony held the phones to his chest and called after her. "Is now not a good time for the grocery store? I can pick the mold off the bread. Cheryl! Cheryl, what's wrong?"

"THANK GOD *you're* normal," Melissa said that afternoon as she flopped onto Ally's couch in a swish of plum-colored satin. "Mother is heading for a breakdown and taking me with her."

Ally, crouched by the VCR, inserted a tape containing the week's episodes of *Coronation Street*. "Did she talk to Tony? I've written out the invitations," she said, indicating several boxes of cards. "We can address the envelopes while we watch TV. That is, if the anniversary party is still on.'

"Who knows." Melissa threw up her hands. "She went over to the house this morning to see him. When she came back she started stripping the wallpaper off my lounge-room wall with her bare hands. I tried to talk to her but she just muttered something about finding a priest before it's too late. Do you think she's turning religious?"

"Maybe," Ally said doubtfully. She rose and picked up the remote off the top of the TV. Then she brightened. "Or maybe they're going to renew their vows."

"Oh, I don't think so, not by the look of grim death on her face as she set about destroying my lounge room." Melissa sat up suddenly, eyes wide. "Maybe she murdered him and wants to confess."

"She hates the sight of blood," Ally protested. "And deep down, she loves him."

"That doesn't mean she couldn't commit a crime of passion." Melissa reached for the bowl of popcorn on the coffee table. "You'd better go over there and make sure he's still breathing."

"You go. I've already been there once and was forced to drink olive oil." Ally sat on the couch and took the bowl away from her sister. "Stop eating all the popcorn."

"*I'm* not going. I hate the sight of blood, too. Do you have any mineral water?"

"In the fridge. I'll call him." Ally reached for the phone on the side table and dialed her father's number.

"Hey, what'd you do to the backyard?" Melissa said from the kitchen. "It seems a lot bigger."

"Ben cut the grass. He flushed out a snake. Scared the you-know-what out of me." Ally paused as her father's garbled voice answered the phone. "Hello, Tony? Are you still breathing?"

"I've never felt more alive!" came his enthusiastic response. "I've found the elixir of life."

"Olive oil?" Ally held her hand over the receiver and rolled her eyes at Melissa, who returned with cold bottles of Pellegrino. "He's in manic mode."

"Water!" Tony exclaimed. "I have enough of the stuff now to turn the outback into an oasis."

"What about Mother?" Ally said.

"Tell her not to worry. I got the bread." A faint beeping ensued and he said, "Sorry, got to go. There's someone on my other line."

Ally hung up. "He says he's got the bread. Looks like she'll get her gallery back after all."

"Who calls money 'bread' nowadays?" Melissa snorted. "He's such a dag some-times."

"At least he's alive and Mother won't go to prison," Ally said, pressing a button on the remote. The screen flickered to life and she pressed Play.

"What did he do to *get* the bread?" Melissa said. "That's what I want to know."

"I don't," Ally said firmly. "If he ends up in jail, we'd be accessories after the fact."

"If he did go to jail," Melissa mused, "Cheryl would be able to return home and I could have my life back." She drank from her bottle. "There's always a silver lining."

"That's not nice," Ally admonished absently as the intro music swelled. "On the other hand…" she cast Melissa a half smile "…Tony did raise us to be optimists." Ally pushed over a box of invitations. "Start licking."

They were halfway through Wednesday's episode when Ben and Danny returned. Ben hovered in the doorway, as if hesitant to intrude.

Ally paused the VCR and glanced at her watch. "You're home early. Wasn't there any wind?"

Ben massaged the back of his neck and studied the floor. "The thing is…"

Danny stuck his head beneath his dad's arm. "The kite got stuck in a treetop. It took us ages to get the kite in the air then we finally did and a tree ate it."

"Tell me where you got it," Ben said. "I'll buy you another one."

"Singapore," Ally replied flatly. "My father brought it back for me when I was ten."

"Oh," he said. "Hell."

Ally struggled with herself. On the one hand there was Melissa and *Coronation Street* on Sunday afternoon. On the other hand there was her lost kite, and Ben looking miserable.

With a sigh she handed over the remote control to Melissa. "You go ahead and watch. I have to get my kite."

"You can't mean it," Melissa said, aghast.

"She's right, Ally," Ben put in. "The kite's stuck in the highest branches, thirty feet up."

"I meant leaving our Sunday afternoon *Coronation Street* marathon," Melissa said. "The tree's nothing. Ally practically lived with the birds when she was a kid. She can climb anything."

Ally went to her room and changed into a roomy pair of shorts and her old running shoes. She retied her hair and clamped the front down with extra barrettes. At the front door she paused and waited for Ben to close his mouth. "Let's go."

CHAPTER SEVEN

IN THE UPPERMOST boughs of an English oak tree Ally clung to a branch and leaned way out, stretching toward a diamond of red silk embroidered with a gold dragon. The branch she stood on was thinner than her forearm and trembled with her every movement. The kite rested lightly in the angle of another branch, the string snagged on a piece of rough bark. If she could just lift the string away from the bark... Ally stretched farther, leaning over open air until only the tips of her toes and her left hand were still in contact with the tree.

"Be careful!" Ben's voice came from down below and very far away.

Ally didn't answer, just blew at the strands of hair that had dared to slip out of place. One of her fingertips touched the string. Just a little farther— Her toe slipped and she clutched the branch, heart pounding. Regaining a firm foothold, once again she reached out…a smidgen more…

"Got it!" She flicked the string off the twig. The kite wobbled momentarily on the branch then a breeze lifted it into the air and it danced away, tugging at the string in Danny's hands.

Elated, Ally rocked back onto flat feet and leaned into the trunk. The bark was rough and dry against her cheek. She'd scraped her knee on the climb up and her T-shirt was half-untucked but she felt great, like a kid again.

"Can you get down?" Ben called, hands cupped around his mouth.

"No worries. I'll be down soon." She was drunk on the smell of warm sap and green leaves and the sound of the warble of magpies. From this height she could see clear to Ballarat, she thought dreamily. When had she given up climbing trees? And why?

Then she realized Ben was hauling himself onto the broad lower limb of the oak. He paused there, scanning ahead to map out a route to come to her rescue. "Stay there," she called. "I'm coming!"

He only grunted in reply and grasped an overhead branch to high-step onto the next bough. Ally descended quickly, her hands working in sync with her feet as she moved intuitively through the maze of branches. She met Ben two-thirds of the way down the tree. Ally dropped easily onto the branch he stood on, facing him.

"I guess you didn't need me. The way you got the kite was dazzling." Ben plucked a leaf from her hair. "You're a different person when you're up a tree."

"No, I'm not." Suddenly she felt intensely self-conscious, cocooned with him in the canopy of leaves. Her face felt flushed, her hair had loosened and her shirt was untidy.

"Yes, you're wild and crazy." His smile was very white, his eyes very green and full of laughter. "Sexy."

The branch beneath her feet was as wide as a footpath but suddenly she felt as though she was bal- ancing on a tightrope. Averting her eyes, she tried to one-handedly tuck in her shirt. She no sooner got a piece of the hem under her waistband than Ben pulled it out again.

"Hey!" she said, startled. "You can't do that." She jammed her shirt back in.

Chuckling, Ben yanked it out again.

"Stop it," she cried, laughing in spite of herself. "I'm a mess and you're making it worse."

"I like you messy. You're more fun." His grin turned wicked and knowing and he leaned in close. "Dirty girl."

Electricity thrilled over her skin, tickling the back of her neck and behind her knees. Then before she knew what was happening, he was kissing her, his lips warm and firm. It was a carefree, impulsive kiss. A kiss of bare brown limbs and hot summer afternoons. Magpies warbled. The air grew heavy. Her heart took flight. She was falling....

"Two little dickey birds, sitting in a tree," Danny chanted from below. "K-i-s-s-i-n-g."

With a groan, Ben broke away. "We'd better go down."

On the ground Ally smoothed her shirt and tucked it firmly into her shorts. She removed her hair tie and recaptured all the wayward strands into a tight ponytail. Messy was all very well but she wasn't a kid and she didn't want to be Ben's "dirty girl." Oh God. Her cheeks burned just thinking about his words, his touch, and the mocking, amused light in his eyes.

Taking a deep breath she walked over to Ben who was watching Danny run halfheartedly across the hill with the kite, well away from the kite-chomping oak. She was a woman with a level head and not an impulsive bone in her body; it was up to her to keep the situation under control. She'd be friendly but just a touch cool, letting him know that while she wasn't going to make a big deal about the kiss, it wasn't going to happen again.

He sensed her approach and glanced her way, his gaze moving swiftly over her. "Back to normal, I see."

"Yes, thank you." She smiled without showing her teeth. "Danny's got the kite in the air."

The kiss might never have happened—except for the awkwardness underlying their excessively polite behavior. Certainly Ben seemed in no hurry to repeat the experiment. Perversely, Ally wondered what had changed his mind about her so quickly. Was she that bad a kisser?

"Fresh air and running around are good for Danny," Ben said, his gaze still on his son. "When he was living with his mum she had him in so many organized activities he had no time for spontaneous play."

Ally watched the golden dragon leap into the air, dipping and soaring until it rose higher and stabilized. "Kids need time to just be themselves."

Ben gave a short laugh. "So do adults. Carolyn also organized me within an inch of my life. Every minute of my few days off were scheduled with things we had to do— chores, friends, even sex."

Ally recalled Saturday nights with George after the late news. She'd have thought a psychiatrist could come up with better foreplay than reports of war and disaster.

"It's no wonder our marriage didn't last," Ben went on. "I was suffocated by her need to control."

Okay, she got the message! No more controlling women in his life. Even she could see she and Ben were fundamentally unsuited. What did *she* want with a guy who cut the lawn like a Spirograph and chased poisonous snakes?

"They say opposites attract but I think that's just wrong," Ally said. "The very thing that makes a person different and interesting at first will be the thing that eventually drives you crazy."

"Exactly," Ben agreed, his all-too-obvious relief allowing him to look directly at her at last. "Chemistry doesn't make for a lasting relationship."

"Chemistry is highly overrated." *So he'd felt it, too.*

Ben nodded. "Half the time you just think you're attracted to someone because it's been a while since you've had sex."

"True," she said, also relieved. Lustful feelings would only confuse her quest for self-awareness. If she was ever going to figure out why Mr. Right eluded her she needed to keep a clear head. *How long had it been for Ben?*

"I can be impulsive," Ben added.

"That must have driven your ex-wife mad," Ally said.

"Often I speak before I think," he continued.

"You give a kneejerk response instead of taking the time to formulate rational comment," Ally elaborated.

"I'm glad you understand," he said.

"Perfectly. The incident in the tree never happened."

"Not that I'm sorry it did. In other circumstances…"

"Another life."

Ben held out his hand. "Friends?"

"Friends." Ally's hand pressed against his warm, callused palm. She told herself the instant sexual buzz was merely a result of abstinence and didn't mean she and Ben had any sort of connection.

Another part of her brain screamed, *Kiss me again.*

But of course *that* wasn't going to happen.

BEN POKED THROUGH the vegetable bin looking for something to make for dinner. He was feeling good after spending time with Danny even though things had gotten a little complicated with Ally. She'd seemed a different person up in that tree. With her eyes sparkling and her hair tousled she was not only attractive but very likable. Luckily, they'd straightened things out.

"How does *supreme de volaille* accompanied by fennel gratin sound?" he suggested.

"Fabulous," Ally said. "Whatever it is."

"Ugh," Danny groaned. "Can't we have tuna casserole?"

"Tuna casserole?" Ben straightened, and shut the fridge door. "Is that what your mother feeds you?"

Danny glanced at Ally, who took on a vaguely guilty expression. "No, Ally made it when you were at work. It's great."

"Your dad's a much better cook than me," Ally said quickly. "I'm sure flannel supremacists will be delicious."

"If you can't remember the name of a dish two seconds after you hear it, you know it's going to taste lousy," Danny explained to her. "It's a rule about cheffy cooking."

"Thanks, Danno." Ben was miffed by his son's lack of support. "There's a rule about kids, too. They have to try new foods to learn to like them."

"Then you should try Ally's tuna casserole," Danny argued. "You could watch her and learn how to make it."

Ben threw up his hands and gave in gracefully, realizing he wasn't going to win this one. "Go ahead, Ally. I'll eat anything you care to make. Do you want help?"

"No, thanks," Ally said, shooing them out of the kitchen. "Go hang out and talk about guy stuff."

Danny jerked his head awkwardly, indicating his bedroom down the hall. "Wanna play Command and Conquer?"

"No, thanks," Ben grumbled, then caught Ally giving him a pointed look whose meaning was impossible to mistake. "I, uh, I'd rather play Gory and Gorier."

"Cool!" Danny said happily, and led the way. Ben followed, knowing he was going to hate it but telling himself he was bonding with his son.

Ally had to call them twice to dinner. Ben's platoon was almost completely decimated but a small band of soldiers were hanging on in spite of Danny's more experienced attack.

"Don't get cocky," he warned his son as they sat down to eat. "The battle's not over yet."

Ally set a steaming casserole dish on the hot mat in front of Ben and handed him a serving spoon. "Go ahead and start. I'll get water."

Danny dug in straight away, making appreciative noises that contrasted sharply with his usual critical reactions to Ben's meals. Ben took a forkful and sniffed, automatically analyzing ingredients. He took a bite and chewed. Salty, cheesy and slightly glutinous but tasty.

He noticed Ally casting him anxious glances and gave her a reassuring smile. "My mother used to make this. Love it."

There *was* something solid and comforting about the combination of flavors and textures. Ben's mind began to turn over. By updating to fresh foodstuffs a good chef could turn the old-fashioned meal into a contemporary classic. Swap tuna for scallops and he'd have a new signature dish.

Suddenly excited, he put down his fork

and got up from the table. If he was quick he might get to the seafood store before it closed. He'd need more eggs to make fresh pasta—

"Where are you going?" Ally demanded, while Danny regarded him with dismay.

"This has given me an idea," Ben said. "I'm going to the restaurant to experiment."

"No, you're not." Ally rapped the table and pointed to his chair. "You're going to sit down and finish your dinner. This is your day off and you're spending it with your son."

Ben was so startled at her abrupt tone he knocked over the wooden pepper grinder, which hit Danny's glass and splashed water onto his plate. "I'm telling you, I could make something really good with these ingredients."

"Oh, thanks," she said, pretending to be offended. "I know I'm not a chef but Danny seems to like it."

"I didn't mean it that way—"

"Never mind about the food," she said more gently. "You've been looking forward to today and it's not over yet. Don't be in such a hurry to rush off."

Chastened, Ben resumed his seat. "I guess I've still got a few tanks Danny could wipe out."

He began mopping up the water with his napkin. Ally was right. He was an obsessive-compulsive maniac who didn't deserve to be a father. Touching her wrist with the tip of one finger he said, "Thanks."

"What for?" she asked.

"For reminding me of my priorities."

"It's my pleasure." Then she smiled, none of this pursed-lip stuff, but a warm, full smile that burrowed straight into his heart, surprising the hell out of him.

WHEN BEN WENT to work Tuesday night he entered Mangos through the front door. He did that every now and then to see the restaurant as a customer did. Tonight the place was packed, every table filled to capacity and every stool at the bar occupied. The love seats in front of the fireplace were jammed with three individuals apiece. Conversation buzzed like cicadas in January and although the ceiling fans whirred at full speed they did little to dispel the heat which surely was at its peak after days of rising temperatures.

At first the impression was of a popular eating place, but as Ben wove his way through the tables he began to realize something was seriously wrong. There were far too many people here. A middle-aged couple at the bar were frowning and glancing at their watches. Dirty plates from the previous sitting cluttered tables where new customers looked over the menu. The guy at the end of the bar had almost fallen off his stool, a hint he'd had time to consume too many drinks while waiting to eat.

Julie, her face flushed and movements harried, was delivering entrées on the far side of the dining room. She cast him a desperate look and hurried over to grab his wrist and drag him out of sight behind the espresso machine.

"Help!" she whispered, eyes wild. "We're overbooked."

"That's not unusual—"

"Except that tonight every single person decided to show up. Then Steve poked his head into the dining room at the wrong time and let a whole swag of people in the front door who didn't even have reservations. He gets furious with me because the wait- staff can't cope. What waitstaff! There's only me and Rico. On top of that I'm expected to act as maître d'. I *told* him we needed more help, but no—"

"Calm down, Julie," Ben said soothingly. "Everything will be okay. I'll send Mick out to bus—"

"You can't spare him, not with all these dirty dishes," Julie exclaimed, letting out a burst of high-pitched laughter verging on hysterical. "Gord put Baz on the grill and Baz is crumbling under the pressure. I had to return three of his salmon steaks because they were overcooked. Gord hit the roof."

"Where's Steve now?" Ben asked, looking around.

"His wife wanted him home because they're having dinner guests," Julie replied, rolling her eyes. "*Excuse me?* We've got two hundred dinner guests."

"Take a deep breath. I'll see what I can do." Ben headed in the direction of the kitchen, pausing at the bar to assure the couple their table wouldn't be much longer. He hoped that was true.

Ben pushed through the double stainless-steel doors and entered Hell's Kitchen. The board was jammed with orders, the temperature was fifteen degrees hotter than the dining room, the decibel reading neared danger levels and the steam coming out of Gord's ears rivaled the hissing of the pots on the stovetop.

"What do you mean the effing salmon is effing finished?" Gord shouted at Beth, who should have been putting desserts together instead of taking Gord's abuse. "It's an effing special and it's only eight o'clock. We can't be out!"

"Baz said we're supposed to get another delivery from the fishmonger but it didn't arrive," Beth ventured.

"Half the orders ended up in the bin because Baz screwed them up," Gord roared, his face a deep crimson. "Where is the little bastard!"

"He's, uh, looking for extra fillets in the walk-in freezer," Beth said diffidently.

"Are you an idiot?" Gord screamed. "We

don't serve *frozen* fish!" He slapped a couple of chicken breasts onto the grill. "Baz's been sneaking my vodka all night. Wait'll I get my hands on his scrawny neck."

Ben tied on an apron and got behind the stove, checking the orders and assessing the situation. Both hands reaching for pans at once, he barked, "Fire on Six. Gord, pull finger, mate, you're in the weeds. Beth, tell Baz to get out here, now!"

Julie burst through the swinging doors. "Table Sixteen is about to walk out because their meals are forty-five minutes late and Table Three spent five minutes abusing me for mixing up their orders," she said. "Pick up on Thirty-four. Gord, where's that chicken?"

"Tell them to hold their effing horses," Gord snarled. "This isn't a fast-food restaurant. If you were doing your job people wouldn't be complaining."

"If *I* was doing *my* job! You're blaming it on *me?*" Julie threw up her hands. "That's it. I've had all I can handle from you, Gord. I quit!"

Just then, Baz lurched out of the walk-in freezer and swayed sideways into a stack of dirty plates Mick hadn't yet loaded into the dishwasher. The dishes crashed to the concrete floor, shattering into pieces that skittered across the kitchen.

Letting out a roar of rage Gord picked up a turnip and threw it at Baz's head. Baz ducked and the turnip hit the remaining stack of plates, sending them crashing, too. Baz stumbled back toward the freezer with Gord hard on his heels.

Ben turned to Julie. "Please, you can't quit!"

"Sorry, Ben," she said, implacable. "I will not work with that man a second longer."

"I'll get Steve to double your salary," he promised rashly.

"Triple wouldn't be enough." She threw her apron onto the serving window counter. As she exited through the back door, she called, "So long, suckers."

Ben glanced around the kitchen. Beth was weeping openly. Mick was sweeping up plates that should have been holding the dozen orders pinned up above the stove. Rico was offloading more dirty plates and handing in another two orders. Gord was stalking back into the kitchen after confronting Baz.

A muffled thumping could be heard from inside the thick walls of the walk-in freezer.

"Mick, go rescue Baz." Ben stood in the wreckage and saw his dream of an idyllic country eatery going up in smoke. He was a chef. He wanted to cook great food, not fix personnel problems. What they needed was someone to step in and organize them all.

He strode back to the dining room. Ignoring the angry questioning faces that turned in his direction, he grabbed the phone off the bar and crouched behind the espresso machine.

"Ally!" he whispered urgently when she picked up. "I need you!"

She was silent, as if not knowing how to react, and his thoughts flew irrelevantly and distractingly to trees. And kisses. Stupid, unforgettable kiss.

"The restaurant's overbooked. Baz is falling down drunk and Gord's on a rampage. The kitchen has fallen into anarchy and the dining room is in chaos."

"I hate chaos," Ally said. "Chaos is bad."

He knew that would get her attention. He paused to wipe the perspiration off his brow with the hem of his jacket. "To make matters worse, Julie's bailed. We're down to one waiter out front and of course, no maître d'."

"I'm sorry," Ally said. "But what's all this got to do with me?"

"We need someone to run the dining room," Ben told her. "Wait tables if necessary. Will you? Please?"

There was a long pause. Ben closed his eyes. She was going to say no. The restaurant business wasn't her field. She was watching her favorite TV show. It was the first Tuesday of the month and she had to dust the Venetian blinds. She—

"I'll just change my clothes," Ally said. "I'll be there in fifteen minutes."

Hallelujah.

CHAPTER EIGHT

"HUNGRY?" Ben asked.

Ally, slumped at a table in the now-empty dining room, glanced up wearily. Everyone had finally gone home. She felt as though she'd never move again but Ben looked as adrenaline-fueled as he had when she'd arrived six hours ago.

"Food?" she said. "At this time of night, or rather, morning?"

"Performing miracles is hard work."

"Now that you mentioned it, I'm starving. A bowl of Gord's roasted pumpkin soup would go down nicely."

"Oh, I think I can do better than that." Ben went behind the bar and got a couple of cold beers from the fridge. Setting a bottle in front of her he took the other one and headed for the kitchen. "Back in half a tick."

Punch drunk with fatigue, Ally stared at the bottle. Beer at 1:00 a.m.? What the hell. She twisted off the cap and took a long slow pull, amazed at how good it tasted.

It had been an exhausting night. She and Rico had been run off their feet and she'd had to juggle bookings in between juggling plates, but the time had flown. Once Ben was at the helm Baz had sobered up, Gord had settled down and Beth had dried her tears.

Seeing Ben choreograph meal preparation during her glimpses into the kitchen had been a revelation and a pure pleasure. He was like bottled energy, adept in his movements, disciplined and firm in his handling of the staff. At home he was laid-back and careless of order but when it came to cooking he was a perfectionist. She smiled, remembering his cheeky wink through the serving window, the accidental touch of fingertips when she reached for a customer's order....

"Your dinner, madame." Ben set before her a plate of coiled spinach linguini topped with seared scallops blanketed in a light creamy sauce and sprinkled with crispy fried shallots. A thin broken line of roasted red capsicum sauce gleamed like rubies around the perimeter and across the top in a dashing zigzag.

Ally inhaled the aromatic steam and began to salivate. "What's this? I don't recognize it from the menu."

"Tuna casserole, Mangos style. It's my homage to home cooking and the new special Steve's been after me for." He clinked his beer bottle against hers. "You're my inspiration."

Ally took a bite of sweet chargrilled scallop and creamy pasta and moaned. "Incredible. Help me out. I'll never finish it all."

Ben picked up another fork and took a bite of her pasta and scallops. "It was incredible how you got all those disgruntled patrons to stay in their seats until we got the kitchen under control."

Ally chuckled. "I told them dessert and coffee were on the house. A little goodwill goes a long way."

"Bold move." Ben gave an admiring whistle. "If I clear it with Steve, would you like to have the maître d' job?"

Ally put down her fork and met his gaze.

"Julie'll come back when she cools down, won't she?"

"I hope so," Ben said. "Even if she does, we still need someone at the front of the house to organize things."

Ally took another bite, giving herself time to think while she struggled with conflicting emotions. Once the crisis that brought her to Mangos tonight had been sorted out she'd actually had fun, but... "I'm hoping to get my old job back at the Cottage Rentals."

"Has your ex-boss asked you back?"

"No," Ally admitted. "Until she does...I'll help out."

Ben raised his bottle for a toast. "Cheers."

Ally touched her bottle to his with a soft *clink*. Below the table his feet shifted and one ankle came to rest against the outside of her right foot, sending warmth sweeping up her leg. Was it an accident or deliberate? To move her foot might seem unfriendly, even prudish. "So, what's in this dish?"

"Scallops and pasta, mostly."

"I meant the sauce."

"Trade secret."

"You used a can of something, didn't you?" she teased. "You just won't admit it."

Ben drew himself upright in mock outrage. "My honor has been besmirched. Filleting knives at twenty paces."

Ally brandished her bread knife. *"En garde!"*

Ben uttered a scornful laugh and disappeared into the kitchen. He returned a moment later, his hands full of large chef knives.

"I didn't mean it," Ally said hastily, holding her hands up. "I know everything you cook is fresh."

Ben flung a knife high into the air. Then another, and another until he was juggling four razor-sharp implements, their steel blades flashing overhead.

"Ohmigod, Ben," Ally gasped, backing away. "Stop it before you slice a hand off."

Ignoring her plea, he slowly circled her as he juggled his deadly batons. Ally crossed her arms over her churning stomach as knives cartwheeled through the air and slapped into Ben's palms, before again being flung on high. Prickles of fear skittered over her skin but she couldn't take her eyes off his face. Her fatigue disappeared and every inch of her felt alive.

Finally he caught the knives one by one. Clustered in one hand like a spiky bouquet, he laid them on the table. "Bet that got your heart rate up."

"You bastard! That was so—" she placed her hands on his chest and pushed him hard "—*exciting*."

Laughing, he caught her by the wrists. His gaze connected with hers and his laughter faded. Instead of fending her off, he pulled her close.

"We weren't going to do this," she murmured.

"If no one sees us, it didn't happen," he said.

Then his mouth was on hers and Ally felt heat flowing through her tingling body. Her knees started to sag and he grasped her by the waist and hoisted her onto a table, sending the cutlery clattering to the floor.

"You're mad," she breathed. "The whole street can see in through the windows."

"A few drunks staggering home from the pub? A freight truck rumbling through town?" His knuckles brushed the curve of her breast where the top button of her blouse had popped open. "Who's going to notice?"

"Someone will," Ally said, unable to contain a moan as Ben's hand slipped inside her blouse and his palm closed around her breast.

He stepped closer, inserting himself between her legs, making her skirt ride up. His pants were rough on the inside of her thighs. She itched to push closer but couldn't get any purchase on the sliding tablecloth. He kissed her again and she gripped his shoulders tightly as the table rocked and scraped against the floor. This was madness. The setting was ridiculous, Ben was all wrong for her but…oh, his kiss.

Headlights coming down the side road directly opposite the restaurant beamed a spotlight straight at their table. In the stark light Ally's naked legs flailed, her bare breast was exposed and Ben's strained face looked sideways at the approaching vehicle. Ally uttered a stifled scream and rolled away from the light, falling off the table to crunch her knee on a fork lying on the floor.

Sobbing and laughing simultaneously, she

huddled under the table, hugging her knee to her chest. The headlights turned and Ally glimpsed a cream-colored Mercedes slow in front of the restaurant before gliding away into the night.

Ben dropped beside her, his arms around her. "Are you okay?" he said, kissing her cheeks and nose.

"No one will see us? Isn't that what you said?" She wasn't laughing now. "That was *George's* car."

Ben rubbed her knee, sober now, too. "Do you want a Band-Aid?"

"I'm not bleeding."

"You're hurt all the same." Ben's hand slid upward to massage her neck with slow, tender strokes. "He's not worth it, you know. You deserve someone who appreciates your warm heart and generosity."

Ally felt herself loosen as Ben's warm fingers kneaded her tight muscles. Tempted as she was to let him go on in this vein, she knew she had to stop him. "I'm not grieving over George."

"That's *good,*" Ben said. "You're being

positive about your breakup. That'll help you get over him."

"I wasn't in love with him anymore." Ally turned around and faced Ben. "I only persuaded myself I was because…well, I don't really know why. I should have told you this before. I was already planning to break up with George the day I found out he was having an affair with his secretary."

Ben's brow wrinkled. "But I thought… You were so upset."

"I was upset with myself for making such a huge mistake by getting engaged to him and then falling out of love," she admitted. "It's happened to me before. I need to figure out where I go wrong before I get involved with anyone again."

Ben searched her face. "You wanted to create distance between us, and having me think you were pining over George helped."

She gave him a small smile. "Also, I was worried about what you would think of me. The whole situation is embarrassing."

"This only proves you *are* vulnerable and not ready for another relationship." He rose and pulled her to her feet. "Let's go home."

While Ben carried the dishes and his knives to the kitchen, Ally reset the table. She was retying her hair in the mirror above the bar when Ben came up behind her.

"If you're not in love with George anymore, why did it bother you that he, in particular, might have seen us kissing?"

Ally slid a hairpin into place and met Ben's gaze in the mirror. "He's bound to make something out of it. You know, I'm acting out, rebelling against my repressed nature or some such psychological gobble-dygook."

A small smile tugged at one corner of Ben's mouth as he studied her face in the mirror. "Are you?"

Ally laughed, and slid sideways out from between Ben and the cabinets. "Of course not. With me, what you see is who I am, through and through. There's no hidden self."

"Right," Ben said. "That's what I thought."

SUNLIGHT FLOODED Ben's room the next morning, bringing him wide awake and gazing at a square of blue sky so bright it hurt to look at it. He'd forgotten to close the curtains last night. He squeezed his eyes shut again and the dancing colors behind his lids were overlaid by an image of Ally, cheeks flushed, lips parted, a deep gleam in her hazel eyes. *So exciting*.

For an intelligent woman, she was a little lacking in self-awareness. But the big news was, she wasn't in love with George. Ben stretched his arms above his head and twisted onto his side. The sheet slipped down his chest and as he recalled their last kiss a low moan escaped him. Where did this spark between them come from? It was as unlikely as it was undeniable. If only he could get her to let her hair down, so to speak.

Nope, no way, he thought, rolling out of bed. Danny was still his first priority, as Ally would undoubtedly be the first to remind him. He was no nearer to bonding with his son than when Danny had arrived. Sure, they'd played a computer game together, but they hadn't *talked* about anything significant. Despite his efforts, that father-son camaraderie he wanted so badly still eluded him.

Ben went down the hall to knock on Danny's door. "G'day, mate. What're you up to?"

Danny swiveled his chair away from the computer. "Mum called again last night. She's back from Bali and wants me to come to Melbourne for the weekend."

Leaving Ben alone with Ally. Great. Lock the wolf in with the sheep and send the shepherd to town. Ben slumped against the doorjamb. "You don't have to go if you don't want to."

"I do want to go. She's got a present for me."

Ben sat on the bed and rubbed his hands over his thighs. "I guess you miss your mum."

Danny shrugged, glancing at the floor. "Yeah."

"You know you can see her whenever you want."

Danny nodded. "Two weekends a month, like I used to do with you."

"Okay." Ben breathed deeply, relieved that he wasn't asking to go back to live with her. "When's she picking you up?"

"If you can drive me there, she'll bring me back."

"All right." Ben rose. "Hey, why don't I buy a couple of those dueling kites and when you get back we can have an air battle?"

Danny grimaced. "Uh, Dad? I pretended to have a good time the other day because I didn't want you to feel bad, but frankly, I'm too old for kites."

"Oh." Ben forced himself to smile. He *had* to find something they both liked to do together. He started to leave, then paused in the doorway. "Where's Ally?"

"She left for work an hour ago," Danny replied.

"I'd better get down there," Ben said, "before she arranges the dry stores in alphabetical order."

When he got to Mangos, Ally was behind the bar spooning maraschino cherries into a little tray. All the other trays were lined up awaiting their turn. Passing behind her to make himself a coffee, Ben could smell her shampoo—pineapple. For some reason it made him think of her hair spread across a pillow, him cuddling her spoon fashion.

"You should get some artwork on these

bare walls," Ally said, mercifully distracting him from his thoughts. "My mother can supply paintings from her gallery. Mangos would get a percentage of the commission and free decoration, and she gets another outlet for her artists. She has the same arrangement with another restaurant in town."

"I'll look into it," Ben said.

A rapping at the front door drew his gaze. A man in a straw hat and bandana stood outside holding a cardboard box. He peered in and, seeing Ally, smiled and waved.

Ally groaned and ducked behind the espresso machine. "Send him away. He's a peddler."

Ben threw her a puzzled glance as he crossed to unlock the door. "G'day," he said to the man. "What can I do for you?"

"It's what *I* can do for *you*," the man responded with an enthusiastic smile. He crossed the room and set his box on top of the bar. "I'm Tony Cummings. Good morning, Ally. Get your papa a bottle of mineral water and a couple of glasses."

Ben looked from the eccentrically dressed, handsome older man to the prim young woman and back to Tony. "You're Ally's father?"

"You mean she hasn't told you about me? I'm Tony Cummings." He pumped Ben's hand with a hearty grip. "Because you're a friend of my daughter I'm going to do you a special deal on a dozen cases of the best extra virgin olive oil you've ever tasted."

"Olive oil, huh?" Ben frowned at Ally.

"I'll get that mineral water." She slid off the stool and headed to the fridge behind the bar.

Tony followed her around the back of the bar as if he owned the place and took a double handful of shot glasses from the shelf below the liquor bottles.

"*Tony,*" Ally said, a warning in her voice.

"Just concentrate on the drinks, *cara,* and leave everything else to me," Tony said, still smiling.

He lined up the shot glasses on the counter then took several bottles from the box and pulled out their corks.

"I believe I've had some of your olive oil that Ally brought home," Ben said.

"If you liked that, you'll love this." Tony

dribbled greeny-gold liquid into a shot glass and held it up to the light. "Look at that color. This is from the south bank of the Murray River, pressed from prime Frantoio olives whose rootstock came from the verdant hills of Italy. Don't rush it, son. Oil this delicious needs to be savored. Take a sip, roll it around in your mouth…that's right. Now clench your teeth and suck in air to make the oil spatter the inside of your mouth. We in the industry call that 'aspirating.'"

"I call it disgusting." Ally banged down a bottle of mineral water in front of her father and went back behind the bar where she polished wineglasses and glared balefully at them.

Ben took a sip, sucked air, coughed and swallowed. "Pungent with a slight bitterness on the middle palate."

Tony beamed. "Your taste buds are clearly well-trained. Both characteristics speak of olives picked early in the season."

"You mean they aren't ripe?" Ally said.

Ignoring her, Tony poured from another bottle and lifted the shot glass to the light. "This one is robust and assertive yet overall, harmonious. The mouth-feel is—" Tony kissed his fingertips *"—unctuous."*

Ben tasted three more varieties and was impressed with them all. "How much do you want for it?"

"Wholesale is twelve dollars per liter. A rock-bottom price for oil of this exceptional quality," Tony assured him. "I've got a thousand liters for immediate sale to a cash buyer."

"A thousand liters! I can't use that much in Mangos."

"You have contacts in the food industry, no?" Tony said, eyeing him shrewdly. "You must know all the top chefs in Melbourne, the food wholesalers and the retailers. A few phone calls and bingo, you've made a tidy profit. You could even sell my oil right here in the restaurant. Keep a few bottles sitting on the counter at the bar for people who want to take home restaurant-quality oil."

"It's an interesting proposition," Ben conceded. Twelve dollars was high but the oil was as good as anything he bought from his Melbourne suppliers. "I'll give you eight dollars a liter."

"Eight dollars." Tony clucked his tongue and started packing his bottles back into the box. "While it would be advantageous for me to make a deal with you here on the spot I have other contacts who would be willing to pay twelve."

Ben suspected Tony was bluffing but he couldn't be absolutely certain. "Why are you so anxious to sell a large quantity all at once?"

Tony glanced around as if to see if anyone was listening, then motioned Ben closer. "I borrowed money on my wife's gallery to invest in the olive grove," he said in a low voice. "This did not please her. If I could get my hands on a substantial amount of money I could give her a handsome surprise at our anniversary party. She might forgive me and come home."

"I see." Ben was silent, thinking. He did have contacts in restaurants and food retail outlets, and had no doubt he could sell the oil. But he didn't want to touch his house fund, a hundred thousand dollars he kept in short-term deposits. Not that he'd had time to go house-hunting since he'd moved here.

"Poor Ally," Tony said reflectively. "She's worried about her mother and I, not to mention our upcoming anniversary party. She's planned the party like a military operation, every detail meticulously accounted for. She would be so disappointed if it didn't take place." Tony paused. "She'd be mightily impressed with any man who facilitated her parents' reconciliation."

Ben glanced over at Ally at the bar. There was no way she could hear what they were saying, but she was watching them closely. "I'd have to talk to my accountant."

"Tell you what I'll do. Pay cash, and you can have the lot for ten dollars a liter," Tony said. "That'll get me out of the dog house and still give you a nice profit."

The deal was too good to pass up. The prospect of making a little money was tempting, and knowing he'd be doing something nice for Ally clinched the matter. Before he could think about it too much, Ben stuck out his hand. "It's a deal."

"Excellent," Tony said, pumping his hand. "I can tell you're a man after my own heart, a man of instinct and lightning-fast decision-making. Come to Cheryl's and my thirtieth anniversary party. Ally will give you the details."

"I'd be delighted," Ben said.

"Tony, may I have a word with you before you go?" Ally loomed over them, frowning.

"Of course, *cara*," Tony said, before adding to Ben, "I'll need the boxes of oil removed from my premises posthaste. And the money deposited into my account, naturally."

"I'll be in touch soon," Ben said, grinning. "Nice doing business with you."

Ally waited until Ben had gone into the kitchen, then turned on her father. "How much of that snake oil did you sell him?"

"A thousand liters," Tony said. "You should be proud of your papa."

"A thousand liters! That's a lifetime supply."

"It's a drop in the ocean in the food industry," Tony said, unconcerned, as he resumed packing up.

Ally paced between the tables. "How does a man of Anglo-Irish extraction acquire an Italian accent? If you were any more Old World you'd burst into 'O Sole Mio' and I'd have to call Cheryl to come and hose you down with Chianti."

"She hasn't done that since before you and Melissa were born," Tony said, a wistful gleam in his eye. Then he frowned at Ally. "Why were you so negative to your poor *papa?* You almost lost me the sale of a lifetime. Luckily, Ben can tell the oil is top-notch even if you can't."

"Stop calling yourself *papa.*" She expelled a sharp sigh of frustration. "Why are you dragging Ben into one of your dodgy schemes when you've already got the money to repay the gallery's mortgage?"

Tony looked genuinely taken aback. "What makes you think I've got the money? Aside from Mrs. Paglioni across the road who bought four liters, Ben's my first customer."

"What!" Ally cried. "Last Sunday you told me to tell Cheryl you had the bread."

Tony stared at her. "I bought a loaf of sourdough. What did you think I was talking about?"

She groaned and covered her face with her hands. "Never mind. At least with the money you get from Ben you can start paying off the gallery's mortgage."

Tony just smiled. Hoisting his box, he slipped through the exit past two young couples arriving for a late lunch, and departed. *"Ciao, cara."*

Ally seated the party of four, took their order and went through the swinging doors into the kitchen. Beth was piping dainty macaroon rosettes onto a pan, Gord was straining a steaming stockpot through a giant sieve into another pot in the sink. Baz had been given a chance to work the grill at lunch, and Ben was reminding him about the importance of *mise-en-place* with regard to the half-dozen squeeze bottles of various sauces lined up on the stainless-steel shelf above the grill.

"Roast capsicum sauce is third from the end, not second, not fourth," Ben said with exaggerated patience as he rearranged them in the proper order. "Chili sauce is in fifth place. Pesto goes here, in first place. Memorize the lineup."

"Yes, Chef," Baz said, frowning hard.

Leaving Baz to refill the sauce bottles Ben

moved to the other end of the bench. He opened a foam box filled with ice chips, pulled out a whole Atlantic salmon and slapped it onto the bench. Then he got out a steel and sharpened his knife in preparation for filleting.

Ally was reminded of her first night of working at the restaurant. Ben juggling knives, Ben's hand on her breast, his mouth hot and insistent… Since that night he'd retreated. They seemed to be following a pattern, two steps forward, one step back, followed by one step forward, two steps back. Right now she welcomed having a breather. If George, who'd seemed so right for her, had turned out to be so wrong, how much *more* wrong would Ben be?

She walked over and personally handed him the order. "I find it amazing you can be so organized in your kitchen and so…random at home."

"At home I like to relax, maintain a semblance of mental health." He whisked the knife back and forth along the steel. "Tony invited me to the party."

"That's fine." Ally picked at a corner of the

foam box. "I'm worried about this oil deal you're doing with him, though."

Ben cut off the salmon head in two brisk strokes and tossed it into a stock pot. "What's wrong with it?"

"You don't even know my father," she said. "How do you know he's not pulling a scam?"

"I assumed since he was your father he'd be trustworthy," Ben said, slicing along the backbone of the salmon. "Are you telling me he isn't?"

"He's my father—I love him," Ally said, then frowned. "But he's put my mother's art gallery at risk to finance this olive farm."

"Starting up a new business is all about risk," Ben said. "Just ask Steve about Mangos."

"It's not just this one time," Ally said. "Whenever Tony starts a new business venture there's great excitement but inevitably his fortunes take a downturn. For instance, when I was in primary school he started an import-export business. He took our whole family to Thailand on a buying trip. We lived like royalty for three weeks, buying silks and sapphires, carvings, batiks, you name it. It was fantastic." She shook her head. "Then we got back and Mother discovered he'd cleaned out the bank account to finance the trip. He had a storeroom full of stuff that he was slowly flogging off piece by piece at the markets while we had to eat rice and beans for the next six months."

"That's not so good." Ben inserted his filleting knife in close to the bone and slid it the length of the fish. "But you survived."

"Barely," Ally replied. "Then there was the time he got into the business of growing hydroponic tomatoes. He bought ten hectares of land and put up five glasshouses. He planted the tomatoes, even got a couple of crops off before he abandoned that."

"What happened?" Ben asked. He peeled off the fillet and started cutting it into even pieces.

Ally shrugged. "Turned out the vegetable mafia at the wholesale market controlled hydroponic tomato sales. Tony couldn't sell his tomatoes because the retailers bought where they were told to."

"That wasn't Tony's fault," Ben pointed out.

"Maybe not," Ally conceded. "But going from the excitement of what seemed like a viable venture to disappointment when he had to sell was devastating. Not to mention the family finances were again in a precarious state."

"Anything else?" Ben asked.

"His furniture business," Ally said. "That was actually successful until the police found out he didn't have a license either to import or to sell. Tony claimed it was an oversight, but who knows?" She paused. "Have you stopped to figure out how you're going to transport the oil, store it, sell it?"

Ben finished cutting up the second fillet and threw the skeleton into the stockpot with the head. He placed the fillets in a metal pan and stored it in the reach-in fridge below the counter. "There's not much to take care of."

"Not much? There's heaps. In a planning vacuum, you-know-what happens."

"What do you mean, 'you-know-what,'" Ben teased, grinning. "Tell me."

"Oh! You're not taking me seriously." She turned her back on him. "Everything's a joke."

"You worry too much," he said. "Sometimes *good* things happen spontaneously, too. You and I, for instance."

Instinctively, Ally felt for her hair clip, to make sure it was tight, then slowly turned to face him. "H-how do you mean?"

"You gave me a place to live. I gave you a job," he said evenly. "Neither of them was planned."

"Oh." Ally found her breath. "Of course. But we were talking about oil."

"The Australian olive industry is taking off in a big way and Tony's oil is good. A little extra money never goes astray. Real estate in Tipperary Springs is more expensive than I realized," Ben said. "I sell the oil, make a profit and I'm able to buy a better house."

"You sound exactly like Tony," she said, disappointed. "How long will it take you to sell a thousand liters?"

"Selling it isn't the problem. I can do that with one or two phone calls," Ben said. "But before I can sell it I need the cash to buy it."

"Oh, great!" Ally exclaimed, and sank onto the step stool. "I've heard this before, too."

"Don't worry, my accountant will think of

something—" He broke off and snapped his fingers, muttering to himself, "That's it! I'll kill two birds with one stone." To Ally, he said, "Danny's going to his mother's this weekend. I'll call an emergency meeting with my Melbourne accountant so we can work out a strategy. Can you recommend a cottage, someplace quiet and private where we can closet ourselves and talk business?"

A strategy. That sounded promising. "Why bring your accountant all the way out to Tipperary Springs? Can't you just talk to him on the phone or go to his office?"

"If I'm asking Ellen to work on the weekend, I have to make it worth her while," Ben said.

Ellen. His accountant was a woman. He was going to spend the weekend in a romantic cottage with her. Ally smiled tightly. "I'll call Lindy and see what's available."

CHAPTER NINE

"His ACCOUNTANT is a gorgeous redhead," Lindy said when she called Ally the next afternoon. "They arrived while I was delivering the basket of goodies to the cottage."

Ally sat abruptly on the stool behind the bar at Mangos. Ben was late and Gord was on the rampage, so she'd called Lindy to find out which cottage he'd rented. Who went on a romantic getaway with their accountant? Was this an excuse to "getaway" from *her*, to put distance between them?

She knew he was focused on Danny. She also knew she shouldn't encourage a relationship when she was no closer to sorting out her heart's desire than she was the night she'd met Ben. But she couldn't help feeling jealous. Not just a touch envious, either, but green-eyed-monster jealous.

"Gorgeous, huh?" Ally repeated. If he was the type to kiss one woman one night and bed another the next she was better off without him, regardless of all the other reasons they shouldn't be together. But it hurt.

"As in, drop-dead," Lindy confirmed.

"Limerick Cottage has two bedrooms," Ally mused. "On the other hand, there's that romantic two-person spa bath."

"Do I detect an interest that's more than merely professional?" Lindy inquired delicately.

"No, of course not," Ally said. "I just want to ensure they've got everything they need. I happen to know Ben's embarking on a new business venture, a risky one at that." Then before she could stop herself, she added, "Maybe I should take over a white board and markers."

"Too obvious," Lindy said, not fooled for a moment. "Don't worry. I'll find an excuse to go back tomorrow morning and check on them."

Ally underwent a brief struggle with her better nature. "They might need more fresh milk or something."

"In other words, you want to know everything," Lindy said. "While I'm spilling the beans, our new manager isn't working out. Olivia is having to come in two or three days a week, just to sort out problems. I think she regrets firing you."

"That's terrible," Ally said, smiling. "I wonder how long before she admits she made a mistake and begs me to come back." A faint beeping on the line told her she had another caller. "Sorry, Lindy. I've got to go."

Ally took a reservation and as she hung up the phone, Ben strolled out of the kitchen, tying on his apron. Ally got out the bag of clean linen napkins from below the bar and started folding. "How's the meeting with your accountant going?"

Ben reached into the fridge and got himself a bottle of mineral water. "Ellen's a whiz," he replied, twisting off the cap. "Just amazing."

"It's unusual to be on such close terms with your accountant that you can spend a whole weekend together." Ally gave him a sidelong glance.

"Oh, she's more than just my accountant,"

Ben said. "I've known Ellen for years. We shared a house back in our student days."

"Like us," Ally said brightly.

Ben smiled. "Not quite."

What did *that* mean? "I'm surprised you could tear yourself away to come to work tonight," Ally went on.

"I can only stay through the dinner rush then I'm going back," Ben said. "Did Steve tell you? Julie's coming back to work starting tonight." Then a party of six came through the door and he headed for the kitchen.

"Good evening," Ally singsonged as she slipped out from behind the bar and glided toward them. "The Pritchard party? Right this way, please."

For the next few hours she was too busy to think about Ben and his relationship—business or otherwise—with his redheaded bean counter. Having Julie return to work was a blessing. By ten o'clock the second sitting had all received their main courses and Ben had left the restaurant.

Ally tidied up behind the bar and tried to tell herself she didn't care. But when all the containers were replenished and all the glasses clean and dry she found herself calling Melissa. She told her sister about Ben and his gorgeous accountant and how Ben appeared to have the worst traits of George and her father combined—a cheater *and* a pie-in-the-sky man. She was building a case against him, but instead of making her feel better that they weren't together, the facts only intensified the hard knot of pain in her chest.

"He's gone back to the cottage," she finished up. "It's probably just business, right?"

Melissa snorted. "I bet the only figure he'll be looking at tonight will be hers. You should have slept with him when you had the chance. Now he thinks you're not interested and he's moved on."

"I don't know that I ever *had* a chance." She paused. "Well, maybe once, in the tree—"

"You were going to do it in a tree?" Melissa was agog.

"No, but he kissed me and called me…" Ally dropped her voice. *"Dirty girl."*

"Ooh, I like that. Anything else?" Melissa asked.

"The other night he threw me over a table in the restaurant and kissed me. We might have gone further if a car hadn't come along and shone its headlights on us. Of all people, it had to be George who happened to drive past."

"Your problem, Ally, is that you're put off too easily," Melissa said. "I'll go out to the cottage and peer through the window to see what he and this so-called accountant are up to. It'll be a snap. Limerick is surrounded by a tall hedge and shrubbery. No one ever bothers drawing the curtains."

"No, Mel," Ally said, horrified. "They'll see you."

"I'll wear Julio's green catsuit and blend in," Melissa said.

"I mean, it's an invasion of privacy," Ally protested. Bad enough that Lindy was taking every opportunity to spy on them.

"I'm not going to *watch*," Melissa said. "Unless there's some really hot sex—"

"Mel!" Ally cried, scandalized. "I forbid it."

"Do you want another George-type experience, where you find out long after the fact that Ben's carrying on with someone else?" Melissa demanded.

"Ben and I aren't even going out," Ally said.

"But you *like* him."

"Yeees." Okay, she admitted it, but only to Melissa, who didn't really count. "I could simply ask him tomorrow if he's romantically involved with Ellen."

"Trust me, my way is better," Melissa said firmly. "You'll know without having to show your hand."

"Mel—" Ally began. But Melissa had hung up.

Was her whole family crazy? If Ben saw Melissa snooping around the cottage he'd assume Ally had put her up to it. Ally had to stop her.

"Julie," Ally said, catching the waitress as she returned from clearing a table. "I have an emergency. Can you and Rico handle the front?"

Julie, her hands laden with dishes, glanced around the dining room. Only two-thirds of the tables were occupied and most of those were on dessert. "Sure, we'll be fine."

Melissa's car was parked a block down the hill from Limerick Cottage. Ally pulled in behind her and walked up the middle of the street to avoid crunching on the gravel shoulder. Her heart was pumping fast and her mind was trying to convince her to turn around. Creeping about in the dark, spying on people was not the sort of thing she did. If she saw Ben and Ellen locked in a passionate embrace she was going to feel even worse than she did now.

Ally slipped inside the tall hedge that surrounded the cottage. The green-painted timber looked gray in the dark and the only light was coming from the spa room, which had floor-to-ceiling windows on two sides. While she stood there hesitating, she saw movement in a shrub. Melissa. Ally had to admit her sister blended in well in Julio's green leotard.

"Mel?" Ally whispered. "Is that you? Come away from there."

Her sister beckoned her over. "They're in the spa bath. Naked."

Ally darted out of the shadow of the hedge and dropped to all fours beneath the shrub. She inched forward, tiny stones and twigs pressing into her palms and knees. "Are you sure?"

"I didn't see them get in but *look*."

Ally parted the branches and peered through. A pretty redhead, her curly hair piled on top of her head, sat in the steaming spa, bubbles rising in frothy mounds around her bare shoulders. Ben wore a dressing gown and was handing her a champagne flute, laughing at something Ellen had said. They looked like a couple in a scene from one of the brochures Ally used to stock at the Cottage Rentals.

Ally felt a sharp stab to her heart. *She* wanted to be the woman in the brochure with Ben. Then the branch she was gripping cracked and she lost her balance, falling sideways to the sound of rustling foliage.

Ben and Ellen turned to the window.

"They've seen us! Run!" Melissa hissed, and backed out of the bushes. Before Ally could even get to her feet, Melissa was dashing for the street, leaving Ally to face the music, just as she always had as a kid.

Ally crawled farther into the bushes with

her bottom facing out and wished she'd worn a dark cardigan over her white blouse.

Ben peered through the spa-room window in disbelief. Had that really been Ally's wide-eyed oval face looking back at him from out of the shrubbery? He set his wineglass on the ledge of the spa. "I'll be right back."

"It's probably just kids," Ellen called after him. "Forget it."

Ben opened the front door and stepped outside. "Who's there?"

The dog across the road started barking. Cautiously he made his way around the side of the cottage. Down low, he spied a heel poking out of the greenery and above it, a smooth round rump. Too tempting.

"Ouch!" Ally cried as he pinched her. She jerked forward and broke another branch.

"What are you doing in there?" Ben asked.

"Nothing," she replied in a small voice.

"*Ally.*"

"Oh, all right." She emerged from between the trees. "I was trying to stop Melissa from spying on you."

"Oh? Why would Melissa spy on me?"

"Why? I'll tell you why," Ally blustered. "She doesn't think it's fair for you to kiss me one night and take your accountant on a romantic weekend a few days later. She thinks you might be a serial cheater and that I should find out sooner rather than later."

Ben crossed his arms over his chest. "How could I be a serial cheater when I'm not involved with anyone?"

"Aren't you?" Ally demanded. "Melissa thinks that if you say you can't go out with women because you're trying to build a relationship with your son, then that should apply to *all* women, including your accountant."

"Melissa's doing an awful lot of thinking about me." Ben was too amused to be annoyed, but he hid his smile. "You can tell her from me that I'm *not* romantically involved with my accountant."

"You were naked in the spa bath. Drinking champagne."

Ben pulled open his loosely tied dressing gown to reveal a perfectly respectable swimsuit. "Ellen's wearing a strapless bathing suit."

"Oh." Ally paused. "And the weekend together?"

"It really is business. We each have our own bedroom."

"You have a perfectly good room in my house."

"Right beside yours, separated by a thin wall that's anything but soundproof. Danny's away. You and I would have been all alone."

"So?"

"So, at night I can hear you undress—"

"You can't!" Ally's hand crept to her throat.

"I can almost feel the whisper of your silk nightie as you slide it over your skin," Ben went on, venting his frustration at the sleepless nights. "Smell your hair where it spreads across the pillow, hear the creak in your mattress when you turn over in your sleep."

Ally gave a breathless laugh. "I had no idea."

"With Danny gone I didn't know if I could trust myself." He moved closer, wanting nothing more than to slide his hands into her disheveled hair and kiss her senseless.

She started to lean toward him when suddenly she pulled away. "Wait a minute! I don't *have* a silk nightie."

"Maybe not," he said, "but I have a vivid imagination."

Ally paced away, her movements agitated. "So you and Ellen really aren't—" She broke off. "Not that it's any of my business."

"Trust me, Ellen's no more romantically interested in me than I am in her," Ben said. "She's already got a partner—a *female* partner."

"Oh," Ally said, surprised into silence. "I guess I jumped to conclusions."

He stepped closer and pulled a leaf from her hair. "You have this strange affinity for trees." He reached up again, this time to remove the elastic from her sagging ponytail, and her hair fell in thick dark waves about her shoulders. "I do love seeing you all unkempt."

"What are you doing?" she asked, grabbing for her hair elastic as if he'd stripped her naked.

Ben sighed. Plunging his hands into her hair really wasn't an option right now. "I'm doing the honorable thing. Stay still."

Her hair was thick and as soft as silk, and it took him a few tries to get it all in one bunch. Then he wrapped the hair elastic around once, twice, in what turned out to be an oddly intimate act. Unexpectedly tender feelings flooded through him when she awkwardly touched her ponytail and rewarded him with a luminous smile.

"Thank you," she whispered. "I'd better go and let you get on with your strategizing."

He wanted to say something to keep her there, but what? That she looked beautiful by starlight? She'd think him a complete dag.

Ally started to move away then paused. She rose on her toes and anchored her hands on his shoulders. She kissed him on the mouth, gently at first, then harder, opening his lips with her tongue. He drew her in, his hands cupping her hips while she slipped her hands under his dressing gown and across his bare chest. His body hardened, blood surging.

"We shouldn't be doing this," she murmured.

This was getting to be a familiar refrain. "You started it."

"No, you did. You touched my hair."

He was too busy kissing to answer. She was soft and warm and desirable and he wanted to make love to her right now.

The front door opened and a woman's voice called, "Ben, what was the noise about?"

It took a moment for his brain to shift gears. "Just a possum," he said over his shoulder. "I'll be there in a minute."

"A possum!" With an outraged laugh, Ally pushed him away.

"I'll introduce you to Ellen," Ben suggested. "Then we'll come back outside and get naked on the grass."

"No, we won't." She moved away and this time didn't pause again until she had the gate between them. "You've got to stop kissing me."

Because she was smiling, Ben was pretty sure she didn't mean it, but it wasn't until she was halfway down the street, hurrying toward her car that he remembered and called out, "*You* kissed *me!*"

And bloody nice it was, too.

"WHAT DID YOUR MUM BRING you from Bali?" Ben glanced at his son next to him in the passenger seat of the U-Haul truck.

Ellen had left early that morning. Since it was Sunday and Ben's day off, he'd rented a truck to take the cases of olive oil into Melbourne. He'd sold the entire consignment to a provedore of fine foods who supplied restaurants all over Victoria. Paolo was always on the lookout for good deals and after tasting the oil, he'd snapped it up.

On the way back from dropping the oil off, Ben had picked Danny up from Carolyn's.

"A puppet." Danny reached into the backpack between his knees and pulled out a traditional Balinese dancing puppet dressed in bright batik silk and an elaborate gold headdress. "I didn't want to hurt her feelings, but what am I supposed to do with it?"

"Hang it on your wall?" Ben suggested halfheartedly, to which Danny made a face. "I guess not. It's nice, though. Maybe Ally would like it in the lounge room."

"Ted gave me a computer game about deep-sea fishing. It's kinda cool." Danny stuffed the puppet back in his bag. "Oh, yeah, Mum said to make sure you get my books and stationery this week because school starts next week."

"I've got the list," Ben said. "You should think about joining a sporting team. Do you like soccer?"

"I dunno," Danny said. "Can I try my new computer game when we get home?"

Ben turned the truck off the highway and onto the road to Tipperary Springs. It was eleven o'clock on a beautiful summer morning and it seemed criminal for his son to be sitting inside in front of a computer. A week from now, Danny would be caught up in schoolwork, making new friends…he'd have even less time for his father.

Back at the house, Ben sorted out Danny's dirty clothes and watched Danny play the game Ted had given him, which simulated the experience of being harnessed onto the back of a deep-sea fishing cruiser out on the open ocean.

"Yay, I got one," Danny shouted. On the screen a marlin leaped out of the water attached to a fishing line.

"Do you like fish?" Ben asked. "We could go to the market and get a nice snapper for dinner. I'll show you how to fillet it—"

"You made me lose it!" Danny recast his virtual line.

"Okay, that's it," Ben said. "We're going to *do* something together. You and me."

"Not now," Danny protested. "Once I get the marlin, the next level is hooking a great white shark."

"Hey, why don't we go fishing for real?" The more Ben thought about it the better he liked the idea. He'd been a keen fisherman as a youth but for the past fifteen years, he'd been too busy for anything but work. "We won't catch a shark, although if we're lucky we might catch a trout. And if we catch one, we're going to cook it."

"But—"

"No buts." Ben rose. "Turn off the computer."

"But—"

"Nuh!" Ben cut him off with an upward slice of his hand. "We're going to have fun together if it kills us."

"Oh, all right," Danny grumbled, and started shutting down the computer.

Wow, it worked. Ben hurried off before Danny could see his surprise. Ben had spent so many years being a weekend father, catering to his son's wishes, that he'd forgotten that parenting meant *he* also had a right to make decisions about how to spend their time.

He found a sporting goods store on Main Street where they rented rods and bought bait and a fishing license. By noon they were standing on the banks of Tipperary Lake, which the clerk told them was well stocked with trout.

On the small sandy beach in front of the boathouse, children played in the water while their parents barbecued lunch. Two teenagers lazily turned a paddleboat in circles in the center of the lake. Hikers could be seen through the trees on the path that circumnavigated the lake.

Ben showed Danny how to attach a worm to the hook and cast the line into the water. A half an hour went by without even a nibble.

"We're never going to catch anything," Danny said.

"Fishing isn't just about catching a fish." Ben leaned back in his deck chair and savored the fine day. Sunlight lit the reeds at the shallow end of the lake where blue-winged dragonflies flitted over the surface of the glassy water. Overhead, a flock of sulfur-crested cockatoos flapped their white wings across the blue sky and screeched as they settled into the upper branches of a gum tree.

Danny reeled his line in and checked his worm. "Do you think Ally's pretty?"

Ben sat upright so fast the folding chair almost collapsed on him. "That worm looks chewed. You'd better put a new one on. Shows the fish are out there, though."

Danny opened the foam box of night crawlers and attached a wriggly worm to his hook. He repeated his question. "Do you think Ally's pretty?"

"Yes, I do. She's a very nice lady," Ben said. "Why?"

"Just wondering." Danny recast his line. "You kissed her in the tree. Is she your girlfriend?"

"I wouldn't go quite that far," Ben said carefully. "We just kissed." Twice, no, three times, each better than the last. "Ally's not looking for a boyfriend and I'm not looking for a girlfriend. We're just friends."

"Mum always pretended she and Ted were just friends," Danny said. "Then I found out he slept in her bed whenever I spent the weekend with you. The next thing I knew they were getting married."

"Did that bother you?" Ben asked. "That they got married, I mean."

"Kinda." Danny shrugged. "They got all lovey-dovey and didn't want me around anymore."

Ben reeled in his line. The worm was gone. "Your mother wasn't trying to get rid of you," he said. "That's not why you came to live with me."

"Isn't it?" Danny raised a skeptical eyebrow.

"*I* wanted you," Ben said. "Your mum agreed that since you were getting older it would be good for you to spend more time with me." He paused. "Even if Ally and I *were* more than friends I wouldn't ever leave you out."

Danny jiggled his rod. "That's what Mum said, too." He was quiet for a long time, and his next question dropped like a lead sinker into the silence. "So you're *not* going to marry Ally?"

Ben stabbed with the hook, missed the wriggling worm, and a bright red bead of blood appeared on his fingertip. "We don't know each other well enough to even think about marriage. Okay?"

Danny nodded, sharp and firm, as if they'd made a pact. "Okay."

Whew! Ben wiped a film of sweat from his brow. He wanted to have meaningful conversations with Danny but it was a darn sight trickier than playing computer games.

Danny wedged his rod between the roots of a willow and went barefoot into the shallows. Ben lay back on the grass and his eyes drifted shut....

A splash woke him, followed by an excited cry from Danny, knee-deep in water. "I got a fish!"

Ben sat up quickly. Danny's rod was bent over, and something was tugging hard on the line, ripples spreading from where it entered the water.

"What do I do?" Danny shouted as he ran to get his rod out of the roots.

"Reel in the line," Ben said. "Don't lose it."

"How do I do that?" Danny tried to wind in the line. The tip of the rod was waving all over the place.

"Stand still," Ben instructed. "Hold on tight. Give the rod a jerk then slowly reel in the line."

Ben got the net, just in case. Danny had probably hooked an old tennis shoe or a waterlogged branch—

A trout broke the surface and fell back into the water.

"It's a fish!" Danny shouted. "I caught a fish."

"Keep reeling it in," Ben said, exited now, too. "Careful, careful…" He waded into the lake up to his knees and grabbed the line, swinging the fish into the net.

"We got him!" Danny was beside himself with excitement, jumping up and down on the bank. "We got him."

Ben staggered back onto shore with the wriggling fish. "Well done, Danny. You caught your first fish."

"Wow!" Danny said, staring at the trout in awe. "I can't believe it. It's a real fish. I didn't think I'd ever catch anything."

"It's a beauty." Ben crouched to carefully remove the hook from the gaping mouth.

"It's big enough to make a nice late lunch for the two of us."

Half an hour later the trout lay cleaned and scaled on a plate. Ben and Danny stood over it, deliberating.

"How do you want to cook it?" Ben asked. "Pan-fried, filleted in a sauce, or baked in the oven?"

"I don't care," Danny said.

"You *have* to care," Ben began, then stopped. Danny just wanted to eat the thing. "Fresh food is best served simply. We'll panfry it in extra virgin olive oil. We have a good supply."

"Can you take off its head?" Danny asked. "I don't want to eat anything that's staring at me."

"Leaving the head on improves the flavor," Ben explained. "See how shiny and clear the eyes are? That's how you can tell it's fresh."

"Uh, Dad? We just caught it," Danny said carefully. "We *know* it's fresh."

"I'm telling you for future reference when you're buying fish in a market."

"Like that'll ever happen," Danny said

with a snort. He went quiet a moment. "I really hate those eyes."

Ben sighed. "Place the blade directly behind the gills, like so," he said, and quickly sliced off the head.

Danny went white. "Is that *blood?*"

"Next time, you can clean the fish," Ben said. "Then maybe you won't be so squeamish."

"Will you make me butcher a hog when we have bacon?" Danny muttered.

Ben laughed, and Danny glanced up at him with a grin.

"Face it, Dad, you're seriously weird," Danny said, getting bolder.

"I'll show you weird." Ben put down the knife, hauled Danny into a wrestling hold and began to tickle.

Danny squirmed out and grabbed the fish head and made its jaws work. "He's going to bite you."

"Have some respect." Ben took the head away from him.

"For you?" Danny laughed, dodging and grabbing.

"For the fish." Ben was smiling, but his eyes were serious.

Danny realized he meant it, and sobered. "Sorry."

"It's okay." Ben put a hand on his shoulder and squeezed. "Find a pan just big enough to hold the trout. It's your fish. You get to do the honors."

Under Ben's instruction, Danny heated the pan, added the oil and cooked the fish, four minutes on each side.

"You don't want to overcook fish," Ben told him, and showed him how to test with a fork for flakiness. Danny watched closely while Ben performed the tricky part of stripping the cooked fillets cleanly from the bones and turning them onto two plates.

"We should save a piece for Ally," Danny suggested.

"She can have part of mine," Ben said, setting some aside.

"Mmm, good," Danny enthused as he ate every scrap of his fillet. "Fishing for real was cool, way better than the computer game." He paused, twiddling his fork, not quite looking at Ben. "Cooking wasn't so bad, either."

At last, Danny was showing an interest! Ben was tempted to leap up and start teaching his son everything he knew. Instead, he forced himself to smile casually. "Yeah, and it really impresses the chicks."

Danny squirmed with embarrassment. *"Da-a-d."*

CHAPTER TEN

"YOUR ANNIVERSARY party starts at four in the afternoon, the DJ will play from seven until midnight," Ally informed her mother late on Sunday afternoon. Ben was out fishing with Danny, and after Melissa had gone home Ally had felt unaccountably restless all alone in the house, so she'd gone to visit her mother at the gallery.

While Cheryl sorted through framed paintings in the studio at the back of the gallery, Ally ran through party plans. "You and Tony will greet the guests together and cut the cake after dinner, together."

Cheryl glanced up from the canvases. "We're not even speaking to each other."

"We've already had positive replies to half the invitations, including your cousins in Queensland who are driving for two days to get here," Ally said. "This party is going to happen and you are going to host it with your husband." Sometimes you had to be firm with parents. It was for their own good.

"Tony's taken over the house with boxes and boxes of olive oil," Cheryl protested.

"That's no longer an issue," Ally replied. "Ben hauled the oil to Melbourne this morning."

"Even so, the house is a mess," Cheryl said. "Tony hasn't cleaned since I've been gone. *I* don't have time, between the gallery and renovating Melissa's house."

"I've hired a cleaning service," Ally said. "I'll pay Danny to mow the lawn and Melissa and I will string up fairy lights in the back garden."

"What if it rains?" Cheryl said. "There's not enough room in the house for everyone."

"My barometer has been fixed firmly on fair for weeks. The forecast is for continuing hot, dry weather," Ally said. "We haven't had rain since the big storm a month ago." The day she'd lost George and found Ben.

"You look tired, Ally," Cheryl said. "Are you getting enough sleep?"

"Probably not," Ally admitted. "Restaurant work requires such long hours. I don't know how Ben and the others do it, day after day, week after week."

Cheryl hauled a large blank canvas out of the stack and leaned it against the wall. It had a triangular tear in the lower left corner. "No one's going to use this now."

"Can't you glue it or something?" Ally asked, peering at the small rip.

Cheryl shook her head. "Do you want it? Be my guest."

"I haven't painted since I was twelve," Ally said.

"You should take it up again," Cheryl told her. "You used to be very good."

Ally glanced at the palette and brushes and tubes of acrylic paint squeezed into crumpled angles, and felt a nostalgic tug which she reluctantly thrust away. "No, thanks." She took both Cheryl's hands in hers. "You've *got* to come to your party. Please say you will."

"Of course, I will," Cheryl said, sighing. "But tell Tony I want the house put back the way it was."

"Okay," Ally said happily. "Now, about

the food. Lindy's mother's catering company is doing a spit roast, salads and desserts."

"You're not getting Ben to cook?" Cheryl asked.

Just hearing his name brought last night flooding back. If she was tired this morning it was because she'd lain awake half the night fantasizing about him. Unlike George, Ben was anything but predictable and she couldn't stop wondering what would happen between them if they ever really let themselves go.

"Ally?" Cheryl prompted.

"Ben'll be there, but not to cook. I planned this event long before I met him. Everything's already taken care of." Ally watched her choose another painting and place it in the growing stack. "Are you putting together a new exhibit?"

"No," Cheryl said. "Ben came in and asked me for paintings for his restaurant. He said it was your suggestion."

"I told him if I had to look at those gray walls another day I'd go out of my mind."

The bell on the front desk chimed to indicate a customer needing service. "I'll just be a minute," Cheryl said to Ally, and went back to the gallery.

Cheryl was more than a minute. Ally peeked into the gallery and saw her mother deep in conversation with a well-dressed, middle-aged couple. Serious potential buyers.

Idly, Ally picked up a tube of cobalt-blue paint lying on an easel and unscrewed the cap. A fat blue worm inched out. Uh oh. She squeezed the tube on the other side hoping the worm would withdraw, but it only oozed out farther.

What was she going to do with it? While she tried to come up with an answer, the worm grew until it curled over. Desperate, Ally scraped it off onto the torn canvas and quickly screwed on the lid. She looked at the large glob of blue against the white for several seconds. Then something made her reach out and smear the paint across the pristine white canvas. Ally blinked in surprise at her own audacity, then smiled with unexpected pleasure.

Her fingertips glistened blue. Pretty. Ally pressed them onto a clear portion of the canvas, leaving dotted prints. Orange would look nice against the blue, she decided, and with the heel of her other hand she smeared an arc of burnt orange sunrise above the cobalt sea. Like a kid in a candy shop, she studied the row of paint tubes. The names were exotic, thrilling even. Cadmium-yellow, alizarin-crimson, viridian, cerulean-blue, burnt-umber.

Ally selected a tube at random and added a blob to the canvas. What the painting looked like didn't matter because no one, barring her mother, would ever see it. She had no plan in mind, nor any idea of what she was doing. All she knew was that smearing the paint around with her hands felt good. She left some colors pure and mixed others, here an intense band of ultramarine, there white swirled into scarlet to form clouds of pink fairy floss. Over there a green that reminded her of Ben's eyes—not the color so much as the feeling of light.

Thinking of his eyes made her think of his lips, which made her remember his kiss. Blushing, she threw herself back into the painting.

Half an hour later, Cheryl came back into

the room. She stopped dead and did a double take. Ally turned to her with a brilliant smile, her upraised hands smeared with a dozen colors.

Cheryl laughed then tilted her head to study the bold sweeps of color. "I like it," Cheryl said finally. "In fact, I love it. What are you going to call it?"

Smiling, Ally shook her head. "Nothing. I'm just mucking around. Throw it out."

Yet even as she dismissed her painting, she felt an exhilaration she hadn't known in years. It was as if her blood had become effervescent. The creative surge stayed with her as she left the gallery and as she stopped at the take-away pizza shop. She was humming all the way home.

"Hello!" Ally burst through the front door bearing two large flat boxes. "Anybody hungry for pizza?"

Danny came running down the hall from his bedroom. "I caught a trout! I caught it myself." He followed Ally into the kitchen. "Try some," he urged, unwrapping the plate on which Ben had saved a piece of fish.

Ally put down the pizza boxes and

forked up a chunk of pink flesh. "That's delicious, Danny."

In the backyard, Ben heard her voice and put down his spade. He toed off his boots at the back door, brushed the loose dirt off his knees and hands and came inside. "Danny cooked the trout, too."

"I'm impressed." Ally gave Ben a smile as she brushed past him to the cupboard for dishes. She glanced over her shoulder at Ben's dirty hands and her smile grew broader. "Making mudpies, Chef?"

"I was digging a herb garden," he said. "Danny, go wash your hands for dinner."

Danny ran out of the room.

Ben soaped his hands at the kitchen sink, unable to take his gaze off Ally. Her eyes were sparkling and her ponytail swung jauntily as she moved. There was a smudge of orange paint on her cheek and her fingers were stained a curious blue-green. She had that rare look about her that he found so irresistible, that bursting-with-excitement glow as if she'd discovered a pot of gold at the end of a rainbow.

He wiped his hands dry and stepped up

behind her as she reached into a top cupboard for dishes. "I'll get those."

"Too late," she said cheerfully as she
pulled plates off the shelf. "You're slow."

"I thought women liked that in a man."
He touched the paint on her cheek with a
fingertip. "What have you been up to?"

"Nothing," she said, unable to repress a
smile.

"Liar." He grinned. "You've been getting
dirty again."

Ally turned away to put the plates on the
table. "I was helping my mother in her
studio."

Ben ran a finger across her temple and
tugged a lock of hair out of her tightly held
ponytail. "Come on, what were you up to?
You can tell me."

Her eyes danced as she ducked under his
arm and opened the fridge door. "You're
playing with fire."

"I'm a chef," Ben said. "I'm used to
getting burned."

"What's burned?" Danny bounded back
into the room, his hands still wet and
dripping. "Not the pizza, I hope."

"For crying out loud, Danny, go dry your hands." Ben jerked away from Ally and turned his son around by his shoulders. "With a towel. Not on your pants."

When Danny had gone again Ben advanced. Ally thrust a jug of cold water into his hands. "Sell any oil today?"

"All of it," Ben said smugly. "Picked up, paid for and delivered." Impulsively he leaned over the water jug, trying to kiss her.

Ally dodged him, circling around to set the cutlery on the table. "You never did tell me what strategy your accountant came up with to finance your oil purchase."

"Ellen set up a limited company in my name and took out a short-term business loan." Ben followed her around the table, distributing the plates, but she was always one step ahead. "So you see, everything worked out."

Ally stopped so suddenly he bumped into her. She faced him, standing very close. "For your sake, I'm glad."

Ben raised his hand to brush her cheek. Her lips were full and slightly parted. He started to lean—

"What's going on?" Danny popped through the doorway.

"Nothing." Ben took a step back from Ally. "That was awfully fast."

Aggrieved, Danny raised his clean, dry hands for inspection. "You're always telling me to hurry up, so I did."

Ally laughed and said, "Let's eat."

It was a mealtime full of laughter. Ally joked around, lively and animated, teasing Danny, making him giggle. Her gaze frequently strayed to Ben and when she caught his eye her smile sent a jolt to his solar plexus. He liked Ally more than he could have imagined when he'd first met her. He found himself wishing she *was* his girlfriend.

His gaze shifted to his son. The afternoon at the lake had tinged Danny's nose with pink and brought out a smattering of freckles on his cheeks. Danny was talkative for a change, full of humor and pleased as punch with himself. Their relationship had made a quantum leap today as they'd bonded over the fish.

In fact, things were going so well with Danny that surely there was no harm in flirting with Ally or stealing the occasional kiss? Then Ben frowned. How much of Danny's good humor was due to Ben allaying his son's fears that Ben wasn't getting serious about Ally?

ALLY RAPPED on Melissa's front door, walked in and did a double-take. The internal wall that separated the kitchen and the lounge room was gone and she was looking at the back of the stove and the inside of a pots-and-pans cupboard.

Melissa hurried out of the short hall that led to her bedroom and stopped short, her purple silk-fringed skirt swinging around her calves. "I thought you were the carpenter."

"Sorry to disappoint," Ally said. "I see Mother has finally gone completely crackers. You should have called me. I would have tried to reason with her."

"I love what she's doing! Everything's so open." Melissa twirled around, lace and bead earrings dangling over her bare shoulders. "Next we're going to knock out the wall behind you and put in bifold doors leading onto a patio."

Ally glanced out the window to try to visualize it and saw Julio casually doing backflips out on the lawn, his bare chest and heavily muscled arms glistening in the sun. "All this great sex is interfering with your brain. Last time I was here you were freaking out at Mother's attempts to redecorate. Now you're into full-scale renovation."

"We've come to an understanding," Melissa explained. "She can make structural alterations but when it comes to color schemes, I'm in charge."

"Let's go over the game plan for Saturday," Ally said. "I'll pick the cake up at 9:00 a.m., then I'll check with the caterers to make sure they're on schedule, pick up my dress from the dry cleaners, pick up the wine and beer from the bottle shop, have a quick lunch then start to ferry the rellies without vehicles from the hotel to the house."

"What's my schedule?" Melissa asked.

"You don't need to do a thing," Ally said. "I've got everything under control. Just be at the house at three-thirty."

"That's not fair," Melissa complained. "You're doing it all. I'm tired of being useless."

"You're not. You helped with the invitations." Ally tried to think of something Melissa could do that wouldn't tax her capabilities. "I know, you can help Mother get dressed and do her makeup. You're good at that."

"That's not a real job."

"Okay, okay. How about if you pick up the cake from the bakery and take it to the house. Can you do that?"

"Of course," Melissa said happily. Then she sank onto the couch and motioned Ally to sit beside her. "Now to the important stuff. I want you to tell me *everything*. What happened the other night?"

"You mean after you ran off and left me?" Ally said. "Ben caught me crouching in the bushes impersonating a hydrangea."

Melissa smiled with anticipation. "And?"

Warmth flooded Ally's cheeks. "He retied my ponytail."

"Ok-ay," Melissa said carefully. "What does this mean? Is he or isn't he sleeping with his accountant?"

"He's not. She's a lesbian. Their relationship really is strictly business."

"I knew it," Melissa said triumphantly. "That's why I left when he came out. I was hoping he'd be overcome by the moonlight and kiss you."

"There was no moon, just a lot of stars," Ally said. "You went to Limerick Cottage thinking you were going to catch them in the act."

"Oh, well…." Melissa waved that off. "Did he? Kiss you, I mean?"

"Actually…" Ally smiled. "*I* kissed *him*."

"Ooh," Melissa squealed. "So what's next?"

"Good question." Ally kicked off her shoes and tucked her feet beneath her. "Oh, Mel, I'm afraid I'm falling for him! When I'm with him I feel as though my blood's been replaced with champagne. It's as if there's this giant electromagnet sucking us together. But he's not right for me. He's spontaneous and unpredictable. Not my kind of man at all."

"He sounds to me like he's exactly what you need right now," Melissa said. "You've got to lose those old thought patterns, Ally. 'Your kind of man' proved to be wrong in the past."

"But what about the future?" Ally said. "The way Ben leaped into this olive oil deal worries me. I mean, it turned out all right this time but what if he's another dreamer like Tony? I couldn't bear to go through what Mother's put up with all these years."

"Mother manages," Melissa said. "You should see her in action with the building contractor. Her combination of sweet talk and steely resolve got him working on my house right away when other people are waiting weeks or months for renovations."

"Yet she can't make Tony do what she wants," Ally mused.

Melissa shrugged. "Maybe that's why she loves him."

CHAPTER ELEVEN

A PAIR OF HANDS covered Ally's eyes, blanking out the throng of relatives and friends milling around her parents' large backyard. She'd paused to watch the DJ setting up on the far side of the pool when *wham!* her vision had been blocked.

"Uncle Brian?" she queried impatiently. Playing guessing games would be just like Tony's practical- joker younger brother from Mooloolaba.

"No," someone whispered in her ear.

She couldn't identify a person from a whisper, not even whether they were male or female. Ben was working the dinner service at Mangos and wasn't expected to arrive until later. Even so, Ally ran her fingers over the hands, feeling for tiny scars. These fingers felt masculine but they were smooth, with longish rounded nails. She sniffed the sultry air. Over the mingled aromas of a side of lamb and a baron of beef slowly turning on the barbecue spit came the faint scent of cloves.

"George!" Wrenching his hands away, she spun around to glare at her ex-fiancé. "What are you doing here?"

"Is that any way to greet a guest?" George pulled an invitation from the pocket of his sports jacket and waved it in front of her. "This was redirected to my new address."

"If you had a shred of decency you would have known not to show up." She glanced around. "Where's Kathy?"

George shook his head reproachfully. "Give me credit for having *some* consideration for your feelings."

Biting rejoinders sprang to mind, but engaging in a battle for the moral high ground with George wasn't worth the bother. "If you'll excuse me, I have things to do," she said, and strode off.

"Where are Tony and Cheryl?" George asked, following her. "I have a present for them."

"They're inside the house, getting ready," Ally said. "You can put your present with the others on the table in the marquee. The bar's in there if you'd like a drink."

"Only if you'll join me," he said. When she hesitated, he added, "Just one, Ally. Please?"

"A quick drink, then." She led the way to the marquee where a bartender was mixing drinks. Buffet tables were laden with cold plates and salads, and another table was piled high with beautifully wrapped gifts.

"This must be some occasion. You look different tonight," George said. "You never wore cleavage for me."

"Actually, I did. You just never noticed. Would you like your usual Bacardi and Coke?" Ally asked.

"I'll have rum and orange juice for a change." When she raised her eyebrows he added, "I like to break free of my routine now and then."

"That shows real growth, George." Ally turned to the bartender. "Rum and orange juice and a chardonnay, thanks."

George sipped his drink and eyed Ally

over the rim of his glass. "I could do without the snarky comments." He glanced around at the milling guests and added, "Can we go somewhere to talk—*alone?*"

"Oh, all right." She led him out of the marquee and across the yard to the finished garage. The walls were covered with sporting memorabilia from football and cricket teams. Dominating the floor space was the magnificent antique pool table that had been in Tony's family for three generations, brought over on a ship from England. There was a couch along one wall but Ally didn't feel like getting cozy with George. She didn't even want to stay long enough to perch on one of the bar stools.

"Well?" she said, tapping her toe on the indoor/outdoor carpeting. "What is it?"

"You've changed," George said, regarding her with a puzzled frown. "You never used to be so hard."

"I'm not hard, I'm just not prepared to put up with your pompous bullshit anymore. For someone who thinks he's so smart you really don't have a clue."

"You're still angry. I don't blame you. The

way I behaved with Kathy wasn't fair." He spread his hands in a gesture of helplessness. "Things got out of control before I knew what was happening."

Ally was silent. She'd never seen George like this before. He must be feeling terrible to act so conciliatory.

"You're a wonderful woman, Ally," he went on. "Kind and sweet and so capable. I never appreciated you."

"Don't worry about it," she muttered. "Water under the bridge."

"No, really," he said earnestly. "I came here tonight to apologize. I'm so sorry. Please don't be angry anymore."

With a genuine apology in hand Ally found it impossible to maintain her righteous indignation. "I'm angry at you, yes, but I'm also angry because I tried so hard to convince myself I was in love with you. I'm…I'm sorry, too," she choked out. "I was unhappy and didn't have the guts to admit I should never have accepted your proposal. I was going to, that day I found you with Kathy, but it was easier to blame the entire breakup on you."

George nodded. "I guess we both made mistakes."

Lulled by his attitude of understanding, Ally went on. "I just wish I knew *why* I keep making the same mistake time after time. I *want* to get married and have children, but as soon as the relationship becomes serious I discover I'm not in love with the man."

"I suspect the answer lies in your childhood," he mused, swinging into psychiatrist mode.

Ally groaned inwardly. She should have known better than to open up to him. She glanced at her watch and started for the door. "The food is going to be ready soon. I have to be on hand to help."

Ignoring her, George went on. "Tell me, what are your earliest feelings about your father?"

Taken aback, Ally checked her stride. "What does that have to do with my love life?"

George paced between the pool table and the couch, finger raised to make his point. "A woman's romantic attachments in adult life are in many ways dependent upon her early

relationship with her father. Your father's un-
orthodox business ventures and volatile personality led you to equate excitement with
negative consequences, thus causing you to
avoid similar such men as an adult."

"Could you say that in plain English?"
Ally said.

"You seek out men who won't cause you
extreme highs and lows of emotion."

"Yes, that's exactly what I do," Ally said.
"What's wrong with wanting emotional stability?"

"Nothing, as long as your subconscious is
not in conflict with your conscious," George
pontificated. "Your early experience with
your father set up a cognitive dissonance
which is played out again and again in your
attempt to negate his influence by attaching
yourself to the opposite personality type."

"English, please," Ally said wearily.

"Your adult need for predictability con-
flicts with your childlike desire for excitement. This you associate with your father,
whom you love and admire despite his irresponsible, if not downright criminal, behavior."

This wasn't much better in terms of jargon but Ally got the gist. She wanted excitement but she needed predictability. He might just have something there.

George continued to pace and muse. "It's a fascinating syndrome. I may write it up as an article in the *Australian Journal of Psychiatry.*"

"Over my dead body," Ally muttered. "Just out of curiosity, what's the 'cure' for this inner conflict of mine?"

George pressed his palms together. "You must purge yourself of the thrill-seeking proclivities of childhood and accept at both the conscious and subconscious levels that the most desirable personality trait in a husband is predictability."

"And how am I supposed to do that?" Ally demanded.

"You must enter the realm of your inner child and see it for the barrier to growth it is. Through psychotherapy, I can help you banish your unwholesome need for exciting male companionship," George explained. "Only then will you truly understand that the right man for you is, and has always been, *me.*"

"What!" Ally exclaimed. "Is that what all your mumbo jumbo has been leading up to? I thought we were talking about me getting *past* you."

"I want you back," George said, abruptly abandoning his professional persona. "I made a mistake getting mixed up with Kathy. She's too demanding—dinners out, perfume, chocolates. And she can't type."

"She's a secretary," Ally said. "Of course she can type."

George shook his head. "I didn't hire her for her office skills."

Ally couldn't believe her ears. "You got your girlfriend to do your typing and took your secretary to bed. Do you see anything strange in this behavior, *Herr Doktor?*"

"I don't understand your hostility," George said, turning petulant. "I thought you'd be flattered that I still want you. You could be everything to me—wife, friend, typist. You wouldn't have to work at the grubby restaurant, getting sexually assaulted by the chef."

"He never assaulted me!"

"I saw you that night, sprawled over a

table like a piece of meat. I could take you away from all that."

"But George, you just told me I have to give in to my inner child's desire for excitement."

"You're misinterpreting my words," George said crossly.

Ally tapped a finger alongside her cheek, deep in thought. Although George hadn't intended it, he'd just given her psychological carte blanche to pursue Ben. "No, George, you're right. I should be spontaneous for a change. It could be fun."

"*Fun* is a relative concept," George grumbled.

"Let me put it in layman's terms for you," she said. "I'm going to have sex with Ben." She smiled and patted George on the arm. "Thanks, you've been a real help."

Leaving George sputtering, Ally strode back to the marquee, grabbed the bottle of bourbon from the startled bartender and tipped it straight into her mouth. The alcohol burned her throat and fed the fire in her belly she'd been trying to ignore for weeks. She was pouring a second shot when someone put a hand on her shoulder.

"Go aw—" she began, then broke off when she spun around and saw Ben standing there in a light tan suit and an open-necked navy shirt, looking incredibly sexy. "Just the man I wanted to see."

"What's wrong?" he said, frowning at the bottle in her hand. "You only drink hard liquor when you're upset."

Ally tossed back a second shot and wiped her mouth with the back of her hand. "Or when I'm gathering my courage." Putting a hand on the back of his neck she stood on her tiptoes and kissed him hard on the lips.

Oh, yes, this was exactly what her inner child, heck, her inner *woman,* had been craving—the indescribable taste of Ben's lips, his arms tightening around her, his heart thumping next to hers. Like a kid with a bag of lollies, she wanted to gobble him up.

Finally she drew back, breathing hard, to see Ben staring at her hungrily.

"What brought that on?" he gasped.

"I have a craving for something sweet," she said.

Ben started to speak but he was interrupted by a commotion on the patio that had everyone moving out of the marquee to join the rest of the guests on the lawn. Tony, in a panama hat and white linen suit, was holding court on the veranda, his arm around Cheryl. She wore a long sleeveless black gown and a massive turquoise pendant.

Ally grabbed Ben by the hand and moved through the crowd to stand beside Melissa, who looked sleek and slinky in a red sequined dress, and Julio, urbanely handsome in a pale suit.

"Attention, everyone!" Tony called. "Thank you all for coming to celebrate with my lovely wife and I thirty years of married bliss."

"Bliss?" Cheryl repeated with amiable skepticism, and then snorted in a most unrefined way. But she was smiling, and that was something, given everything that had occurred over the past month.

"Cuddlepie, you know I adore you." Tony kissed her and turned back to the crowd. "I admit I'm not always easy to live with and Cheryl's put up with a lot over the years. My anniversary present will make up for that."

Surprised and delighted, Cheryl threw her

arms around him. "Darling! You paid off the mortgage on my gallery."

"Better than that." Tony pulled a mobile phone out of his pocket and made a quick call. A moment later, the rumble of an engine was heard and everyone looked to the driveway at the side of the house. A black sports car pulled up with Tony's brother Brian behind the wheel.

"Happy anniversary, sweetheart," Tony said. "This is your brand new Audi A4 cabri-olet!"

A collective gasp went up from the crowd at the shiny black convertible with a tur-quoise interior wrapped up in an enormous red bow.

The blood drained from Cheryl's face as she stared at it, her body frozen in shock.

Ally, worried her mother would collapse on the spot, ran over and put an arm around her. She could feel her trembling. "Mother! Are you all right?" Ally glared at Tony, then said in an angry undertone, "Are you mad?"

Tony's smile never wavered. "She's always wanted a sports car."

Cheryl drew in a deep breath and pulled

away from Ally. She stood very straight and with a brilliant smile she kissed Tony on the cheek. "Darling Snugglepot, what a surprise!"

"Anything for my Cuddlepie," Tony responded jovially.

Cheryl, her arm around him, turned to smile at their guests, who were applauding with drunken gusto.

"Ally, Melissa!" Uncle Brian held a digital camera in one hand and with the other he motioned them sideways. "Move next to your folks. I'll take a family photo."

Ally found herself next to Cheryl. "Your forbearance is incredible, Mother. I don't know how you do it."

"Ally, sweetheart, this is a wonderful party," Cheryl said, smiling for the camera. "Everyone's come so far and you've done so much work to make it a success."

Melissa leaned across Ally to speak to Cheryl. "Did Ally tell you *I* picked up the cake? And I helped address the envelopes for the invitations."

"Yeah, thanks, Melissa," Ally hissed. "You sent one to George."

"I did not!" She paused. "Did I?"

"Shh, girls, behave," Cheryl said. "Melissa, you did a wonderful job, too. I take it you two had no idea about the car?"

"Of course not," Ally said. "I'd have made him take it back."

"I think it's fabulous," Melissa said.

Uncle Brian made them shuffle places, and Ally wound up on the other side of her father. She forced a smile and muttered through her clenched teeth, "What were you thinking? Now you must be even deeper in debt. The money you got from Ben for the oil couldn't possibly have paid for that whole car."

"It covered the deposit," Tony replied out of the side of his mouth. "In a few more months the harvest will be in and there'll be more than enough money to pay off both the gallery and the car."

"How are you going to make payments until then?" Ally demanded.

"Big picture, Ally." Tony slid his arm around her and gave her a squeeze. "Concentrate on the big picture."

"You're unbelievable."

"Smile," Tony urged. "Your mother wants you to be happy. Look, *she's* happy."

"You think?" Ally said.

Finally, Uncle Brian ran out of space on his digital camera and the photo session came to an end. Ally watched her mother exclaiming over the many special features of her new convertible. It was true, Cheryl had always said she'd like to own a sports car—but like this?

Ben found Ally and put an arm lightly around her shoulders. "Let's dance."

He led her onto the tiled patio surrounding the pool. Underwater lights cast a blue glow around the waterline and reflected on the faces of the people dancing and talking in the warm dusk. Thunder rumbled in the middle distance, but a few bright stars were still visible. Fairy lights twinkled through the trees.

"Everything's gone like clockwork as far as I can tell," Ben said as they moved to the slow music. "You can relax and enjoy yourself."

"I *am* enjoying myself."

"Then erase that little frown between your eyebrows. Nothing can go wrong with your plans now."

"It's not the party," Ally said. "I'm worried about my parents. Tony could have paid off at least part of the mortgage on the gallery. Instead, he blew all the money on an extravagant, meaningless gesture."

"Extravagant, yes. Reckless, perhaps, but I wouldn't call it meaningless," Ben said. "He was trying to show your mother he loves her. That has to count for something."

"I don't know," Ally said, unconvinced.

"You need a break from solving your parents' problems." Ben pulled her closer to whisper in her ear, "Tell me more about that sweet tooth."

Ally gave a low chuckle. "George thinks I should quiet the clamoring of my inner child by sleeping with you."

Ben's eyebrows rose as he drew back to see if she was joking. "George wants you to go to bed with me?"

"Well, not precisely. He wants me to go into therapy, but I prefer a more—" she slid her fingers inside his jacket "—hands-on approach."

"Why, Ms. Cummings, are you flirting with me?" She blushed and Ben grinned.

"I know your priority is Danny and that's fine," Ally went on, more seriously. "We don't have to get, you know, emotionally involved."

"Let me get this straight…you want to sleep with me as therapy?" He pretended to think about it. "I don't know. If I'm going to get naked I need something more personal."

Ally considered that. "How about, I like you and I think you're really hot?"

"Better." Ben gave her a smile. "I always suspected you had a wild and crazy streak. In the interest of mental health I'm willing to have sex with you."

"Hmm," she said. "If *I'm* going to get naked I could use a little more enthusiasm."

He pressed his hips against hers and let her feel his enthusiasm. When he spoke next to her ear, his warm breath raised prickles on the back of her neck. "I want you more than anything."

Ally melted into him. "I knew the first time we met that you were after my body."

Ben smiled against her temple. "Your prescience is amazing." He danced her into the darkest corner of the patio, away from the crowd. "Danny is at his mother's this weekend."

Ally's heart was beating very fast. She could feel Ben's heart pounding, too, and pressed closer.

"Ally...?"

"Yes." It wasn't a question; it was an answer.

He bent his head to kiss her, feather-soft, on the lips, then again, with more pressure and warmth. Ally felt her heart expand. She slipped her other arm around his neck and they stood motionless, one kiss merging into another.

Finally Ben broke off, his breathing ragged. "Do you have to stay until the end?"

Ally glanced around. The sky was completely dark now. The crowd had already thinned; some of the older guests had gone home early. Cheryl was sitting among a group of her women friends on the veranda; Tony was talking to the men outside the marquee. The party-hardy types would carry on into the wee hours. She'd done her best to make the evening a success. There was nothing more she could accomplish. "Let's go home."

Lightning flashed over the hills as they

drove across town, windows down to let in the warm breeze. Ally counted the seconds until the low rumble of thunder vibrated the sultry air. The storm was closer, but any rain would likely pass to the south.

The house was dark and quiet. Ben pulled her into his arms, kissing her breathless. Ally tugged free, moving away with a laughing backward glance over her shoulder. Ben followed on her heels.

Ally's bedside lamp glowed softly next to the dark crimson duvet piled high with pillows. She turned to Ben, nervous and excited by the intent look in his eyes.

"I've wanted to do this for such a long time," he said, and began removing her hairpins. The pins rained on the hardwood floor with tiny pings, bouncing and scattering. Her hair slipped down in soft thick clumps.

"I have a container for those," Ally whispered.

"Later." He plunged both hands into her hair and pushed it back to press kisses on her face and neck. His long fingers sifted through the silken strands then let her tousled hair fall about her bare shoulders. "I'm going to mess you up and tumble you down," he murmured as his hands moved over her body. "I'm going to unbutton you, unzip you. I'm going to make you mine. *Dirty girl.*"

Her bones were melting, her heart was racing, her vision was reduced to a blur of dark eyes and golden skin. She kept thinking she ought to be more playful but the feelings overwhelming her were too intense. Laughter faded to a soulful moan as he slowly tugged down her dress then stepped out of his pants. Trembling, she clung to him, skin on skin, fiery hot. Oh bliss, pure bliss.

Without warning, the bedside lamp flickered and went out. Lightning illuminated their bodies through the curtains as Ben pulled her onto the bed. She glimpsed a length of thigh, his mouth on her breast, his passion-filled gaze. Thunder drowned out his huskily murmured words, her inarticulate cries. A few raindrops spattered with sudden force against the windowpane. The pleasure-ache deep inside became a throbbing insistent drive until at last she heard him call her name and answered with his.

Afterward Ben lay on top of her, heavy and warm, his face buried in her neck. Ally smoothed her hands down his back and he rolled to the side, pulling her with him so they were face-to-face. Wordlessly, she gazed into his eyes, unable to summon the easy banter with which she'd started this game. To her relief, Ben didn't seem to feel the need to talk, either. Wrapped in each other's arms, they drifted into a satiated slumber.

Ben's eyes blinked open when the table lamp came on suddenly. Had minutes passed? Hours? Wind blew through the trees, but still there was no rain. Groggily, he reached over to switch off the lamp then, seeing Ally, he stopped.

She was lying on her stomach, her face shielded from the light by his shoulders. Her mouth was soft and swollen, her hair a tangle on her pillow. Her bare back curved to a slender waist, the flare of her hips just visible beneath the sheet. His gaze rested on the fullness of her left breast where it flattened against the mattress.

His body hardened as he looked at her. At

last, she'd unleashed the passionate side she kept hidden under those prim white blouses and straight-as-an-arrow skirts. From where he lay, the therapy would seem to be a success. But as for not getting emotionally involved, for him, at least, it was too late.

How was Danny going to feel about Ben's relationship with Ally? He couldn't just spring it on the boy after assuring him nothing was going on. No, he would have to ease into it gradually.

Ally's eyes opened. She pushed herself up onto her elbows. "What happened? Why is the light on?"

Ben leaned over and kissed her slowly and very thoroughly. "The power came back on."

Her gaze drifted down his naked body and her mouth curved in a slow smile. "So I see."

CHAPTER TWELVE

SOMEONE WAS SHAKING him awake. Ben grunted and tried to bury his head beneath the pillow, but it was yanked away. He scrunched his eyes against the light.

"Ben," Ally said. "Wake up. Danny's back."

"He's not due back till noon." He pulled Ally into his arms and tried to settle back to sleep.

"It's quarter past twelve," she said, struggling free. "Carolyn's car just pulled into the driveway."

Ben's eyes snapped open. Sure enough, he heard the crunch of tires on gravel coming to a halt followed by the slamming of car doors. Seconds later, the front door rattled as Danny tried to open it. Then Danny turned his key in the lock.

Ben muttered a curse and rolled out of

bed. He pulled on his jeans, not bothering with his boxers, then paused, head cocked as the sound of voices drifted down the hall. "Carolyn's come in, too. If she asks, we'll pretend nothing happened between us."

For a moment, Ally looked taken aback. Then she said, her voice brittle, "That should be easy. We've been doing that for weeks."

Ben glanced her way as he dragged on his shirt and began feverishly buttoning. Her arms were crossed over her stomach and that pursed-lip smile was back.

"Don't take this the wrong way," he said. "Last night was amazing. I just don't want to be caught sneaking out of your room under the disapproving glare of Danny's mother."

"Hey, I was the one who said we wouldn't get emotionally involved, remember?" Ally gave him a peck on the mouth and smiling brightly, patted his cheek. "I'm fine."

"Dad?" Danny called from the hallway outside Ben's bedroom. That was followed by a creak as Danny pushed open the door, which had been ajar. "He must have gone out."

Ben paused, his hand on the doorknob. All he had to do was stay put until Carolyn left.

"Wasn't he supposed to take you fishing?" Carolyn asked. "Typical. He never keeps his promises."

Ben cursed under his breath. Now he had no choice. He opened the door and slipped through, shutting it behind him. "Good morning, Carolyn. Danny, are you ready to catch a trout?"

"Hey, Dad. What were you doing in Ally's room?"

"I, uh, was…fixing her closet door," Ben said, rubbing the back of his neck. "The… hinge was loose."

Carolyn's gaze raked him up and down, taking in his misbuttoned shirt and rumpled hair. "I bet you're really handy with a screwdriver."

"Go put your bag away, Danny, and change into your old clothes," Ben said. "We'll have breakfast—I mean *lunch*—then go to the lake."

Danny nodded, and disappeared into his room.

"I *do* keep my promises to Danny," Ben said to Carolyn as soon as their son was out of earshot. "Quit running me down in front of him."

"Maybe you keep your word to him but you haven't kept your promise to *me,*" Carolyn said, with a jerk of her head toward Ally's door. "You told me, no women."

"Exactly, no *women.* There's only Ally."

"You said, and I quote, 'There won't even be *a* woman. Whatever spare time I've got I'm going to focus on Danny.'"

"What did you do, take notes?" he demanded, hands on his hips.

Carolyn put her nose in the air. "I don't need to. *I* have an extremely good memory."

"Dammit, Carolyn. I didn't say I'd be a monk."

"You don't need to flaunt your sexual encounters—"

"It's not an 'encounter.' I live here," he said, getting madder by the second. "Anyway, what about you and Ted?"

"Ted and I didn't sleep together when Danny was in the house until we were married."

"Bully for you. He still knew what was going on. And Danny *wasn't* in the house last night—"

Ally's bedroom door opened and she emerged dressed in a crisp white sleeveless blouse tucked into a pencil-slim, charcoal-gray skirt. Her hair was pulled back in a French braid so tight it stretched the skin at the corners of her eyes. The braid appeared to be secured with every one of the pins he'd removed last night, plus another dozen. Even her choice of brooch, a Scottish thistle, contributed to her prickly, buttoned-up appearance. The sexy woman of last night might as well have been a figment of his imagination.

"Good morning," Ally said pleasantly. "Carolyn, I presume." She held out her hand for his ex to shake. Then, without quite looking at him, she added, "Thank you, Ben, for repairing my closet door. I'm sure I'll have no more trouble with it."

"Ally, Carolyn knows—" Ben began.

"Excuse me," Carolyn butted in before he could continue. "Are you telling me Ben *didn't* spend the night in your room?"

Ally looked at her and smiled her tight-lipped smile. "I wasn't aware I was telling you anything. But if you're *asking*..." She let the word hang, emphasizing Carolyn's rudeness, then finished on a mildly incredulous note. "Do I *look* like Ben's type? Or he, mine?"

Was Ally covering for him? Or subtly letting him know last night was a once-off, a failed experiment? Ben tried to catch her eye but she was determinedly keeping her gaze averted.

"Not really." Carolyn frowned uncertainly. "But—"

"I'm late," Ally went on, the matter settled. She rubbed at her inner elbow then stopped, dropping her clenched hand to her side. "Carolyn, nice to meet you. Ben, I'll see you later at the restaurant. I'm stopping off at Melissa's first."

Ally brushed past Ben and made a sharp right turn to the lounge room instead of the kitchen. No breakfast? Ben followed, barely hearing Carolyn telling him she was going to say goodbye to Danny. The front door shut behind Ally. Ben stared in disbelief. She'd gone out without eating or brushing her teeth. Worse, she hadn't tapped her barometer.

The door opened again. Ally came in, glared at him, then rattled the glass on the barometer with a couple of sharp jabs. Still itching at her elbow, she departed a second time. Ben went to the window to see her reverse her car out of the garage, only to be blocked by Carolyn's car. That stopped her for a second. But then she backed over the pansy border and onto the lawn, digging ruts in the dry grass, then looping around Carolyn's car before bumping onto the road toward town.

Ben swore in admiration. Was there no end to Ally's hidden depths?

Carolyn came into the room, still remonstrating. "Cleaning up your language is another promise you've broken."

"Danny won't turn into a hardened criminal if he hears his father curse once in a while." Ben glanced pointedly at his watch and opened the front door. "I've only got a couple of hours before I have to be at Mangos. You'll have to excuse me if I'm going to keep my promise to take Danny fishing."

"All right, but I'm warning you." Carolyn stood on the steps and wagged her finger. "If I hear *anything* that makes me doubt your ability to look after my son—"

"*Our* son. Goodbye, Carolyn." Ben shut the door and leaned against it, wondering about Ally. What the hell was going on in her head now?

MELISSA WAS LYING on the couch with an icepack on her forehead, nursing a hangover when Ally got there.

"I need breakfast and a toothbrush," Ally announced without preamble.

"There's a new toothbrush in the bathroom which you may have after you make me a Bloody Mary," Melissa said. "With a raw egg and a dash of Worcestershire Sauce."

"A little under the weather, are we?" Ally said, not unsympathetically.

Melissa moaned and closed her eyes.

Ally walked through the open space where a wall used to be and went to the fridge for the ingredients of Melissa's drink. Since she'd been here last, bifold doors had been installed in the exterior lounge-room wall that led onto Melissa's new deck. Cheryl was out there speaking to the carpenter. His hands were planted on hips slung with a tool belt, and his tanned and leathery face wore a resigned but respectful expression.

Ally handed Melissa her drink. "What's Mother doing here? Didn't she stay at Heronwood last night?"

"Unfortunately, no," Melissa said. "She's been rushing around doing things ever since she got up. It's making me quite ill."

"Where's her new car? Is she really as excited about it as she seemed last night?" Ally put a couple of slices of bread in the toaster.

"She left the car at the house," Melissa replied. "She *said* she couldn't drive after she'd been drinking. Luckily for us, Julio doesn't drink when he has a show the next day." Melissa groaned again. "Bring me some extra-strength paracetamol, too, thanks."

Ally got her the painkillers and sat on the couch with her toast and a cup of tea.

Melissa swallowed the tablets along with the contents of her glass, then lay back on the couch and shut her eyes. "Better. Thanks." She opened one eye. "You and Ben looked pretty cozy last night."

Ally shredded the crust off her toast. She'd suddenly lost her appetite. "Everything was fine until his ex-wife dropped Danny off at home this morning. Ben shot out of my bedroom so fast you'd have thought his pants were on fire."

Melissa pushed herself up higher on her cushion. "You slept with him! Way to go, Ally. How was it?"

"Wonderful." Ally allowed herself a brief dreamy smile before expelling a gusty sigh. "Until he pretended he'd been in my room to fix my closet."

Melissa grinned. The color was coming back into her cheeks. "Your very own Handy Andy."

"Very funny," Ally said. "I understand why Ben wouldn't want Danny to find him in bed with me unexpectedly, but the way he brushed me off made me feel as though I didn't belong with him. And I suppose he's right."

"He isn't your usual type," Melissa said. "But that's *good.*"

"No, it's better that we're not shouting it from the rooftops," Ally decided, convincing herself even if Melissa looked dubious.

"After all, I'm not falling in love with him or anything."

"You said you liked him," Melissa reminded her.

"I'm attracted to him. That's all," Ally said. "He doesn't really know me. He always makes me out to be this wild and crazy person. Which I'm not."

"Are you sure?" Melissa said, sipping her drink.

Cheryl came in, dusting off her hands. "Hello, darling," she said to Ally. "How are *you* this morning?"

"No hangover, at least." Ally got up to hug her mother. "I'm surprised to see you here. I was hoping last night would spark a reconciliation between you and Tony."

"Not a chance after what he did." Cheryl moved restlessly about the room, stopping here to straighten a cushion, there to tidy a stack of magazines. "I was furious with your father last night. I just couldn't say so in front of all our friends and family. How could he *do* that to me! I mean, honestly, a sports car!"

"Take it and don't ask questions," Melissa advised.

"The car is out of this world, but the gallery has to come first," Cheryl went on. "Where did he get the money to even pay for a deposit? If he borrowed more on the gallery I'll kill him with my bare hands."

"No, he didn't do that," Ally assured her. "He got ten thousand dollars from selling olive oil to Ben."

Cheryl stopped suddenly and stared at Ally. "You mean he had money and he didn't put it toward paying off my mortgage?"

"Uh-oh. You didn't know about that?" Ally exchanged a guilty look with Melissa. "I shouldn't have said anything."

Cheryl shut her eyes, hands clenched by her sides, her lips moving as she silently counted to ten. Or maybe she was shooting for one hundred.

"Mother?" Ally said. "Are you all right? I'm sure he meant well."

When Cheryl opened her eyes they glittered with tears, but her smile was as cold as ice. "He *always* means well. This time he's gone too far. I'm divorcing him."

She stalked outside onto the deck and started throwing offcuts of wood the carpenter had left lying around into a card-board box.

"Does this mean she's going to be living with me forever?" Melissa wailed, clutching her head at the noise.

"Probably," Ally said. "You'd better ask the builder to include another bedroom in your renovations."

A car pulled into the driveway and Ally went to the window. "Oh, no! It's Tony, driving the sports car. That's it, I'm out of here."

"Ally, where are you going? You can't leave me here alone with them," Melissa screeched from the couch. "You're the peacemaker in the family."

"I haven't done a very good job so far!" Ally grabbed her purse and hurried out the door before she got involved in the inevitable fracas. "I have to go to work."

Ten minutes later she pushed through the front door of Mangos and stopped dead, gaping, her personal problems blown right out of her mind. All of the original artwork she'd seen her mother extract from her collection had been hung on the dining-room walls. Landscapes of the Australian bush, a mixed-media collage, a couple of portraits, an acrylic painting done in the naif style, plus one wildly colorful abstract.

Horrified, Ally went closer and peered at the lower left-hand corner, looking for the tear in the canvas, not that there was any doubt it was hers. Sure enough, the flap of canvas was there but the paint had glued it into place. The picture had been framed and a discreet, typewritten card from Cheryl's gallery proclaimed it 'Untitled, acrylic on canvas.' The price listed was $3,500.

Ally stepped back to look at the painting again and felt a jolt when she recalled how she'd been consumed with thoughts of Ben while she'd splashed paint around. The joke was on her. The painting actually was about something—the feeling that had been growing inside her for weeks.

Head over heels.

She gave a short sharp bark of laughter that might have been a sob. That was it. She was taking it down.

Ally dragged a chair over to the wall and stood on it, but she wasn't high enough to lift the painting off the hook. Getting down, she moved the chair away, stripped the linen cloth and place settings from a table and dragged it next to the wall. She climbed onto the chair and from there onto the table. It wobbled dangerously as she leaned over and struggled to unhook the painting.

Ben came around the corner from the kitchen in his starched white chef jacket. "What are you doing?"

"Taking…this…painting…down," she grunted. "You…can't…sell…it." She succeeded in getting the one meter by two meter painting off the hook, her arms stretched to maximum, but it was too big and unwieldy for her to step off the table while holding it. "Can you give me a hand?"

Ben crossed his arms over his chest. "Put it back. I like it," he declared. "Landscapes are all very well for the tourists but I prefer something more modern. I'd buy it myself if I had the money to spend on artwork."

"You wouldn't if you knew who the artist was," Ally said. The table rocked beneath her feet. The heavy painting nearly pulled her off balance and stuck behind it, she couldn't see a thing. "Ben," she said, desperation creeping into her voice. "I can't hang onto this much longer."

"Who is the artist?" Ben asked. "Turn it a little so I can see the signature."

Ally started to shuffle around, then realized how ridiculous this was. "There is no signature."

"I didn't even notice," Ben said. "So who painted it?"

"Mother's playing a joke on you and she has a bizarre sense of humor," Ally said. "This painting wasn't meant to be for sale and certainly not for such an exorbitant amount of money." She felt the frame start to slip in her hands. *"Are you going to help me or not?"*

Ben reached up and took the weight of the painting. Ally lowered it into his hands with a relieved sigh, then clambered to solid ground. She straightened her skirt and tucked in her loosened blouse. *"Thank* you."

Ben put the painting on the table. *"Now* will you tell me why Cheryl shouldn't put this up for sale?"

"I painted that picture," Ally said.

"You!" Ben stared at her. "I didn't know you were an artist."

"I'm not! Can't you tell?" Ally exclaimed. "I was just having fun. If you look closely, you'll see the canvas is ripped."

Ben went right up to the painting and poked at it with a finger. "You're right. We'll just mark it down." He took the pen that was on his white jacket and stroked through the last zero to make the price $350. "Satisfied?"

"No!"

He stroked through another zero. $35.

"It doesn't matter how low you price it, I don't want that hanging on the wall," Ally said. "It's too personal. Too…messy. Those are my emotions splattered all over the canvas and hanging in public for everyone to gawk at."

"Isn't that what art is supposed to be about?" Ben asked. "That painting gives me a good feeling. It makes me…happy. The painting radiates happiness."

"Really?" Hearing the wistful note in her voice she added gruffly, "Interesting. But that doesn't make it art."

"Explain it to me," Ben said. "I don't understand non-representational painting. You said those were your feelings. What were you thinking about when you painted it?"

"Nothing in particular." She glanced at her watch. "Look at the time. I'd better get organized."

"Come to the kitchen first." He beckoned her to follow him. "I made you something."

"I'm not hungry," she protested.

"That's okay," he said. "Just have a taste."

Baz, Gord and Beth were taking a break, sitting on lidded buckets or sacks of potatoes, eating pasta and chicken. They mumbled greetings when Ally walked in.

"Is it linguini?" she asked, discreetly feeling her waistband.

"Nope, something better," Ben said, pulling a ceramic dish from the warming oven. "Chargrilled prawns with tomato and feta and just a hint of chili." He stabbed a fork into one and offered her the savory morsel.

Ally leaned forward and took the prawn between her teeth. It was spicy and juicy, fresh and flavorful. "Mmm," she murmured. "More."

He fed her another. "Am I forgiven?"

She stopped chewing. Her eyes locked with Ben's. "What for?"

"Don't pretend you weren't annoyed this morning when I didn't acknowledge us."

Ignoring the fork and his comment, Ally picked up a third prawn with her hand just so she could lick her fingers. "You should put this on the menu."

"That's the plan." Ben glanced toward the other cooks who were busy eating and bantering among themselves. "Seriously, are we okay?"

Ally sighed. Ben was more than okay, he was sensational. Herself, she wasn't so sure about. Her track record with serious relationships was so poor she didn't trust herself not to hurt him.

"From the way you reacted this morning, it's obvious you're not ready for a relationship." She smiled and touched the front of his jacket. "But we like each other and that's something to feel good about."

"I panicked this morning," he said. "Danny's important to me. I can't risk losing him."

"I know Danny's important," she replied. "I wouldn't want to come between you."

He slid his hands around her waist and kissed her neck. "I'm going to tell him about us—in general terms, of course."

Ally stepped sideways, dodging him. "Baz is looking."

"Who cares? Just say you're not angry with me."

"I'm not angry," she insisted, then held up her hands in a gesture of minor concession. "Okay, there was a brief moment when I was hurt...but my feelings weren't logical and now I'm over it. Honestly. We had really great sex and that was that," she said. "Everything else is the same."

"Wait a minute," he protested. "We had phenomenal sex and everything's *different*."

She took a step back from him and wagged her finger. "Just don't do anything silly like propose or else I'd have to break up with you and we wouldn't have any more of this great sex."

Ben laughed and shook his head. "I used to think you were kind of uptight. Now I realize what a great sense of humor you've got. Don't ever change, Ally."

"I mean it," she said. "Let's just go on being really good friends who have really great sex."

"Works for me. For now." Ben offered her the dish of prawns and when she waved it away he walked over to Gord and Baz, still chuckling.

Ally watched him go. *Don't ever change,* he'd said.

If only she could.

CHAPTER THIRTEEN

BEN KNOCKED on Danny's door and went in. His son was on the floor, surrounded by piles of exercise books, pens, pencils, plastic rulers and erasers, and he was labeling everything with a black marker. His new school uniform, gray shorts and a sage-green polo shirt with the school crest over the left breast, was draped over the back of the computer chair, ready for the morning.

"Are you looking forward to your first day at school?" Ben asked, sitting down on the bed.

"Yeah, I guess," Danny said with a small shrug. "I won't know anyone, though."

"You'll make friends quickly, don't worry." Ben handed him a printed sheet of paper. "I signed your consent form for the soccer team. Don't forget to hand it in."

Danny took it and put it in the front zipped pocket of his new backpack. "I need a lock for my locker."

"I meant to pick one up today and forgot," Ben said. "Tomorrow, I promise. Come by Mangos after school and remind me. I pumped up your bike tires and greased the sprockets. You're pretty much all set."

"Except for this," Danny said, indicating the piles of books left to label.

"I'll give you a hand." Ben sat cross-legged on the floor and reached for a notebook and a black marking pen. They worked in silence for a few minutes while Ben thought about how to bring up the real reason he'd come in here tonight.

"You know that time we were fishing and you asked me if Ally was my girlfriend and I said no?" Ben said finally.

Danny looked up from the ruler in his hand. "Yeah?"

"Well, I like her. I *really* like her," Ben elaborated, feeling unaccountably nervous. "The way a man and a woman like each other."

"You mean sex?" Suddenly, Danny seemed a lot more interested in the conversation.

"Not just— What do you know about sex?" Ben demanded. He'd always thought himself sophisticated and mature enough to handle a frank discussion with his son when the time came. Now he was beginning to wonder.

"Dad, I'm twelve years old," Danny said matter-of-factly. "Is this The Talk? Because if it is, don't worry. Mum's already explained everything."

Carolyn had more balls than Ben had given her credit for. And *he* was way behind the times. "Right, well, that's good. If you ever have any questions about what she told you, or anything else, don't hesitate to ask."

"Are you and Ally going to get married? I know you slept in her bed."

"I can't put anything over on you, can I?" Ben stalled while he wondered how to explain. Should he say it was too soon, that he didn't know her well enough? The trouble with that was, it made their relationship sound casual which wasn't how he felt about her. "Marriage is a big step," he said finally. "I'm not sure Ally's ready."

"Mum kept saying she didn't want to get

married again, then Ted asked her and wham, they were getting married."

"Is that right?"

Ben remembered Ally's joking comment that he'd better not propose. *Had* she been joking, or was it a clue to the direction her thoughts were moving in?

Danny finished labeling his ruler and started in on a box of colored pencils. Ben thought he'd forgotten about him and Ally until Danny glanced up and said, "Do you love her?"

Ben pictured her wide smile, her funny little ways. "Yes, I do. I love Alley." Just saying it sent a warm glow through him.

"Well, then, if you do want to marry her, I don't mind."

Ben smiled and reached over to squeeze his son's shoulder. "Thanks, mate. That means a lot to me."

THE FOLLOWING WEEK Ben, Danny and Ally drove up the highway past Wombat Hill to the Sunday Market, a collection of stalls selling arts and crafts and local produce. The goods for sale were all local and unique.

Some, especially the jewelry, was of exceptional quality.

They meandered beneath brightly colored market umbrellas, occasionally separating to pursue individual interests before joining up again farther down the aisles. Ben browsed old car parts and old books, bought a jar of homemade chutney and chatted with a man selling handmade wooden rolling pins about the best shape for rolling dough.

Ben came to a jewelry stall where silver and enamel earrings, bracelets and brooches were laid out on black felt cloth. In a locked glass case were gold rings set with precious stones, fine enough to grace any city jewelry store. An exquisitely worked ring in a graceful design set with a champagne diamond caught his eye. It seemed made for Ally—contemporary but with a touch of the traditional.

During the week they'd fallen into a pattern of coming home from the restaurant and going straight to bed together. But since the morning Carolyn and Danny had caught them, Ally had insisted Ben sleep in his own bed to avoid awkward explanations.

"Just once I'd like to wake up with you

instead of running off like a thief in the night," he grumbled.

"You woke up with me the first time," Ally said, disentangling her legs from his. "Look what happened."

"What *did* happen?" Ben demanded. "After a brief period of angst everything was resolved. Carolyn knows we're having a relationship. So does Danny. But we're still sneaking around."

"Not sneaking, being discreet," Ally argued. "It's one thing for Danny to know we have feelings for each other and another thing to have it shoved in his face. You and he are only just starting to bond. We need to tread lightly until your relationship with him is solidified."

Ben had gone back to his own bed, telling himself he ought to be grateful she was so understanding. But the truth was, he was getting impatient. He'd been single for five years and he'd dated a lot of women, but he'd never met anyone he cared for enough to settle down with, until Ally.

She'd changed since he'd first met her, more and more she was becoming the woman he'd always suspected she was. If he'd been giving advice to Danny he might have said you don't make love to someone a few times then ask them to marry you. But the way Ally constantly surprised him, he might live with her for a hundred years and not completely know her.

Ben moved on to another stall but his mind kept flicking back to the ring. Being engaged would bring their relationship into the open and move it forward. He loved their nights together, but he wanted their days to be spent as a couple, too. Retracing his steps, he found himself standing in front of the jewelry stall.

"I'll take that one," he said to the woman behind the table and pointed to the champagne diamond. This was going to max out his credit card, but Ally was worth every penny.

Ben concluded the transaction and tucked the ring box into his shirt pocket, well pleased with himself. As he moved off, he heard a man call his name. He turned to see Tony in his Italian peasant clothes presiding over a stall displaying his olive oils. In front of the row of slender green bottles was a basket of bread chunks and small dishes of olive oil of varying shades of yellow-green.

"More oil?" Ben said. "I thought I took it all off your hands."

"I had a few cases left so my manager and I have been experimenting with infusions," Tony said. "Lemon, garlic and chili, rosemary and thyme. Try some."

Ben dabbed a piece of bread in the oil nearest him and popped it into his mouth. "Very nice. By the way, the bloke who bought your oil has had retailers asking for more. I gave him your name so they could contact you directly."

"Excellent. I've got another proposition for you," Tony said with a most charming smile. "Until now, olives from the grove have gone to a neighboring farm for processing, entailing extra costs. With the new grove of young trees I've planted it makes economic sense to upgrade my facilities by installing an olive press so I can process the oil onsite. Cut out the middleman and maximize my profit. I'm looking for private investors."

"Why not ask the bank for a loan?" Ben said.

"Bah, they have no vision, these men of mammon." Tony dismissed them with a wave of his hand. "You, Ben, you know an opportunity when you see it."

Ben dabbed another chunk of bread in a different oil. Beautiful. "How much are you after?"

Tony tilted his head to one side as if eyeing Ben up and working out how much he was good for. "Oh, say, a hundred grand?"

Ben choked on the bread and thumped his chest to push it down. "A hundred thousand dollars!"

Tony clicked his fingers. "Peanuts in the grand scheme of things, my boy. With a new press, maybe next year a bottling plant, I can go national. International!" He leaned back in his metal chair and spread his arms wide. "There's no limit, except to the imagination."

There certainly seemed to be no limit to Tony's confidence in himself and his product. But a hundred thousand dollars? Ben quickly ran through his options. He could take out another loan through the company Ellen had incorporated for him, but he'd have to service it by drawing on his house fund. Ellen would probably say it didn't make sense to pay interest when he had all that money sitting there doing nothing. The downside was, if the return on the olives was less than Tony anticipated, there would be consequences for his and Danny's future.

Ben dabbed bread into the third and last infused oil and ate it, aware of Tony's bright gaze fixed to his face. He let the flavors roll over his tongue. For oil this good, the risk just might be worth it.

"Take a bottle of each," Tony said. "I want you to have them, no matter what you decide. If you're interested we need to act soon to be ready for this year's harvest. I'm going to California next week to an international trade show for olive growers. I'll need to order that press before I go."

"I'll think about it," Ben promised, accepting the bag Tony offered him. "I'll talk to my accountant."

Ally came up beside him carrying a ceramic lamp with a vivid blue glaze. "Uh-oh, last time you spoke to your accountant you spent ten thousand dollars in an afternoon," she said. "How much is Tony doing you for this time?"

Ben glanced at Tony, who coughed and turned away, apparently possessed of a sudden burning need to cut up more bread. He looked at Ally. "He wants a hundred thousand dollars to invest in new pressing equipment."

"What!" Ally shrieked.

Ben heard Danny calling to him from two stalls down where used computer games were for sale. "Dad! Can you come here?"

"Excuse me," Ben said quickly. "I have to go. Thanks for the oil, Tony. I'll be in touch."

"*Arrivederci.*" Bread knife in hand, Tony waved him off.

"Coward," Ally muttered, then turned to her father. "You don't know when to stop, do you? Why are you buying new equipment when you don't have a reliable water source?"

"*Cara,* if I turn timid now, everything I've been through so far would be for naught," Tony said. "We get nothing in this world unless we follow our dreams with faith and determination. Remember, think of the big picture."

"Your dreams are Mother's nightmares," Ally said.

Tony scraped the cut up pieces of crusty

bread into a wooden bowl. "Has she driven her new car yet?"

"I have no idea," Ally said. "I'm afraid to go around to Melissa's anymore. Who knows what I'll find. I've a good mind to inform Ben how precarious the situation is with you and your olive grove."

"You need to spend money to make money," Tony insisted. "With Ben's investment, I can buy a new press, get a higher profit, plant even more trees and have more oil to sell. It's a great plan."

"It's a terrible plan!" Ally exclaimed, throwing her hands up. "Like all your plans, there are too many factors outside your control. What if you don't get as much water as you hoped and the crop fails?"

"Why, then I'd think of a new strategy." Tony smiled winningly. "There's always a way out, Ally."

Sometimes his unfailing optimism enraged her. He had no right to be so confident, not when he *had* failed in the past. "*Nanna* didn't have a way out," she countered. "Unless you call death an exit strategy for a hard life."

"Nanna?" Tony's smiled wavered. "Why are you bringing her up?"

"Don't you remember the year you re-mortgaged our house and we lost it and ended up living in a caravan with no heating?" Ally reminded him. "Nanna got double pneumonia."

"You're holding Nanna's death against me?" he said, incredulous.

If she could have blamed it on anything or anybody other than her beloved, larger-than-life father she would have done so in a heartbeat. But she couldn't. "Who else?"

"You're being a little harsh," Tony said, looking wounded. "You were only a child, Ally. You don't know what went on."

"I know all I need to know," Ally said. Oh, what was the use talking to him? People were jostling her, trying to get to the oil. Tony's attention was wandering and she'd had enough. "I've got to go. See you later."

"Give my love to Cheryl," Tony called after her, his smile wistful.

Ally found Ben concluding a transaction which netted Danny two used computer games and a joy- stick. "If you're done let's head back to the car," he suggested.

As they slowly made their way through the tide of people back to the parking lot, Ally said to Ben, "I hope you won't let Tony suck you into his crazy scheme."

"It's not so crazy." Ben checked to see that Danny was still with them and put a hand on his son's shoulder, steering him through the crowd. "Tony's put a lot of effort into his olive oil business. It could pay off big."

Ally moaned and shook her head. "You don't know my father. Even if he makes money off a scheme, he immediately throws it away on some other crazy project. It's a form of gambling. He's addicted to the rush of high stakes and risky return. I'm warning you, don't get involved."

"I don't know, Ally. The olive oil industry is really taking off. Any money invested is a legitimate tax deduction. This is an opportunity too good to pass up."

"An opportunity too good to pass up," Ally repeated. "How many times have I heard that? Can you even borrow that much?"

"I was thinking of using my house fund," Ben said.

"You could be making a mistake that will cost you that family life you say you want," Ally warned.

"I'd only be delaying buying a house," Ben said stubbornly. "If this year's crop is as good as Tony expects I could be ready to buy in six to eight months."

"You don't understand," Ally said, frustrated. "Tony has no water license of his own for irrigation. Without water he can't guarantee the size or quality of the olive crop."

"I know about Tony's water situation. He explained it to me at the party. He's got an ingenious system and it seems to be working without a hitch," Ben said. "I'm prepared to take the risk."

"You're both crazy!" Ally groaned. "When this all goes pear-shaped, don't forget I warned you. If Tony goes down so will you. In fact, you'll probably sink faster together."

"Has he ever let anyone down, really?" Ben asked. "He seems very confident he's going to get the money to pay off the gallery."

"He's always confident. That's how he

gets people to trust him with their money. Tony *has* let someone down—my Nanna— his mother. She lived with us until she died when I was ten. Tony had taken out a second mortgage on our home to finance some dodgy business venture and the deal went bad, Tony went bust and we lost the house. We spent that winter living in a tiny unheated caravan. That year was wet and cold. Nanna got double pneumonia and died, all because Tony's grandiose plan to make a million dollars failed."

"I'm sorry about your grandmother," Ben said. "But this is different."

Ben's mobile phone rang and he answered it. "Steve, what's up? You're sure? We'll be there right away." Ben clicked off. "Steve got a tip-off that I. Lemke is heading for Mangos today."

When Ben and Ally got to the restaurant, Steve was fussing about like an old man, sending Julie out for fresh flowers for the bar and getting in everyone's way in the kitchen. Gord was cursing a streak and the rest of the staff were dancing around each other as they feverishly prepared for lunch service. The atmosphere was wound tight, the usual laconic banter replaced by tense mutterings.

"When's he coming?" Ben took a clean apron from the laundry bag, tied it on then tucked a hand towel into the waistband. "Lunch? Dinner?"

"Don't know," Gord said, pouring a cask of shiraz into a large tray of roasted bones. Sweat beaded his brow and his red hair was damp at the roots. "Our orders are to be ready for him at any time."

"Ben," Steve said, popping up in front of the serving window. "I want you to make him your scallop dish. Even if he doesn't order it, send it out anyway, compliments of the house."

Ben looked up from his list of prep tasks that started with boning rabbits for a terrine. "How will I know who to send it to if we don't know what he looks like?"

"That could be a problem," Steve agreed, stroking his silver goatee. "He books under an assumed name. Rumor has it he's middle-aged, medium height and weight, brown hair and eyes—in other words, nondescript."

"Then he should be easy to pick out among

the yuppies with their three-hundred-dollar hairstyles and designer clothes," Ben joked.

"Apparently, he's a master of disguise," Steve went on. "He doesn't want anyone to know he's a restaurant reviewer so he'll be served as an ordinary customer. Sometimes he's on his own, sometimes in a couple or a group. I've heard he's shown up wearing fake mustaches and beards, glasses, wigs. He never looks the same twice."

"Then how does anyone know he's even been there?" Baz piped up.

"We'll have none of your drunken babble today," Gord grumbled. He gave the bubbling wine and bones a shake and pushed the roasting pan to the back of the stove.

Ben noted with relief that despite Gord's comment, Baz was completely sober. "Everything has to be perfect today," Ben said to Baz, more for Steve's benefit than because today was different from any other day. "Not one plate leaves this kitchen without either me or Gord inspecting it. Got that?"

Baz snapped to attention. "Yes, Chef."

During the busiest part of lunch service Julie stuck her head through the serving window and said she thought Lemke was in the restaurant. "Single on Table Seven. He ordered carpaccio, cheese soufflé, kingfish and mushroom risotto."

Ben exchanged a look with Gord. "Two entrées and two mains for one diner? Sounds like a food reviewer to me."

Gord peered around the corner into the dining room. "That's got to be him. Look at the fake glasses."

Ben stood behind him and looked over Gord's head. The man at Table Seven seemed of medium height as far as Ben could tell, with brown hair, but he was rather more than medium weight. "How can you tell the glasses are fake?"

"He went to scratch his eye and jammed a finger straight into the glass, as though he'd forgotten it was there," Gord said.

"Maybe he just got them for reading and isn't used to them," Ben suggested.

"Maybe he's a doofus," Julie said, shaking her head at their guessing games.

"The glasses are fake, I tell you," Gord insisted.

Steve grabbed Julie's arm. "When you

wait on him be attentive but not obsequious, knowledgeable but not overbearing. This is I. Lemke, I'm sure of it."

"He could be Babar the Elephant for all I care," Julie said. "I give *all* our customers polite, efficient service." She turned on her heel and left.

Steve shooed Ben and Gord back to the kitchen, rubbing his hands together. "Chef's hat, here we come."

"Baz," Ben called above the clatter of Gord slapping the risotto pan on the stove. "Carpaccio and kingfish. Send the fish out first. This is for Lemke."

"Lemke," Baz repeated. "Yes, Chef."

"No, no, no," Steve said, flapping his hands. "Scallops first."

Ben went to the reach-in fridge and poked around in the tray until he found the plumpest scallops. Steve hovered. Ben gritted his teeth and tried not to take any notice. He put some reduced fish stock on to heat for the cream wine sauce, and while the scallops seared he plunged a serving of fresh spinach linguini into a pot of boiling water.

Everything was done in minutes. Ben

drained the pasta and swirled it on the warmed plate, carefully ladled the perfect amount of cream sauce over it, then placed the caramelized scallops on top one by one with his fingers. Another light glaze of cream sauce, followed by the roast capsicum sauce… He reached for the squeeze bottle only to grasp at empty space.

"Where's my roast capsicum sauce?" Ben yelled. *"Baz!"*

"Sorry, Chef." Baz leaped around Gord and held out a bottle of dark red sauce. "Here it is."

"What did I tell you about *mise-en-place?*" Ben growled. "Never, never—"

"Mess with your meez," Baz finished abjectly.

"Hurry!" Steve said, about to wet himself in an agony of anxiety. "Oh, let me do it." He grabbed the squeeze bottle and squirted Ben's signature *M* on top and droplets around the outside of the plate.

Ben turned on Steve, outraged. "You might be the owner but I'm the boss in this kitchen!"

Steve wiped the plate rim with a napkin and waved Julie away. "I'll deliver it personally."

Certain steam must be coming out of his ears, Ben stalked to the walk-in freezer and pressed his forehead against a container of homemade ice cream.

"Chef?" Gord's gruff voice came to him through the frozen mists. "You'd better get back out here before that effing sod cooks the whole meal."

Ben sighed and brushed the frost off his eyebrows. "Coming."

The last party with a lunch reservation was arriving just as Steve was setting down the plate of scallops at Lemke's table. Ally crossed her fingers that Lemke would give Mangos a favorable review, and went to greet the couple who were looking around expectantly.

The woman was heavy-set but attractive with spiky brown hair and dark eye makeup. Her husband had a jovial smile and he looked as though he enjoyed a glass of wine or three with his meal.

"Mr. and Mrs. Leonard?" Ally said pleasantly. "Right this way, please."

Ally led them to Table Eighteen by the window and handed them menus and a wine list before removing the extra place settings. "Are you here for the weekend?"

Mrs. Leonard smiled and replied, "We came up from Melbourne for the day and had a lovely walk around the lake. We're *starving*."

"I know you'll love the food we serve at Mangos. Ben Gillard is our chef and he's wonderful," Ally said. "Enjoy your meal. Your waiter will be with you shortly."

Ally went back to the reception desk to survey the room. She noted which tables were close to finishing, which were ready for the next course and which looked as though they were settled in for the afternoon.

Julie took the Leonards' order then came back to the bar for the wine. "They like their grub," she confided as she uncorked a bottle of sauvignon blanc.

"They did say they were starving." Ally got wine- glasses out and inspected them for fingerprints before putting them on a tray. From across the room she saw Lemke look over and wave. She nodded at him and said to Julie, "Better go see what he wants."

A moment later, Julie returned bearing the

plate of scallops, barely touched. She rolled her eyes as she passed Ally and headed for the kitchen. Ally put down her cloth and followed, standing well back. Steve watched anxiously, chewing his hangnail. Julie set the plate down on the serving counter. One scallop had been eaten and a bite taken out of a second.

Ben cursed softly. "What's wrong with it?"

"He said the sauce burned his mouth," Julie replied. "He couldn't even taste the scallop."

Ben dabbed a finger into a red droplet and touched it to his tongue. This time he cursed aloud, using words even Gord probably didn't know. "Baz! You handed Steve the wrong bottle," he roared. "Instead of roast capsicum sauce he squirted on lashings of pureed red chilies!"

Ben slammed the offending dish of scallops into the rubbish bin, plate and all. "Of all the dumbarse mistakes, this takes the cake."

CHAPTER FOURTEEN

ALLY DIDN'T STICK around for the bloody aftermath, but hurried back to the front of the house. Steve came out and apologized profusely to Lemke, who ate the rest of his meal without complaint, but everyone knew the damage had been done. Somehow, the lunch service passed.

Instead of the usual buzzing chatter among the crew, the kitchen was filled with deathly silence. Ben wore a thunderous scowl while Baz crept about trying to appear inconspicuous. Steve was slumped on a chair with an icepack pressed to his temple and Gord's face looked like a ripe tomato and clashed horribly with his carroty hair. Beth quietly went about her desserts and even Mick was loading dishes in the dishwasher, so they barely made a sound.

Ally felt sorry for Steve because he'd wanted that chef's hat so badly, and she felt awful for Baz who copped the brunt of everyone's fury. But she felt worst of all for Ben, whose reputation had been wrongly tarnished.

At last the restaurant began to empty. The final customers to leave were the Leonards. Ally noticed they hadn't finished all their food, nor did they wait for Julie to present their bill. Instead, they came up to the reception desk to pay. "I hope everything was all right," Ally said.

"All of it was excellent," Mrs. Leonard assured her with a smile. "Our eyes were bigger than our stomachs. We need to get back to the city, so if we could have the bill...?"

"Of course." Ally rang up their meal and passed over the docket.

Mr. Leonard reached into his pocket for his wallet. His hand came back empty. Stricken, he looked at his wife. "I must have left my wallet in my other pair of pants."

"Walter, how could you?" Mrs. Leonard frowned, and started searching in her purse. "Do you have any cash?"

"I have no wallet, remember?" Mr. Leonard replied. "You'll have to use your credit card."

"You know I don't like doing that," she muttered, opening her purse. "I've only got forty-five in cash. That's not enough."

Mr. Leonard turned to Ally. "I'm very sorry."

Ally was beginning to wonder if this was a scam, when Mrs. Leonard sighed and handed over her credit card.

Relieved, Ally ran it through the machine and passed across the duplicate receipts and a pen for Mrs. Leonard to sign. She signed her name in a cramped hand that caught Ally's attention because there appeared to be too few letters.

"Thank you, Mrs.—" Ally read her signature as a pretext to checking it against the credit card. "Isabel Lemke." She stared at the woman. "Are *you* I. Lemke?"

"Shh." Isabel Lemke glanced around to make sure no one was listening, then whispered, "Only to my friends."

Ally waited until the couple had left, then hurried into the kitchen, eager to tell Ben. She found him wiping down his station.

"Guess what?" Ally said, bouncing on her

toes. "The customers who just left are the Lemkes. Isabel Leonard is a pseudonym for I. Lemke. Steve and Baz didn't blow it after all. She loved your food!"

Baz and Beth cheered, Gord mumbled some good-natured obscenities. Ben's tense frown melted into a weary smile and he tossed his wrung-out cloth into the sink. "It just goes to show you shouldn't get worked up about these things."

"Steve!" Ally called as the owner arrived to see what all the excitement was about. She retold the story, launching him into renewed visions of glory.

"Ally, come with me." Ben pulled her away from the jubilant crew and around the corner into the dry stores area. He dug into his pocket for a small box. "I wanted to give this to you this morning but I got sidetracked."

Ally reached for the box automatically, then snatched back her hand, confused and flustered. "What is it?"

"Nothing dangerous," he said, smiling.

"I mean, I hope it's not a—" She broke off, aware she'd put her foot in her mouth.

"Ring?" Ben supplied. He snapped open

the case and the diamond sparkled. "Look, I know this is sudden, but I'm serious about you."

Ally couldn't speak, her heart was pounding too hard and there was a huge, painful lump in her chest.

Ben took her hand. "Try it on." Before she knew what was happening, he was sliding the ring over her finger. His hands were trembling and his breath was warm on her forehead.

Ally stared at the perfectly cut gem, her mind a jumble of confused emotions. "It's beautiful but I…I can't accept it. I'm sorry." She tried to pull it off and started to get frantic when it wouldn't come.

"Ally." Ben took both her hands in his. "I love you. I want to marry you."

"Don't! Please don't say any more," Ally cried, pulling away. Finally, she got the ring off and she pressed it into his hand.

"Tell me what's going on," Ben demanded, his fist closing around the diamond. "I don't understand you."

"I'm not ready for marriage." Ally itched at a fresh outbreak of eczema on the inside of her elbow. "Neither of us planned on getting involved."

"Maybe not, but it happened," Ben said, searching her face. "I thought you cared about me, too. It was you who took our relationship to the next level."

"I *do* care about you. And yes, I wanted to make love but I didn't think this development through to its logical conclusion. We should have stuck to being landlady and tenant. Adding employer-employee made things even more complicated. Then we became lovers. Now you want to add husband and wife to the mix," she went on, becoming more agitated. "I can't keep all these separate roles straight."

"Listen to you," he complained. "You compartmentalize your feelings. You tidy up your emotions into neat little boxes so you never have to look at the jumbled up mess inside. News flash, darlin', life *is* messy. Glorious highs followed by tragic lows. Pleasure and pain, joy and woe. You're not living, you're just going through the motions."

Ally clamped her hands over her ears so

she didn't have to listen. "It all happened so fast with us. Too fast."

"Who says fast can't be good? Maybe that shows we're meant to be together," Ben said. "Dammit, Ally, you don't break up when things are going well."

Were they breaking up? Had it come to this already? Ally felt her world crack open. She was burning every bridge she crossed—powerless to stop herself. Falling in love was scaring her to death. Imagine if she agreed to marry him and a week or a month or a year later she realized she couldn't go through with it. And yet she couldn't bear to let him go out of her life. "I didn't say I wanted to break up. Why can't we go on as we are?"

"Because I'm tired of pretending we're not a couple. It's like being in limbo," he said bitterly. "Either we're heading toward something permanent, or—" he met her eyes "—we recognize there's no possibility of a future together."

The silence seemed endless as Ally desperately tried to think of a way out. Finally she whispered, "Maybe that would be for the best."

Ben thudded a fist against the stainless-steel door of the walk-in freezer and paced away. Head down, he said in a cold, hard voice, "Danny and I will move out right away."

Ally felt as though her feet had been knocked out from under her, leaving her with nothing solid to hang on to. *Head over heels.* She spun around and pushed through the kitchen doors, almost knocking over Rico coming from the dining room.

She crouched behind the bar and looked in the cabinet for…something. There must be *something* she needed. She felt her eyes overflow and grabbed a paper cocktail napkin off the lower shelf. There, she knew she needed something and that was it. Fiercely, she dabbed away the tears.

She loved him, therefore she had to give him up. The tragic absurdity of their situation struck her, and for a moment she didn't know whether she was laughing or crying. This was exactly the sort of thing that happened when unpredictable people came along and upset her routines.

"Ally?" Julie stood above her, the phone Ally hadn't even heard ringing in her outstretched hand. "Melissa's on the line. She's at Ballarat Hospital. She wants you to come. It's an emergency."

Ally rose, smoothing down her skirt, feeling her hair to make sure it was in place. "Tell her I'm leaving now."

As long as she was burning bridges she might as well set fire to the lot. She marched back into the kitchen and stood beside Ben, who was prepping for the dinner service.

"Summer's over and the tourist trade is slowing," she said. "Julie can handle the front until you find someone else."

Ben slammed a cleaver down onto a whole squab, neatly slicing it in two. Without looking at her, he asked, "What are you saying?"

Ally took a deep breath. "I quit."

Not a single emotion registered on his face. He picked up a filleting knife and started deboning the bird. Finally he said, "That's probably for the best."

Ally turned to go, then paused. "I noticed you took my painting down after all. Where is it? I'd like to have it."

"You're too late," Ben said shortly. "It's been sold."

ALLY HURRIED into the Ballarat Hospital and followed the signs to Outpatients. Melissa was sitting in the waiting room, one foot resting on the plastic chair opposite, reading an old copy of *Who* magazine.

"Melissa," Ally called, rushing over. "Are you all right? What's wrong with your foot?"

Luckily, Melissa was so concerned with her own problems she didn't notice Ally's swollen eyes.

"Ally, thank God you're here." Melissa tossed the magazine aside and peeled back the bandage covering her big toe. "Look! Isn't it awful?"

Ally squinted at the toe. It appeared perfectly normal to her. "What exactly is wrong?"

"My toe has been bleeding on and off for days. This morning it wouldn't stop. I knew I hadn't cut it so it freaked me out and I came directly to the emergency room." Melissa paused dramatically. "The podiatrist says I have *wild flesh.*"

"I beg your pardon?" Ally laughed despite Melissa's tortured expression. "Wild flesh?"

"That's how Dr. Horstmann translated it from German, because he didn't know the

English term. It's raw tissue that grows un-bounded by skin." Melissa shuddered, making her beaded earrings vibrate. "They don't know what causes it and there's no stopping it except by *cutting it out*."

"Will you need stitches?" Ally asked.

"Well, no," Melissa admitted. "But Dr. Horstmann can't say for sure that it won't come back."

"I still don't really see what it is you're talking about." Ally crouched down on the floor and peered closer. "Can you point out this so-called 'wild flesh'?"

"There!" Melissa indicated a thin crescent of dark red spongy tissue at the base of her toenail. "Ugh. It's so gross!"

"That little thing?" Ally said. "I could take that out with my nail scissors right now." She started to fish in her purse for her manicure set.

"Don't you dare." Melissa swiftly tucked her foot under the chair. "I thought you came to give me support."

"I did," Ally assured her. "But the food reviewer came today and everyone was bouncing off the walls with nerves. Then Ben and I…" She dragged in a deep breath.

"Never mind that now." Summoning her sense of humor, she wiggled her fingers in Melissa's face and said in a spooky voice, "You've got *wiiild flesssh.*"

"Don't *say* that. It creeps me out." Melissa dabbed at her eyes, smearing her already-smudged makeup.

Ally looked at her sister, puzzled that she wasn't seeing the funny side. "Is something else wrong?"

"No." Melissa maintained a doleful silence for ten seconds then wailed, "Yes! Oh, Ally! Julio's gone to Adelaide with the Cirque du Soleil to continue their Australian tour."

"You always knew he'd move on eventually," Ally said gently. "You told me yourself Julio was a short-term prospect."

"Yes, but I didn't know I was going to fall in love with him," Melissa said, sighing heavily.

"I'm so sorry." Ally hugged her and burst into tears. "Love sucks."

"Ally?" Melissa said, drawing back in consternation.

They didn't get further than staring at each other with tearstained eyes. The nurse, a short, pretty woman in her early thirties, came out of a door to their left. "Melissa Cummings? The doctor will see you now."

"I'll come in with you," Ally told Melissa, putting her arm around her sister.

"Thanks." Melissa blotted her moist eyes and limped over to where the nurse was waiting.

"Don't worry," the nurse said cheerfully. "The whole procedure won't take more than a few minutes."

"Really?" Melissa said, frowning. "I thought it was much more serious than that."

"No worse than trimming your cuticles," the nurse assured her. "It's a common procedure."

"You're very brave," Ally murmured encouragingly to Melissa during the injection of the local anesthetic. When the doctor brought out a scalpel Melissa bit her lip and shut her eyes. Ally squeezed her sister's hand. "You could write to Julio. Maybe he'll be back this way someday."

Melissa gave a short hopeless laugh. "We can't communicate with written language. He knows only a few words of English and my

Spanish is nonexistent. No, it's over. My only consolation is that he's as broken up as I am."

"All done, Ms. Cummings," the doctor said to Melissa as he pushed back his chair. "Change the bandage in a couple of days and wear sandals until it's healed."

"What! That's it?" Melissa said. "I was talking, and missed it!"

"Be grateful. Thank you, Doctor." Ally rose and gave Melissa her arm to exit the hospital. "Can you drive?"

"I suppose so since it's not my right foot," Melissa said. "Does this bandage make my foot look big?"

"Your foot couldn't look big if it tried." Ally paused and added, "I'm sorry about Julio."

At being reminded, Melissa lifted her chin and blinked rapidly. "It's okay. I'll get over him."

Ally steered her sister to the visitors' parking lot and helped her into her car. Instead of carrying on to her own car, she got in the passenger seat and twisted to face Melissa. "Do you think I have a commitment phobia?"

"I thought only men got that."

"I'm twenty-nine years old," Ally said. "I want to get married and start a family before it's too late. More importantly, I want to love a man and be loved. Yet as soon as I get close to marriage I sabotage myself."

Melissa moved her seat back for more leg room and propped her foot on the console. "What do you mean?"

"As soon as a man wants to spend the rest of his life with me, I lose interest or get scared," Ally said.

"Has Ben proposed?" Melissa asked, clutching Ally's arm.

"He gave me a ring—or rather, he tried to. I wouldn't take it. I'm afraid of talking about marriage or even saying 'I love you' in case it jinxes the whole relationship."

"But why are you so worried?" Melissa said. "Ben's a great father. He'd make an equally great husband. You two are good together."

"I couldn't accept his proposal," Ally said, scratching at her inner elbow. "It's like the kiss of death to any relationship I'm in. If I say I'll marry the guy, the next thing I know

I'm trying to figure out a way to end it. Look at George."

"You didn't want to marry George," Melissa pointed out. "He's a philanderer."

"Yes, but I didn't know that until *after* I wanted out," Ally said.

"That's because he was also boring," her sister reminded her.

"He was stable and predictable which is what I want."

"*Do* you?"

"Doesn't everyone?" Ally demanded. "How can you even think about starting a family if the guy isn't going to be a responsible partner?"

"That's important I suppose, but to tell you the truth, it's not the first thing that comes to mind when I'm weighing whether I like a man," Melissa said. "I'm asking questions like, does he make me laugh? Can he bend over backward and touch his heels?"

Ally rolled her eyes. "Be serious."

"Okay," Melissa said. "You keep saying you 'should' do this or you 'shouldn't' do that. What about doing what feels right?"

"I don't know what that is!" Ally exclaimed: "I'm so confused. I'm constantly examining my motives and feelings and I still don't understand what's driving me."

"That's because you're trying to use logic to solve an emotional problem," Melissa said. "Remember those instincts I was talking about? Get in touch with your gut feelings."

"George more or less told me I needed to confront my inner child and tell it to grow up," Ally said. "I interpreted that to mean I should give in to my not-so-subconscious desire to sleep with Ben. George said that would get it out of my system, but I just want more and more."

Melissa threw up her hands. "So go for it. What are you waiting for?"

Ally stared at her. "If it's that simple, why did I just break up with the best man I've ever known?"

Melissa stared back. "Good question."

"DAD, WHERE'S MY OTHER pair like this?" Danny said, coming into the room holding one blue sock and one brown sock.

"In your drawer. If you folded them the

way Ally showed you, you wouldn't have to ask," Ben replied, sorting miscellaneous bits and pieces into shallow woven baskets on the kitchen counter. AA batteries, odd screws and other hardware in one basket; pens, paper clips and erasers in a second; elastic bands and bread bag ties in another. In each basket he'd placed cardboard dividers to separate out the various different items.

"Don't you think you're getting a bit anal about all that junk?" Danny said, sitting on a chair to don his mismatched socks.

"'A place for everything, and everything in it's place,'" Ben said, absently. He turned to the corkboard to pin up Danny's school notices and permission slips from left to right in order of when they had to be handed in. Just being Danny's buddy wasn't enough; he had to also be a father his son could rely on.

"Come on," Danny begged. "We've got to get to the lake before the fish stop biting."

"All right." Ben relented and grabbed his car keys from the hook beside the door. "Let's go."

Once in the car, Ben drifted into a daydream

about Ally. It had been three weeks since they'd moved out of her house. At first he'd been angry at the way she'd ended their relationship. Then he'd realized that she was unhappy, too, and he was partly to blame for their breakup by forcing the issue with that damned ring. Danny talked about her all the time, which made it difficult for Ben to forget how it felt to kiss her and hold her….

"Da-a-d, you're doing it again," Danny said.

Ben glanced sideways. "What do you mean?"

"You sighed," Danny said.

"No, I didn't." He paused. "Did I?"

"You were thinking of Ally, weren't you?" Danny asked.

"I don't need a reason to sigh," Ben replied. "Sensitive New Age guys like me sigh all the time."

Danny rolled his eyes. "Da-a-d. New Age is so *old*. Girls like the he-man type now."

"Oh, they do, do they?" Ben looked at his son curiously. "How would you know that?"

Danny shrugged his skinny shoulders and stuck his chin in the air. "I just know."

"I tried the proactive route," Ben said. "It

blew up in my face." For now, he'd give her space, and trust that sooner or later she'd realize what they had together. Sometimes it took a he-man to be patient.

ALLY PUSHED ASIDE several weeks' accumulation of newspapers and flyers on the kitchen counter and tried to remember if it was Egg Day or Muesli Day. Ben had gotten her mixed up with the delicious and ever-changing meals that he whipped up in minutes. Oh, who cared what day it was? She grabbed a handful of crackers and a drying hunk of cheese. She hadn't done the dishes since Thursday and there was no space on the cluttered counter to cook anyway.

It was great being on her own, though. She was getting back to her routine and *loving* it. Without Danny's socks cluttering up her washing machine she'd soon be sorting her clothes into whites and colors again. Now that Ben had his shaving gear and manicure kit out of the bathroom containers she'd have her hair stuff and cosmetics reorganized in no time.

She picked up a coaster that had somehow

made its way into the kitchen and carried it back to the lounge room, only to glance vaguely around, wondering where it was meant to be. Eventually, she gave up and tossed it onto a side table. Yessir, being on her own meant she could arrange her life and her surroundings exactly as she pleased.

Control of her life included control over her heart. Maybe she ached for Ben a little bit, but she'd forget what it was like to make love with him in a thousand and fifty years or so. Forget how it was to wake in the morning, gaze into his eyes and feel her heart fill.

No more chocolate tarts at midnight, no more red dragon kites getting caught in trees on blue-sky afternoons, no more whirling blades and breathless kisses. From now on she'd watch *Coronation Street* with Melissa on Sundays and come home to a clean and tidy house. Just as soon as she got herself together and cleaned up the mess.

Someday she would figure out what kind of man was right for her. She would get married and have the children she'd always wanted. Right now she was feeling relieved at another lucky escape. Wasn't she? Yes, of course, she was. She *always* felt relieved when she broke up with a man.

But she didn't want to think about that right now. The only true bright spot in her life at the moment was knowing that someone liked her painting enough to take it home and hang it on their wall. The twenty dollars she'd earned from the sale barely covered the cost of the paint but that wasn't the point. For years, she'd sublimated her creative side in safe outlets like home decorating and kooky brooches. It was time she sat down and had a long heart-to-heart talk with that inner child of hers.

CHAPTER FIFTEEN

"WHEN WE GET THE MONEY from the oil we'll buy our own house," Ben promised his son. They were driving north to check out Tony's olive grove. Maybe he ought to have had a look at the operation before he'd released the funds from his account to Tony's, but until now he'd been too busy to get away from the restaurant.

"I liked living at Ally's house," Danny said.

Ben stifled a sigh and injected as much optimism into his voice as he could. "We'll find something even better."

"How long will we have to stay at the apartment?" Danny asked. "It's so dark and the roof still hasn't been fixed."

They were back living above the restaurant. The big bare rooms did seem gloomy after Ally's bright and cheerful home. At least the rent was low, a bonus considering he was now in debt up to his eyebrows.

"I've talked to the rental agent. They're onto it," Ben assured him. "We're okay for now. There hasn't been a drop of rain in two months."

After passing through forested hilly country they'd come to open flat land that stretched dry and brown all the way to the Murray River. Here, north of the dividing mountain range, the vegetation was parched and withered and the bare dirt was cracked where dusty flocks of sheep had nibbled the straw-like grass to the roots.

Good thing Tony had water futures sewn up in the area or the grove of young olive trees he'd planted would be in serious trouble right about now.

ALLY WENT THROUGH the door into the Cottage Rentals and was hit by a wave of nostalgia so strong she stopped dead. *This* was where she belonged. Lindy glanced up and uttered a squeak when she saw Ally. Ally put her finger to her lips and continued to Olivia's desk.

Olivia was focused on her computer monitor as she skimmed through a summary of the bookings for the weekend. Ally cleared her throat.

Olivia slowly tore her gaze away and swiveled her chair around to face Ally. "May I help—?" she began, then her eyebrows rose in thin black arches. *"Hello."*

Her expression wasn't unfriendly and Ally took heart, quickly reminding herself not to beg unless absolutely necessary. "I'd like my job back."

Olivia folded her arms over her bony chest. "Why should I give it to you?"

"Because I can do it better than anyone." Ally paused. "Even you."

Unblinking and unsmiling, Olivia stared at her for a whole minute. Finally, she let out a deep sigh. "I hate to admit it, but you're right. You can start next week."

Ally simply nodded, not letting Olivia see her elation. She gave Lindy a discreet thumbs-up, and left. Slowly but surely, she was getting her life back.

She continued on to Melissa's house and found her sister and mother in the driveway, staring in silence at the Audi sports car. "I thought you were going to make Tony return it," she said to Cheryl.

"He refused," Cheryl replied. "Apparently he's searched for years for the perfect gift for me and now that he's finally found it, I have to keep it."

"It does match your outfit," Melissa said, glancing at Cheryl's black pants and beaded black tank top. "*All* of your outfits, in fact."

"You don't think it's too much black?" Cheryl asked.

"Not with your blond hair. And the turquoise interior matches your eyes," Melissa said.

"The car *is* gorgeous," Ally had to admit.

"I'll bet it handles like a dream," Melissa added.

"I'm *not* driving it," Cheryl said. "That would be tantamount to accepting it."

"You've let it stay here for weeks," Ally said. "I think you've accepted it."

"We could sit in it awhile," Melissa suggested.

Ally slid a hand along the polished exterior, then opened the passenger door to stick her head in. "I love that new car smell."

"Mother?" Melissa raised an eyebrow.

Cheryl crossed her arms over her chest and turned her back. "You girls go ahead. I'm not touching it."

Ally slipped into the leather bucket seat. "Wow."

Melissa ran around to the other side and got in behind the wheel, running her fingers over the control panel. "It's got all the options."

"It'll be repossessed any day." Cheryl stuck her chin in the air. "I refuse to get attached."

"Did Tony say how he was going to keep up payments?" Ally opened the glove compartment to look inside.

"He told me not to worry about that," Cheryl said, sniffing. "He treats me like I'm a child."

"Or a queen." Melissa got out again. "*Come on,* Mother, at least see what you're giving up. What harm can it do?" She paused and added persuasively, "Tony never has to know."

Cheryl hesitated, fingering the tiny beads on her top. "Well, maybe just a peek."

Ally exchanged a grin with Melissa, who hopped in the back.

Cheryl leaned her head inside the driver's side and smoothed a hand over the soft turquoise interior. "You can't beat real leather."

"The seats are even more comfortable than they look," Ally said. "Adjustable lumbar, too. You could throw away the cushion you use in your old sedan."

Cheryl pulled back, suddenly suspicious. "Why are you girls so adamant I like this car? Has your father gotten to you?"

"No!" Ally said. "I don't blame you for being angry at him. Buying this car was completely irresponsible."

"You have to admit, it's a more romantic present than a mortgage repayment," Melissa insisted. "Mother, you've worked your butt off for years. You deserve something utterly gorgeous and luxurious."

"Not if it means losing what I labored so hard to achieve," Cheryl argued.

"I agree," Ally said. "Mel, we're getting carried away by the materialistic allure of a flashy sports car." She opened her door and started to get out.

"Shut up, Ally, you love it as much as I do. Get in, Mother," Melissa urged. "You know you want to."

Cheryl bit her lip. "If I get in, it doesn't mean I'm keeping it."

She slid into the driver's seat and gave a deep involuntary sigh as she sank into the leather. She gripped the wheel and swung it back and forth. She checked and adjusted the rearview mirror. Finally, she reached for the keys in the ignition then paused to glance sternly at each of her daughters in turn. "If I take it around the block, it doesn't mean I'm keeping it."

Ally grinned and fastened her seat belt.

"Woo hoo!" Melissa said. "Put the roof down."

BEN TURNED OFF the highway onto a narrow country road that stretched ahead in a long straight line toward a band of magnificent old river red gums, before taking a sharp left and continuing parallel to the river beside rows and rows of silvery-green trees dotted thickly with green berries. A little farther along they came to a plantation of saplings barely a meter high.

"Are those the baby olive trees?" Danny asked, craning in his seat to get a good look at the grove.

"They must be," Ben said. Was it his imagination or did they look wilted? No, surely not. Tony and his farm manager wouldn't let them die after all the work and money that had gone into planting them.

Ahead, he spotted the white milk can mounted on a post that marked the entrance to the farm. Ben slowed and turned onto a long gravel driveway that led to an old farmhouse and, set farther back, outbuildings. Past the house was an open carportlike structure that sheltered a tractor and miscellaneous equipment. Next to that was a concrete building with large plastic crates stacked outside.

Tony emerged from the building clad in a pair of dungarees and a faded blue singlet, his red kerchief knotted around his neck. "Welcome to Cummings Estate, home of premium extra virgin olive oil," he said expansively. "Ah, young Danny. Come for a look around, have you?"

Danny nodded. "Can I sit on the tractor?"

"Go for it," Tony said. "Just don't abscond with the agricultural accoutrements."

"Huh?" Danny said, puzzled.

"Don't drive off," Ben translated.

Tony motioned Ben into the shed. "Let me show you the facilities. Note the concrete walls and insulated roof to maintain a cool temperature on even the hottest summer days."

"Impressive." Ben followed Tony through the door. Inside, he stopped dead. The cavernous interior, roughly twenty meters long by ten meters wide, was completely empty.

"Along this wall we'll install the state-of-the-art olive press." Tony strode about, gesturing with broad sweeps of his arm. "Over here we'll put the stainless-steel holding vats—"

"Whoa, Tony," Ben said, halting the flow. "Where *is* the new equipment? I thought it'd be up and running by now."

"The press is on order from Italy," Tony explained. "These things take time."

Ben was nonplussed. "How long?"

Tony shrugged. "Two to three weeks, provided it doesn't get held up in customs. The point is, we have plenty of room." He swept an arm wide. "This building is big enough to house a bottling plant."

"But will you be set up in time for harvest?" Ben persisted. "With all that money tied up in equipment, if you have to pay to get the olives processed at the local plant then the return will be lower."

"Don't you worry," Tony assured him. "The equipment will turn up and everything will be fine. Come out to the grove. We're picking today."

They left the building and walked along a rutted track between rows of olive trees. Danny hopped off the tractor and ran after them. Through the trees Ben could see a dusty white ute hooked up to a flatbed trailer on which sat two crates. Using short plastic rakes, pickers stripped the olives off the flexible branches and into a funnel-shaped net that surrounded the tree. When the small bin at the base of the funnel was full, the contents were tipped into one of the large crates on the trailer.

Ben's gaze swept the rows of trees stretching into the distance. "Harvesting will take forever if you do it all by hand."

"I've arranged for a contractor with a mechanical harvester but in the meantime, this grove is ready to be picked." Tony pulled down a branch so Ben could examine the thumbnail-size berries which were beginning to turn from green to yellow. "Koroneki olives. Beautiful flavor, this oil."

"I see the irrigation system is underground," Ben said, noting the black plastic pipes running off an upright tap at the end of the row of trees and disappearing into the dry earth.

"Of course," Tony said. "To minimize evaporation."

"You've done well to obtain a steady supply of water during this hot, dry summer," Ben commented. "From what I've read I understand saplings need regular irrigation in their first year to survive."

Tony shot him a glance and looked away, neither confirming nor denying Ben's statement.

"You *do* have a water supply," Ben said. "Don't you?"

"Currently, no," Tony admitted. "With so little rainfall this summer my sources dried up, so to speak, heh, heh. Since the middle of last month no one's had any excess water to sell and I'm still waiting for a license to draw irrigation water from the Murray River."

"You haven't had water for nearly eight weeks?" Ben asked, appalled.

"Don't worry," Tony said. "The adult trees are drought resistant."

Perhaps, but the financial loss of five hundred kalamata saplings would have to be paid for before Ben saw a return on his investment. He'd sunk his house deposit into this olive grove. "You could have told me that *before* I signed over the money."

"That I didn't is a token of how certain I was—and still am—that everything will work out." Tony clapped a hand on Ben's shoulder. "One good rainfall in the next few weeks and the young trees will be fine."

Ben felt a slow rage begin to build. "What does your mate in the meteorological department say about the possibility of rain?"

"He's a cautious sort of bloke," Tony said

carelessly. "Doesn't like to stick his neck out."

In other words, more dry weather ahead. Ben felt sick to his stomach.

"You've got to think long term, look at the big picture," Tony went on, as they continued walking through the trees. "We'll get that water license, install that olive press, build that bottling plant. Maybe we'll plant grape-vines. The wine industry is booming…."

Ben tuned out, unable to listen to another word. What would happen if things *didn't* work out? He lived in a leaky apartment, had a debt he couldn't service. How would he take care of Danny? How long before Carolyn insisted on regaining custody? He felt like such a fool, especially after Ally had warned him. Why hadn't he listened to her?

"I'm going," he said, cutting into Tony's rhapsodical vision of his farm's future. "I've seen enough."

A FEW DAYS LATER Ben slipped out of the res-taurant during the between-service lull and went to Danny's school to watch his son's soccer game. He got there a few minutes after the game had started.

Danny's team wore green shorts and gold jerseys; the away team was dressed in red and blue. Positioned in right defense, Danny kicked at a tuft of dry grass while the action took place at the far end of the oval.

Ben walked around the soccer pitch to where the other parents stood in the dappled shade of a few straggling gum trees. As he got closer, his heart picked up its pace. Ally was there. She wore a white blouse and dark skirt with her hair pulled tightly back. He hadn't talked to her since the day she'd quit her job at the restaurant. He'd contrived to move out while she was out then he'd left his house key on her desk while she was at lunch.

There was no way he could avoid her, so he walked up and stood beside her. "What's the score?"

Ally turned, startled to see him. Their eyes met and she smiled hesitantly. "One nil for us."

He'd forgotten how clear her skin was, how warm her smile, how bright her eyes. Odd, really, considering how much time he spent thinking about her. Ben cleared his throat. "I'm surprised to see you here."

Ally kept her gaze fixed on the play at the other end of the field. "Danny comes into the office to see me sometimes after school. He asked if I wanted to watch his game today." She paused. "Occasionally I bring him tuna casserole for dinner when you're busy in the restaurant."

"Ah," Ben said. "That explains a few things."

"I thought you knew," Ally said. "I'll stop if you don't like it."

"No, I appreciate your thoughtfulness."

He was saved from further awkward conversation when the opposing center forward got control of the ball and kicked it at breakneck speed down the field toward Danny's goal, followed closely by the rest of the team. Danny stood frozen in a kind of half crouch as the center forward came directly at him. Ben held his breath, waiting to see how his son would handle the situation.

Danny began to run slowly toward the other player. The center paused briefly and drew his leg back to kick the ball into the goal. In that instant, Danny scurried forward and deftly knocked the ball away from his opponent. He ran with it for a few meters then passed to his offensive wing who took it away back down the field.

Ben let out a whoop and turned to Ally in his excitement. "Did you see that? He stopped that kid from getting a goal."

Ally beamed at him. "He's doing fabulously well."

Ben held her gaze a moment longer, wanting to revel with her in his pride at Danny's accomplishments. There were so many things he wanted to tell her. "Did you hear? Mangos was awarded a chef's hat."

"Congratulations! It's all due to you," Ally said. "Steve must be over the moon." She paused. "I'm working at the Cottage Rentals again. Oh, but you must know," she added quickly, obviously remembering the key he'd placed on her desk.

"I'm glad for you," Ben said. "Karen, the new maître d', is working out well, although everyone misses you."

"Say hi for me. Are you and Danny still fishing?"

Ben nodded, aware of a hard lump in his

chest when he spoke to Ally about his son. He'd had such hopes they could be a family. "It's become a weekly ritual, Sunday afternoons."

"That's great." Ally's cheeks turned pink and she scuffed her toe in the dust. "I miss him."

Ben heard the catch in her voice and the pain localized in his heart. Did she miss *him,* too?

There was something else he had to get off his chest. "I hate to say it but you were right about your father. I can't believe I was taken in so completely. The olive press, the expansion plans, the whole thing sounded so plausible."

"Therein lies Tony's genius," Ally said, shaking her head. "His schemes *could* work and they often do, frequently enough to re-inflate his belief in himself, at least. What was it this time—no water, no equipment?"

"Both," Ben admitted. "He's gone off to California to attend a trade show on olive growing and spread the joy of Cummings Estate olive oil."

"Did you lose very much?" Ally asked quietly.

"I won't know until the crop is harvested and the oil sold but I'm betting I won't be buying a house this year." Ben shrugged. "I've learned my lesson."

"Don't feel bad," Ally said. "Tony has a way of being very persuasive. Once you start seeing dollar signs it's hard to rid yourself of the urge for the quick buck, the big money. God knows, Tony's never lost that urge. But don't give up hope. Sometimes, against all odds, he pulls the rabbit out of the hat."

"We need another torrential downpour for that to happen," Ben said. "What's your barometer saying these days?"

"Fair," she replied apologetically. "I know that's not what you want to hear." She gazed up at the hard blue sky. "We could all use a break from the dry weather. Your herb garden is the only thing thriving around my place."

"You've watered it, then?" Ben asked.

Ally gave him a quick smile. "Seemed a shame to let it die after all the work you put into it. If you ever want to pick some, just help yourself."

The soccer game moved down to their end and they stopped talking to watch for a few minutes. Ben snuck glances at Ally. Her hair was tightly pulled back from her clearly defined features. His fingers itched to remove the pins and watch it fall in soft waves to her shoulders.

"I'm back on the rental market," he announced casually. "Have you found new tenants yet?"

Ally let a long silence elapse. "I've only got one bedroom available now. I'm turning yours into a studio."

"Oh," he said, aware of that pain in his chest again. "Good for you."

What had he expected, that she'd beg him to come home? Yes, as a matter of fact, he had. He'd been so sure that once they'd had time apart she would realize how she felt about him. Instead, she'd taken steps to make sure he couldn't come back.

"Ben?" she said tentatively. "I'm sorry about how things turned out."

He glanced at her but she was staring straight ahead, biting her lip. "Never mind," he said. "Another life."

A whistle blew and the soccer game was over. Danny came running up to them. Dust covered his hands and face, but he was smiling from ear to ear. "We won! Two to one!"

Ben clapped him on the back. "You were great!"

At least he had Danny. After a rocky start, they'd bonded. Danny spent less time on the computer and more time with Ben, just hanging out, talking guy stuff. Ben watched his son turn to Ally and saw her laughing face light up.

Now if only he and Danny had Ally.

"PUT THE EASEL here by the window," Ally said to her mother. Ally opened the curtains in Ben's old room and sunlight flooded in, turning the walls from azure to robin's egg blue.

"You've got paints, brushes, canvases, thinner." Cheryl checked off the materials she'd given Ally from her studio and finished with an indulgent smile. "When you're ready to display your work, call me."

Ally laughed. "This is strictly for my own

amusement. Whoever bought my painting at Mangos must have had too much wine with dinner."

"That painting was a bargain," Cheryl said.

"Yeah, once I crossed two zeros off the price," Ally said. "Why can't you tell me who bought it?"

"Because I don't know. Steve was very vague about it. Whoever it was paid cash and didn't leave a name."

"I suppose it doesn't matter," Ally said. "The main thing is, I'm excited to be taking up art again."

"You used to love to draw and paint," Cheryl said.

"Tell me more about when I was a girl," Ally begged. If George was right and the answer lay in her childhood, she needed more information.

"You had such a wonderful color sense," Cheryl told her. "You were passionate about your favorite things and had grandiose ideas for a little girl—you're more like your father than you realize, you know. You were passionate about your dislikes, too, but we didn't notice those so much because you had such a sunny disposition."

Ally, arranging her tubes of paint on a worktable, glanced up. "You make it sound as though I've lost that sunny disposition."

"You're a little more…set in your ways. You don't like surprises or changes to your routine." Cheryl smiled when Ally stared. "Don't look at me like that. You must know that about yourself."

"Yes, of course," Ally said. "I just don't remember being different from who I am now."

"You're still cheerful," Cheryl said. "Just not as happy-go-lucky as you were as a child. Or as prone to wild ideas. That's not so strange or terrible. Everyone grows up."

Did growing up mean growing sad, or becoming less resilient? Ally didn't like to think so. "When did I change?"

Cheryl was quiet, thinking. "If I have to pinpoint a time I'd say it coincided with your grandmother's death. You were very close to her and her passing hit you hard."

"I remember," Ally said, her voice somber. "She'd still be alive if it wasn't for Tony and one of his wild schemes losing us our house that winter."

"Are you talking about the year we lived in the caravan?" Cheryl glanced at her in surprise. "It wasn't Tony's fault we lost the house. There was a severe downturn in the economy. A lot of people went out of business."

"What about Nanna?" Ally persisted. "She never would have gotten pneumonia and died if we hadn't been in that caravan."

"Nanna was seventy-eight and suffered from dementia. Even before we moved to the caravan she would leave the house and wander outside in the rain in slippers and a thin housecoat," Cheryl said. "You probably don't remember because you were so young. We tried to keep those things from you and Melissa so as not to scare you. Tony wanted Nanna to go into a care facility but she refused and he didn't have the heart to make her leave the family. He was still trying to persuade her when she got sick and had to go into the hospital instead."

"I didn't know that." Ally dropped to the bed, her mind churning with self-recrimination. "I gave him a hard time about Nanna. Why didn't he tell me the real story?"

Cheryl sat beside Ally and put an arm around her. "Probably because deep down he blames himself for not being able to protect his own mother. It's hard when the child has to become the authority figure to their parent. He really did try." She sighed and shook her head, smiling. "In spite of his faults, he's a good man."

"You sound as though you still love him," Ally said.

Cheryl shrugged helplessly. "I always will even if we end up not married anymore. I wish he'd think a little harder about the consequences of his actions but he wouldn't be Tony without the grand gestures and the flamboyant style." She sighed. "We've had so many wonderful times together. I haven't filed for divorce yet. I'm going to give him one last chance."

She obviously didn't know Tony was again in dire straits, possibly the worst thus far in his long and colorful career. As frustrated as Ally got with her father she couldn't imagine her parents not being together. Yet they were such different people she found it difficult to understand how they'd stayed together. She said as much to Cheryl.

"We've survived as a couple with a great deal of tolerance and mutual respect," Cheryl said. "We see our differences as complementary rather than oppositional. Most of the time, that is. But all the tolerance and respect in the world doesn't make a true marriage unless you have that magical intangible called love."

Cheryl drew back and searched Ally's face. "What's happening with you and Ben?"

"Nothing," Ally said, suddenly feeling empty. "I saw him at Danny's soccer game and we caught up on news but that's all. Part of me wants everything to go back to how we were when he lived at my place. I know we can't do that, yet I can't seem to go forward. I still don't trust my judgment when it comes to men. There's too many people's happiness at stake and I don't mean my own."

"Relax. Don't try so hard to fit everything into neat little boxes," Cheryl said. "You can't love someone else until you love yourself. Do that and you'll know who the right man is." She rose and brushed the creases out of her black slacks. "I'd better get back to the gallery."

Ally walked her out and stood on the steps to watch her climb into the Audi. "Are you going to keep the car?"

Cheryl laughed, looking younger than her fifty-three years. "I guess I have to now that I've been driving all over town in it."

CHAPTER SIXTEEN

ALLY SAW HER MOTHER out then went back to
her studio. She positioned her easel to catch
the maximum amount of natural light, then
stood there staring at the blank canvas. She
thought of painting the view from the
lounge-room window but that seemed too
tame.

*Once upon a time there was a little girl
who loved to climb trees, who perched on the
highest limb and dreamed big dreams.*

Ally smiled to herself, remembering. Big
dreams and crazy schemes. Like spending
the night in the massive fig tree in the vacant
lot down the road from the caravan park,
because she'd wanted to paint the inside of
the tree in early morning light. She'd told her
mother and father she was staying at her
friend Diana's house, but instead she'd

climbed the fig tree and hauled up a blanket, her sketchbook and watercolors in a bucket on a rope. She'd been too excited to remember to bring something to eat.

Her mind lost in the past, Ally picked up a tube of burnt umber and squeezed a blob onto the canvas. Another blob of Davy's gray and one of viridian, and with sweeping upward strokes she began to block in the huge spreading branches of a Moreton Bay fig tree.

Talking to her mother had stirred up all sorts of memories. She could recall exactly how she'd felt wedged in the fork of a branch, the wet bark slippery beneath her fingers. That's right, it had started to rain. It was cold, too. Winter. Ally shivered remembering how she'd huddled in the dark in her thin wind cheater, so determined to see her adventure through.

Something else nagged at her, a blurry memory of Nanna, her white hair plastered to her head, eyeglasses spotted with rain, thin cardigan over a flimsy nightgown and mud-spattered slippers. Her frail voice rising with the wind, calling on Ally to send down the bucket. And when she'd raised it again, what did she find but a bacon and fried egg sandwich wrapped in tinfoil.

Ally's fingers slipped, smearing the paint. Had *her* childish escapade been the cause of Nanna's pneumonia? No, Cheryl had said it herself, Nanna was always going out without protection against the wet and cold. But perhaps she'd subconsciously blamed herself, just as Tony did.

Ally moved away from the canvas and tried to recapture the exhilaration of climbing foot-sure and devil-may-care through the glowing green toward the luminous blue sky. Nanna would have encouraged her in that, she realized. After all, Nanna had helped her spend the night in the tree instead of telling her parents. Ever since Nanna's death she'd been playing it safe, focusing on one tiny portion of the whole.

Ally shut her eyes and looked at the big picture.

ALTHOUGH her barometer had barely budged in weeks, Ally tapped it every morning out of habit. There was nothing wrong with habits, she'd decided, as long as they weren't vices, and some vices weren't bad in moderation. She'd quite taken to gluttony.

Tap, tap. Yawning, she was about to turn away without looking when she caught a movement of the needle out of the corner of her eye. The pressure had dropped thirty millibars. The needle rested on Change.

It was about bloody time.

She heard the rumble of thunder and looked out the lounge-room window. A storm was visible on the horizon, advancing quickly on Tipperary Springs. With rain on the way she would have to mow the backyard, something she'd been putting off for weeks.

Ally went to her room and put on a long-sleeve shirt buttoned at the wrist, then pulled on a pair of long pants and tucked the cuffs into thick socks. At the back door she slipped her feet into a pair of high boots and pulled on leather gloves. She brought a broom and a cricket bat out of the laundry-room closet and went outside to leave her weapons on the veranda. If she saw so much as the tip of that snake's tail while she was cutting the grass—

She blinked and looked again. Yesterday morning the grass had been halfway up her calf. Today, it was cut short and the edges neatly trimmed. Then she noticed the zigzag pattern of the mower across the grass. There wasn't a straight line in the entire backyard. Ben must have mowed the lawn yesterday when she was at work.

That he would still do this for her after she'd hurt him made her want to cry. Instead, her heart swelled as she looked around her yard and saw all the positive changes he'd made. The herb garden, the cleaned-up junk pile, the old shed cleared out.

Maybe it was time *she* cleaned up the mess inside.

CHERYL PULLED into the driveway of Heronwood. The white paint on the restored Victorian home was brilliant against a backdrop of dark clouds and vivid green camellia bushes. In the humid air, the scented jasmine that climbed the posts and twined around the filigree trim gave off a heady scent. Cheryl sighed. So many memories.

She climbed out of her gorgeous black

convertible—the repo men would have to dynamite her out of it if they wanted to take it. Glancing at the sky, she pressed a button to raise the roof.

Then she got her suitcase out of the back seat and marched up to the front door, jingling her keys purposefully. While Tony was away in California she would reclaim what was rightfully hers.

Before she could put her key in the lock, the door swung open. Tony was standing there, his arms spread wide as if he'd been expecting her. "My love."

"You bastard," she said, and stepped into his embrace.

Some time later, Cheryl sat up in bed and looked around. "You got rid of the white board and put my painting back. And the Balinese statue is in its place. I was going to do all that while you were away."

"Without my knowledge and consent? Good thing I returned a few days early and arranged things the way I wanted." Tony stroked a hand down her bare back. "Why did you come home?"

Cheryl leaned over the side of the bed for her

purse and took out a recent mortgage statement from their bank. "I was picking up the mail while you were gone and saw that the mortgage had been paid in full on the gallery."

Tony opened his mouth to speak. "I—"

Cheryl stopped him with a kiss. "I don't want to know where you got the money. Just tell me it wasn't anything shady."

"The money came from an impeccable source." Tony put a hand over his heart. "I swear."

"Good." She sank into the pillows and faced him. "Promise you won't ever put my gallery at risk again."

"Cross my heart." He looked sincere, but then he always did.

"What did you do with the computers?" she asked. "Not in my sewing room, I hope."

"I moved my office out to the garage," Tony said.

"The garage?" she said. "There's no room for anything in there but a bar fridge and the pool table."

He gave a half smile and shrugged. "Kept the bar fridge. Sold the pool table."

"You sold the pool table?" Cheryl felt his forehead with the back of her hand. "Are you sick? Have you lost your mind? That was your grandfather's. Aside from the sentimental value it was worth a fortune—" Understanding dawned. "Oh, Tony!" She flung herself on top of him, smothering him with kisses.

"It's only a piece of furniture," he said, hugging her. "But if you're in a grateful mood, you can..." He whispered in her ear. "Then I'll..."

By the time Cheryl was aware of her surroundings again the room had dimmed and a cool breeze was blowing through the screened window. "The change has come." A moment later she heard the first heavy drops hit the leaves outside. "Is that rain I hear?"

Tony lifted his head, listened, then smiled at her. "That, my love, is the sound of good fortune. The reason I came home a few days early was because I got a call from my mate in the meteorology department that a major storm was on the way." He kissed her, then sat up and swung his legs out of bed. "If you'll excuse me, I've got to go check the Internet. Water futures will be selling like hotcakes."

TORRENTIAL RAIN poured down for three days and four nights. For drought-stricken northwestern Victoria the deluge was almost Biblical in proportion. Ally didn't even try to see Ben before it stopped. She wasn't about to wash up in his gutter looking like a drowned rat a second time.

The day before, Melissa had braved the elements to watch *Coronation Street* with Ally. They ate popcorn and drank red wine and commiserated about their love lives.

"I got a letter from Julio," Melissa said. "A postcard, really. Lots of love hearts and flowers."

"Why don't you go to Adelaide and see him?" Ally suggested, holding out her glass for a refill.

Melissa poured. "Do you think I should?"

"Why not? Think big, that's my new motto," Ally said. "You can fly there in an hour, or hop on a train in Melbourne and be there tomorrow night. The circus will be there for a few more weeks, right?"

Melissa nodded, her expression brighter. "My boss was just asking me when I wanted to take holidays—" She broke off, shaking her head. "What's the use? It'll only delay the inevitable. Once they're done in Adelaide Julio will be off to Perth. Then Singapore, then Kuala Lumpur. I can't follow him around the world."

"Why not?" Ally asked. Admittedly, her brain was fuzzy after two glasses of shiraz, but the plan seemed perfect. "Your house is fully renovated and there are plenty of people looking for long-term rentals."

"Like Ben and Danny," Melissa said. "I saw Ben going into the real estate agency yesterday."

"You can't have them," Ally said. "I've got plans for Ben and Danny."

"You're as bad as Tony." Melissa smiled. "By the way, I saw him and Mother tooling down Main Street in her new convertible. I think they've made up."

Ally raised her glass and clinked with Melissa's. "Hooray."

The morning of the fourth day dawned clear and crisp. Overnight, it seemed, the long hot summer had come to an end and autumn was here. Ally gazed out the lounge-room window at the roofs of the town, brightened by the yellows and oranges of the deciduous trees mixed in with the eucalypts, and felt a stirring in her soul.

It was Monday, Egg Day. Every fiber of her being rebelled against the monotony of eating the same thing every second day, week after week, year after year. Some habits she would do well to break. When she thought of the wonderfully delicious meals Ben had prepared for her she wanted to go over there and ask him to make her breakfast.

Well, why not? He'd always encouraged her to be more spontaneous.

BEN AWAKENED to someone banging on the door. "Take it easy," he mumbled, dragging himself out of bed. He glanced at the clock. For crying out loud, it was seven in the morning!

He swung open the door. Ally stood there, looking unbelievably fresh and pretty at this ungodly hour in a tweedy green-and-pink cardigan. Beneath that was a matching pink cotton knit that clung to the curves of her breasts and to her slender waist. There was something else different about her, he thought blurrily, something he couldn't quite put his finger… Now he had it. Her thick brown hair framed her oval face and swung around her shoulders in gentle waves. "You've let your hair down."

She pushed it back, self-consciously. "Do you like it?"

"Very much." He stepped aside. "Come in."

"It's Egg Day," she announced, and handed him a carton of free-range eggs. "Can you make me a mushroom omelet?"

She'd gone mad. Okay, fine. He'd take her any way he could get her.

"There should be some chanterelles left in the cool room downstairs," he muttered.

"Not chanterelles," she said. "Pine mushrooms."

Ben came fully awake, all his chef's sensibilities on high alert. "Do you know where to find wild pine mushrooms around here?"

"Tony used to take Melissa and I when we were kids," Ally said. "After a big rain, a good crop always comes up in the pine plantation west of Tipperary Springs."

That was all Ben needed to know. "Danny's at his mum's. I'll be ready in ten minutes."

A half hour later they were walking through the quiet, needle-carpeted pine forest. Ben stooped to pluck a golden mushroom and brush off dirt stuck to the gills. He held it to her nose so she could breathe in the earthy scent of autumn. Ally, clutching a double handful of the large, misshapen mushrooms to her chest, dropped them into the woven basket. "It's like finding treasure."

At the top of the hill they paused in the stillness of the forest. Ben put down the basket and pulled pine needles out of her hair. "I don't know how you do it," he whispered. Then he cupped her face in his hands. "Why did you come here today?"

She met his gaze. "I miss you. I want to be with you. Ben, I'm so sorry for the way I acted. I've sorted some things out in the past few weeks. I've been such a fool. Can you forgive me?"

"There's nothing to forgive." He kissed her deeply and thoroughly and in a way that suggested he was through with waiting. At last he drew back, but he didn't let her go. He gazed into her eyes and asked, "Is it a He-Man you want?"

"A He-Man?" she repeated, wrinkling her brow. "Is that a superhero or something?"

"No, I mean a macho, full-speed-ahead-and-damn-the-torpedoes kind of guy," he explained.

"I don't want some jerk bossing me around and telling me what to do, if that's what you mean," she said. "Why?"

"Oh, nothing." He smiled and released her face. "Just something Danny said."

"I like a man who knows his own mind but gives me space to make up mine," she said slowly. "A man who sees to the heart of people and loves them for who they are, not who they think they should be." She smiled up at him. "A man who makes me laugh."

Ben was smiling back at her now. "How about a man who can cook? That's got to be worth something."

Still grinning, Ally ignored that and went on, "Can you bend over backward and touch your ankles?"

Ben's eyebrows shot together in a frown. "What!"

"Just kidding," Ally said, laughing. "That one was Melissa's." She put her arms around his neck and pulled him to her in another long and dizzyingly sweet kiss.

Ben grinned with satisfaction. "Let's go home. I'll make you the most delicious omelet you've ever tasted."

"How many psychiatrists does it take to change a lightbulb?" Ally asked, skipping ahead in front of him.

"I don't know," Ben said. "How many?"

"Only one, but the lightbulb has to *want* to change. The joke is, if the lightbulb wants to change, it doesn't need a psychiatrist." Ally laughed uproariously.

"That makes no sense at all," Ben said calmly. He shifted the basket to his other hand and put his arm around her shoulders. "But I'll take your word for it."

In comfortable silence they walked back through the woods to the car. Ally snuck glances at him, loving the way his cheeks were ruddy with the cold and his hair gleamed in the morning sun. The two of them together couldn't have felt more right. Three of them, really. Danny was a bonus as far as she was concerned.

Back at his apartment, she propped her chin in her hand and gazed at him in a delirious kind of happiness and wonder as he sautéed the mushrooms in butter.

"What is it?" Ben said. "You've been staring at me for an hour now. Do I have dirt on my nose, butter on my shirt? What?"

"I love you," she said.

Ben gave the mushrooms a flip. "Everyone loves the guy making the food."

"No," she said slowly. It was important he know she was serious. "I *love* you."

He froze for an endless unblinking moment. Then the pan clattered out of his loosened grip onto the burner. With two giant strides he was lifting her from her chair and wrapping her in his arms. "I love *you*."

He kissed her cheek, her neck, her hair.

"Ben, stop…"

"I'll never stop. You said you loved me," he proclaimed triumphantly. "You can't unsay it. It's too late. There's no turning back."

"I don't want to turn back," she said, "but *Ben*…the mushrooms are on fire."

"Why didn't you say so!" Ben ran back to the stove and turned the gas off. Then he sat down, pulled Ally onto his lap and kissed her. "Tony called yesterday. The olive press arrived and with all this rain the saplings will survive. The whole harvest is looking very promising."

"Thank goodness!" Ally put her arms right around Ben and squeezed hard. "Oh! Oh! I'm so relieved."

"Hey, take it easy," Ben said. "I still have my shares in Mangos I wasn't going to touch. There was no way I was going to risk everything."

"No, but *I* did." Ally said. "I took a second mortgage out on my house so Tony would have enough money to pay off Cheryl's gallery."

"What!" Ben exclaimed. "You didn't!"

Ally nodded. "I couldn't let my parents get divorced. They love each other too much. Tony was willing to sell his pool table but that wasn't going to be enough so I helped him out."

Ben shook his head in wonder. "That was gutsy of you."

Ally shrugged. "You convinced me that his olive oil was worthwhile and Mother convinced me that Tony was." She paused and smiled wickedly. "I must admit, taking such a risk was rather thrilling."

"Tony's talking about starting a vineyard," Ben said. "Maybe you'd like to invest in that."

Ally considered the prospect. "He came through on the olives."

"I was kidding!" Ben said. "Don't even think of it. We have no more money to spare on pie-in-the-sky schemes."

"Vines planted now will be producing in three or four years," Ally argued. "The Australian wine industry is booming. You've got to look at the big picture, Ben."

"I *am* thinking big picture. I'm thinking house, family, children," Ben said. "You know, you're more like your father than you realize."

Children, he'd said. Could that mean he still wanted to marry her? Oh, she hoped so but she couldn't take anything for granted, ever again. "I've finally come to terms with myself, thanks partly to you," she said. "You jolted me out of my routine."

"I knew there was a dirty girl inside that prissy miss." Ben sifted his fingers through her hair. "I couldn't rest until I'd set her free, or at least got a good look at her."

"You seduced me with food," she accused, laughing.

"I didn't hear you complaining," he said. "Come, I want you to see something." He pulled her to her feet and down the hall to his bedroom.

"Are you going to show me your etchings?" she teased.

Ben smiled. "Something like that." He covered her eyes, guided her to the threshold then took his hand away.

Ally gasped. Over his bed was her painting, the one with the rip in the canvas. "*You* bought it!"

"My theory was, that's your love for me up there. Whenever I got depressed about us I'd look at that painting and think, those feelings are too strong for her to repress forever." He grinned. "Besides, it was marked down something like a thousand percent. Too good a deal to pass up."

He went to his dresser and took something from a carved wooden box. Turning to her he opened his hand and in his scarred and calloused palm was the diamond ring. "I want you to be absolutely certain this is what you want."

The lump in her throat was too big to speak around so Ally simply nodded. She'd never been more certain of anything in her life.

With trembling hands, Ben slid the engagement ring on her finger. "I'm getting a license tomorrow morning," he said. "We'll get married tomorrow afternoon. I'm not taking any chances."

Ally gazed at the ring on her finger and felt nothing but happiness. "What will Danny say?"

"Danny will be delighted," Ben said. "He already gave me his permission to marry you."

Ally laughed and went into Ben's arms. After that, she couldn't say anything more because he was busy unpinning and unbuttoning her. By the time he was finished she was completely undone.

And she loved it.

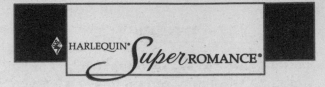

...there's more to the story!

Superromance.
A *big* satisfying read about unforgettable characters. Each month we offer *six* very different stories that range from family drama to adventure and mystery, from highly emotional stories to romantic comedies—and much more! Stories about people you'll believe in and care about. Stories too compelling to put down....

Our authors are among today's *best* romance writers. You'll find familiar names and talented newcomers. Many of them are award winners— and you'll see why!

If you want the biggest and best in romance fiction, you'll get it from Superromance!

Emotional, Exciting, Unexpected...

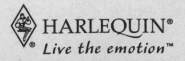

HARLEQUIN®
Live the emotion™

HARLEQUIN®
Presents

**The world's bestselling romance series...
The series that brings you your favorite authors,
month after month:**

Helen Bianchin...Emma Darcy
Lynne Graham...Penny Jordan
Miranda Lee...Sandra Marton
Anne Mather...Carole Mortimer
Susan Napier...Michelle Reid

and many more uniquely talented authors!

Wealthy, powerful, gorgeous men...
Women who have feelings just like your own...
The stories you love, set in exotic, glamorous locations...

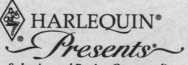

HARLEQUIN®
Presents

Seduction and Passion Guaranteed!

Harlequin Historicals®
Historical Romantic Adventure!

From rugged lawmen and valiant knights to defiant heiresses and spirited frontierswomen, Harlequin Historicals will capture your imagination with their dramatic scope, passion and adventure.

Harlequin Historicals... they're too good to miss!

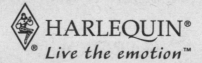

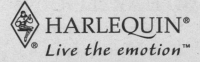